The
Handmaid of
Desire

~

Other Books by John L'Heureux

Quick as Dandelions

Rubrics for a Revolution

Picnic in Babylon

One Eye and a Measuring Rod

No Place for Hiding

Tight White Collar

The Clang Birds

Family Affairs

Jessica Fayer

Desires

A Woman Run Mad

Comedians

An Honorable Profession

The Shrine at Altamira

The

Handmaid of

Desire

~

a novel by
John L Heureux

This is a work of fiction. Names, characters, places, and incidents either are the product of the author's imagination or are used fictitiously. Any resemblance to actual persons, living or dead, is entirely coincidental.

Published by Soho Press Inc.
853 Broadway
New York, NY 10003

Library of Congress Cataloging-in-Publication Data

L'Heureux, John
   The handmaid of desire : a novel / by John L'Heureux
      p.   cm.
   ISBN   1-56947-073-1 (alk. paper)
   I. Title
PS3562.H4H36   1996
813' .54—dc20   96-20632
                                                              CIP

First Edition
10   9   8   7   6   5   4   3   2   1

for Joan Polston L'Heureux

"The author is dead and his intentions are irrelevant."
—*Michel Foucault*

~

"Literature is the cemetery of communication."
—*Maurice Blanchot*

~

"Don't come crying to me."
—*Anton Chekhov*

Part 1

~

1

The flight attendant, serene in her Donna Karan pants suit, stopped halfway down the aisle. She frowned briefly and then allowed a business smile to play on her face as she pointed an accusing finger at Olga. Her fingers were long and white and on the accusing one she wore a turquoise ring, a terrific gift from her Denver boyfriend, a Thomasite priest.

"Your seat belt," the attendant said, admiring her finger with its big ring.

"Turquoise is lucky," Olga said.

"Oh God, you know!" the attendant said. "Isn't it wonderful!" She looked again at the ring, forgetting her role as flight attendant and becoming for the moment simply what she was, a lucky young woman with a husband and a lover. She bent over and held out her hand to give Olga a better look.

"Lucky," Olga said, her fingertips barely touching the mottled blue-green stone. "Unless it's from a monk. From a monk, turquoise is not lucky. This is true."

"A monk?" The attendant yanked her hand away and hid it behind her back. There was something wrong here. This woman was peculiar. Dangerous maybe. Besides, she had an accent. The attendant stared at Olga for further signs of craziness. Olga stared back, innocent, or maybe just stupid. "Your seat belt," the flight attendant said in a firm voice. "You've got to fasten it."

Olga reached for the belt, perhaps fastening it, perhaps not. "I'm doing my job, only," the attendant said, conciliatory now. "It's the law."

Olga smiled.

The flight attendant stood there in the aisle. She was troubled, uncertain what to do next, tempted—for no reason she could see—to throw herself into this woman's arms and weep and ask forgiveness. One last chance.

As the flight attendant moved away, hand to her hair, Olga added, "Take care with that ring."

Olga had her notebook at the ready, but she did not bother to jot down the flight attendant. The flight attendant was irrelevant. Who could care about this silly woman with her priest lover and her anonymous husband? She mattered to God, of course, if there was a God, and to her lover and maybe even to her husband—but not to Olga, not now, and not in the future, at least not in any narrative conceivable at this point.

Olga sat back to consider the multifariousness of human nature and to endure the flight.

～

The plane landed in San Francisco at the appointed time. There had been delays, of course, first in New York, then in Denver, but good tail winds and good luck had brought the plane in at exactly 3 p.m.

Inside the terminal a small crowd had gathered, pressed against the velvet rope. Everybody was looking for some one person. Professor Zachary Kurtz would be looking for Olga, so his letter had promised, but nobody approached her even though in her black rain cape and floppy hat she was highly visible. She smiled impartially at everyone, at no one, as if she were a Hollywood star at a premiere. She touched her dark glasses with her free hand and gave the crowd this smile which, if they wanted to, they could understand. Several people turned and looked at her, and Zachary Kurtz also looked. Someone pointed and said, "Isn't she that actress? The homely one that does those serious parts?" "Where?" someone said. And then she was gone.

It was Friday afternoon, rush hour, when luggage is always delayed but Olga's luggage was at the carousel, waiting for her. And, for her, a cab stood ready at the curb, even though rain was falling and important executives stood about, diminished, cursing. Olga ignored them and got into her cab.

"I want to go to the University, to the faculty club," she said.

"S. F. State? U. S. F.? Berkeley? Which?"

"*The* university," she said. "I know it's a distance, but not to worry."

The cab driver examined her in his rear view mirror. He could not place her accent, which surprised him because he was a student of comparative literature and spoke five languages reasonably well.

"That's gonna be nearly fifty dollars, lady," he said.

"Forty-one," she said, "and a few pennies. But I'll *pay* you fifty providing you don't talk. I have my thoughts to do."

"Sure thing," he said. "What part of Europe you from? Eastern? Belarus?"

He said, "I thought I heard an accent."

He said, "I'm from Denver myself, but I study languages. My name is Daryl," he said.

Olga said nothing.

"I just wondered about your accent?" he said, his brows up.

Suddenly Olga took off her dark glasses and leaned forward so that her head was almost touching his bushy red beard. In the mirror he could see her face clearly and he could see the hard expression in her eyes. He did not wait for her to speak.

"Okay, lady," he said. "You're the boss."

"Yes," she said, and put her dark glasses on again.

Just outside the city the rain stopped and they drove in silence through the lion-colored foothills toward the green fastnesses of the university. Olga was seen studying the distant mountains as the driver shot her occasional furtive glances in his mirror. She was his age, thirty, maybe more. And she had just the trace of an accent. Rumanian? At some point she took off her glasses and her floppy rainhat and he could see her black hair pulled straight back and knotted in a large bun. Very severe. Very middle European. Though she wore no expression whatsoever, her face seemed somehow tragic. Or perhaps menacing. She sat swathed in her black cape, impassively staring at the speeding landscape, thinking what?

Olga was thinking of the next hours, of her new book, of her task here at the university. Her task was to rescue some lost souls from the effects of their scandals, satisfy a few passions, answer some importunate prayers, and, on the side, to teach a little course in feminist drama and another in literary theory. She did not feel tragic and certainly not menacing; she merely looked that way because she was contemplating the final end of all things and the path that led there. She was wondering what form her invention would take.

As the cab turned smoothly into the long avenue of palm trees leading to the heart of the campus, and thus to the faculty club, Olga unsnapped her collar and in one deft gesture slipped the cape off her shoulders and from under her body. She pulled a large pin from her hair, and then three small ones; as she shook her head, her long black hair cascaded about her face and shoulders. The cab driver, sneaking a glance in his mirror, was astonished to see that his formidable passenger had completely disappeared and in her place sat this young woman with lots of black hair and a yellow skirt and sweater. The cab lurched to the right and then to the left, but it did not upset Olga who continued removing all traces of lipstick with a tissue. From her large leather handbag she took a pair of beige shoes with flat heels and exchanged them for the black pumps she had been wearing. She ran her tongue over her lips, her long fingers through her hair; she sighed as if she were at last ready to begin.

When the cab pulled up in front of the faculty club, the meter read forty-one dollars and eleven cents. The driver checked the meter and then checked Olga yet one more time. He took her bags from the trunk and would have carried them into the faculty club for her, but she would not let him. Instead she handed him a worn fifty dollar bill and waited for him to leave. He reached in his pocket for change.

"Don't do that," she said. "We made a pact."

"Well, thanks," he said and got into his cab. But he did not drive away. He sat there watching as Olga, ignoring her luggage, went up the stairs, light and quick, a schoolgirl in a yellow outfit with a leather handbag slung over her shoulder. How could he have thought she looked tragic? Or menacing.

"Daryl's the name," he called out. And, to Olga's surprise, he added, "Be seeing you."

She stopped then. At the start of a book you could never be certain which characters would eventually come to matter. She cautioned herself to keep an open mind. She went on.

~

The young man behind the desk at the faculty club looked as if he had just alighted from his surfboard. He had blond hair and a thick blond mustache and his face was bland and handsome. His features were straight and, in that sense, perfect. His blue eyes and white teeth, his square shoulders and narrow hips: all of it was Californian, scrubbed clean of any imperfection or impediment. He stood, whole and—in a way—wholesome, completely comfortable inside his body.

Olga took all this in, noting with a pang that on his smooth brow nothing had been written, ever.

The young man leaned across the desk as if he had been waiting for her. "How ya doing?" he said, interested, and hinted things with his eyes.

Olga stood with her hands clasped in front of her, passive, accepting but not returning the eyes.

"Everything cool?" he said.

"Well, um, I'm new here," she said, demure.

"A transfer?" he said. "I'm Peter. I can show you around, right? What dorm are you in? Are you in a dorm?"

"No," she said. "I'm not in a dorm," and she slipped him a tentative smile.

He liked that. What he could see from behind the desk looked fine. She had a terrific little body and her face was pretty good, especially when she smiled, and best of all she wasn't taller than he was. He was six feet, but lately all the girls seemed to be gaining on him.

"Grad student?" he said. That would be cool too. "I'm a senior myself."

She looked down, modestly. "I'm going to teach here," she said.

A teacher. His mind raced ahead: had he said anything too forward, had he got himself in deep doodoo, had he just screwed himself by laying the groundwork to screw her?

"But only this quarter," she said. "Only two courses."

"Let me guess," he said, backing away a bit, feeling for the solid ground of student-teacher talk. "Science, right? Statistics? Computer engineering?"

"Feminist drama," she said, "and a little course in theory."

"Aw-right!" he said, in recognition. "So you must be Professor Kominska, right?"

She nodded.

"Foucault? Are you teaching Foucault?"

"Up to a point," she said.

"To me, Foucault is a god. I mean that's really what he is, a god."

"Up to a point," she said.

"So," he said. "Like, this is really something. I mean, I'm in your course and everything. If I'm accepted. But Zachary said I was. Accepted. Practically, I mean."

Her face darkened and she began to look like a professor.

"Zachary Kurtz, but he lets some of us call him Zachary. He's the best teacher in this university, really, and he said you'd let me in. Well, he said he'd talk to you about it."

She only looked at him.

"I mean, it's up to you, Professor. I wouldn't want to seem presumptive." He chewed the corner of his thick blond mustache and gave her the eyes again.

She thought for a moment. Could she, could anyone, print some message on that brow? "Presumptuous," she said, "not presumptive. What is your name, since it is assumed we're going to be in class together."

He relaxed. Maybe he hadn't gone too far. Maybe he wasn't in deep doodoo. Who knows, he might even get to screw her.

His name was Peter Peeks, he explained. Not as in mountain peaks but peeks, like a spy. She looked at him. It was a joke, he said, though he could see from her reaction that it wasn't a very good one, and hey, he wished they could begin all over again because he knew she was a very famous professor and she taught the really newest kind of literary theory and he really wanted to take her course, and now that they'd gotten off on the wrong foot he felt like a complete asshole, if she got what he meant. Right?

"A good beginning," she said, only half-aloud because she was thinking and she wasn't sure where Peter Peeks fitted in, if indeed he fitted in at all. The bit about spying was good, but might turn out to be useless.

"Well, Mr. Peeks," she said, "let us deconstruct . . . in the Aristotelian manner: I was told to go to the faculty club and pick up keys for my apartment in Faculty Terrace. *Atqui*, this is the faculty club. *Ergo*, where are my keys?"

"Far out," he said. "Excellent." He began rummaging in the top drawer of the desk. "Keys," he said, and he pulled out a small box of loose keys, none of them with identifying tags.

Olga reached across the desk and picked up an envelope propped against the lamp. On it was written "Keys for Professor Kominska, Faculty Terrace."

"You're not much of a spy," she said.

"Jeepers," he said, "we're off on the wrong foot. Don't be hasty about this, Professor. I sincerely believe you're gonna end up liking me. A lot."

Olga laughed, because truly he was sincere. And truly presumptuous. And because, if she decided he mattered after all, his youth and innocence and sheer animal energy might prove both practical and fun, sin being beside the point.

And so, at his insistence, she let Peter Peeks carry her bags the short distance from the faculty club to Faculty Terrace. He used the time constructively, informing her of the income, personal habits, and dispositions of a great many of her neighbors, insofar as he knew them; where he did not, he simply made it up, working from gossip and a rather limited imagination.

Meanwhile Peter's friend, Scott, was also using the time constructively. Scott pushed the lesser drugs on campus, but more recently had moved up to cocaine. At the moment—because of cash flow problems—Scott found himself unable to pay his supplier, and so he was sitting at the faculty club desk waiting for Peter Peeks to return and give him some good advice and maybe some money. He smoked a joint and waited. He was about to light up again when the telephone rang. Scott had begun to feel expansive and so he answered the phone.

"Listen," a voice said, very annoyed. "I want to know if Olga Kominska has arrived. Has she arrived? Is she there?"

"There's nobody here," Scott said.

"Don't be smart with me," the voice said. "This is Zachary Kurtz and I want to know if Olga Kominska is there. She was due in on the three o'clock flight, and either she wasn't on it or else she missed me. And I want to know if she's there. Or not."

"There's nobody there," Scott said. "Here, I mean."

"*You're* there! Is this Peter Peeks? Who the hell is this, anyway!"

Scott drifted off for a minute. He didn't know Zachary Kurtz but he knew about him. He was brilliant, everybody said, but touchy, touchy, with a tongue like a razor blade.

"Hello? Are you there?"

"Oh yeah," Scott said, drifting back, "but I don't work here, Professor Kurtz. I'm just robbing the place."

Scott began to laugh at that, delighted with the craziness of the idea, of actually saying it to somebody—it would be so great in a film—and then he realized that it wasn't a bad idea at all, and so he hung up and did it. He started with the Power Mac 7500. He disconnected the monitor and carried it out to his car. He came back for the keyboard and the CPU, and again for the laser printer. He lit up a joint and looked around, enjoying his high. After a while he took down and rolled up the rather good McKnight that brightened the foyer. He selected an umbrella from the drying rack; it was a big umbrella, with red and white stripes, and he liked it. He opened it, closed it. Excellent. He put it aside for the moment. After a brief search, he located and emptied out the petty cash box. Enough for a small pizza anyhow. He shrugged, looked around the place indifferently, lit one last joint, and left, twirling his new umbrella as he went.

As a consequence of this little robbery, executed almost accidentally, Peter Peeks would be fired that same evening. But his firing was hours away and no grim thoughts troubled his optimistic mind as he turned from Apt. 94, his arm still tingling from Olga's touch.

Peter Peeks had no place in this story—he was as irrelevant as the flight attendant or the chatty cab driver—but Olga had been tempted by that empty brow, that lithe young body, that perfect California face. Peter Peeks did not belong, but she had decided she would fit him in.

"I'll be seeing you," she said, her hand upon his arm, planning.

~

Alone, Olga examined the apartment. Two bedrooms—or a bedroom and a study—a single bath, and in the living room a wall of glass that opened on a tree-lined street. The furniture was Academic Modern: a little leather, a lot of brass and glass, a sofa of Haitian cotton. White walls, a creamy carpet, some Stella prints, two Klees, a Kandinsky. Junk copies.

And so, once again and not for the last time, she was about to begin. Of making many books there is no end. She sat down on the sofa and covered her face with her long hard hands. She had to get some rest. She had to put aside her feelings of insecurity and unreadiness. She had to slow down the process of perception. If only she could stop, for just an hour, for just a moment.

But her mind continued ticking. Foucault insisted that the individual was dead, the author invisible, reality a fabrication. Why, then, could *she* not cease to be? For even twenty seconds? Still, that was not the problem. The problem was: how to begin?

She lowered her hands to her lap and lay her head back against the

2

Nothing happened next, and nothing happened later that night—except a fall of rain, except voices from the swimming pool—and Olga went to bed an anxious woman, confused by her new surroundings, troubled, insecure. Could she perform this task? Write this book? Was it all some dreadful, glittering mistake?

She woke on Saturday, however, very much her old self. She had unpacked her clothes, and now she unpacked her books, her notes, her various work utensils. She had brought black pens in two definitions: fine point and very fine. Pencils, Mohawk, No. 2 1/2. A stack of notebooks—bound, not looseleaf—of European size, 6x8. A pencil sharpener, a rubber eraser, cellophane tape, a pile of yellow sticky pads, and a notebook computer with accompanying jet printer. She was ready to begin.

But nothing happened. Nothing came to her.

She waited.

She sat at her desk and continued waiting. She was accustomed to this process, though of course she could not stand it. Why, then, did she bother?

She waited.

She opened her notebook and read the entries. They were dull, dead, except for a quotation from John Calvin she had copied out on the flight to California. "God will speak to us with great blows from halberds, with great blows from pikes and harquebuses: we will not understand a word, the language will be most strange."

She thought about this for a while and then drew a large X through the quotation. God was not her subject. Nor goodness. Nor, for that matter, language.

What was her subject then?

She read her most recent entry. "In the English department of that university . . ."

The telephone rang.

"Zachary Kurtz here," he said. "I guess you missed me at the airport yesterday."

"I took a cab," she said.

There was a silence on the phone.

"I never depend on the kindness of strangers," she said.

There was more silence.

"I'm hanging up now," she said.

"Hold on," he said. "Hold on. Jesus."

She held on.

"We've gotta talk here. We've gotta get together. How about I come by this afternoon and fill you in on the department, and courses, and your role here, et cetera. Three? Three-thirty?"

"No, I don't think so."

"How about we meet at the coffee shop?"

"I have my thoughts to do."

"Pardon me? Listen . . ."

"I'm ringing off now," she said, and rang off.

She put Zachary Kurtz out of her mind at once. She wanted to work. She wanted to write. But she could not tap into her subconscious where all the interesting things went on. She paced up and down the living room. She wrung her hands, twisting her fine mechanical fingers into knots. She was a failure, a fake. She had been deluding herself all along.

Peter Peeks came knocking at her door.

"What is it?" she said from inside.

"It's Peter Peeks," he said, trying to look through the peep hole. "Can I come in?"

"No," she said.

"I lost my job," he said. "I was fired."

"Come back tomorrow," she said.

"Can't I come in?" he said.

For just a second, she was tempted. "Tomorrow," she said.

She left the door and went back to pacing up and down the living room. After a while Peter Peeks went away.

"I'm doing my thoughts," she said aloud to the room, but she had no thoughts and she was doing nothing.

She paced. She called upon the gods. She cursed. And then, defeated, she gave up. She set her alarm clock and lay down for a nap.

When she awoke, she took a long bath and there in the tub, as sometimes happened, she became invisible and drifted off into the dark landscape of her subconscious, making scenes, inventing characters, asking, exploring. She came back to herself in time to dry off, to make up, and to dress for this evening's reception.

A single sentence hung suspended in her mind—"In the English department of that university there was a small number of certifiable fools"—and, seeing it suspended there, felt very good about it. Hopeful. Then exhilarated.

What a difference a single sentence could make.

She took out "certifiable," thus giving the fools larger, more generous possibilities.

She was ready to go, glamorous suddenly, and full of confidence. She smiled at herself in the mirror. Let the earth tremble.

3

In the English department of that university there was a small number of fools, but Robbie Richter was not one of them. Or at least he did not consider himself one of them. He was the same age as the fools—they were all in their fifties—and he had been around as long as any of them, but his dedication to literary theory had lifted him from the fool category where his age and accomplishments would quite naturally have put him. He was a theorist, as productive and avant-garde as any of the young theorists. He was not a fool.

He was a nervous wreck because he was hosting this party, but by no means was he a fool.

These ruminations were provoked by Cynthia's telling him to hurry up with his dressing. "You're getting to be like one of those fools," she said. Easy for her to say. Cynthia could get bathed, made up, and dressed in ten minutes flat. Cynthia wasn't even human, which was, of course, why he loved her.

"Hurry *up*, Robbie," she called from downstairs, "the caterers are at the blessed door!"

The caterers were here to provide a suitable welcome for Olga Kominska: shrimp, pate, brie, English stilton, the usual stuff with sausages and bacon, and, by way of exception, two hundred miniature sandwiches. And booze, of course, lots of it. Zachary Kurtz had arranged everything. The reception was being held at Robbie's house because he lived in Faculty Ghetto in the old center of the campus and because he had this big lawn where large crowds could stomp around and drink and because, after all, he was Robbie Richter and everybody loved him. The entire English department had been invited, fools and theorists alike, and they would all come because they were pleased and relieved that Olga was now among them.

"Robbie! For heaven's sake!" Cynthia called from below.

"Coming, coming," Robbie said, but at that moment their dog Ozzie, half-terrier, half-dachshund, lifted his stout little leg and peed on Robbie's trousers, soaking the cuff and staining his new shoes.

"Oh, Ozzie, poor little baby," Robbie said, and knelt down to comfort the dog. Ozzie snuggled up to him and gave him kisses. "Oh, what a good dog, what a pretty little dog. And what a pretty belly you've got, it's a fat belly," and here he planted a loud kiss on Ozzie's belly, which caused the dog to squirm wildly and squirt a little more pee on Robbie's trousers.

Downstairs he could hear the rattle of glasses and the banging of trays. The department was paying for all of this, thank God. Zachary had seen to that. Wonderful Zachary.

Zachary Kurtz had been among them only three years, a bargain import from Cornell, but he had seen at once where the problems were and had persuaded Robbie that the future lay with him, the Big Z. Robbie said the name aloud, "Zachary," and felt that little tremor in his breast. He loved Zachary. Robbie was sufficiently secure in his own sexuality not to be disturbed by this odd love he felt; he knew it was principally intellectual; he knew it was founded on admiration for Zachary's strength of character rather than anything merely physical and base. What he loved about Zachary was his stern intelligence, his dedication to scholarship, his determination to make this English department into something new and wonderful that had never been seen before. Then too there was his youthful aggressiveness, his ruthless commitment to professionalism, and also his cute little mustache. Cynthia had accused Robbie of having a crush on Zachary, which was silly, because Zachary was nearly twenty years younger and besides, Zachary was above such things.

"Robbie! I mean it now!" It was Cynthia, getting impatient.

"Coming," he said, shouting toward the stairs. He took off the pee-stained trousers and put on his work corduroys. They were baggy and old, but what else could he do?

He heard voices on the front walk, nervous laughter, the sound of people arriving. And then he heard Cynthia crooning her welcome to Zachary. Zachary!

Robbie went to the mirror for one quick look at himself before going down to his guests. He looked fine, given his limitations. He was short, but Zachary was short too; in fact almost all the young Turks were short. Robbie leaned closer to the mirror. Actually, he looked pretty good for fifty-three. He was losing his hair, it was true, and he was not very distinguished-looking to begin with, and he always had bad breath, but his innate goodness and his astonishing mind made him a very attractive person, he felt.

He started down the stairs, smiling, because there in the foyer stood Zachary Kurtz.

"Zack," Robbie shouted, and moved to shake his hand, a bad habit left over from associating so long with the fools, who always greeted each other like long-parted friends.

Zachary nodded to him and moved off to the patio and the drinks table. Rebuked, Robbie started after him.

"You've got guests, Robbie," Cynthia said, and Robbie turned back to see Gil Rudin standing in the doorway trying to get around his hugely pregnant wife Betz who was going belly to belly with Rosalie Kurtz. Dueling babies. Betz Rudin was due to deliver first and Rosalie resented that.

"Betz," Robbie said, "you look gorgeous," and he kissed her. Then, since Rosalie was married to Zack and deserved primacy of place, he said, "And you look even more gorgeous, Rosalie," and kissed her too.

"Very subtle," Gil Rudin said. "Very tactful, Robbie."

The three women laughed at that, as if Robbie were a fool, and Gil Rudin let out one of his snorts, a breathy grunt that expressed both amusement and contempt. Gil was a star in the department, a seminal thinker, but he was a famous womanizer and he had buckets of

Hollywood money and floppy blond hair and Robbie hated as well as respected him. Seeing Robbie's discomfort, Gil snorted again, unnecessarily, and Robbie blushed and made for the patio.

"Gil makes me crazy sometimes," he said to Zachary, "with that snort of his."

"He's a star, what can I tell you?" Zachary said. "They tend to snort."

"He thinks he's superior," Robbie said.

"He is superior," Zachary said.

"All that Hollywood money," Robbie said.

"The money has nothing to do with it," Zachary said.

Robbie turned to the bartender. "I want a large scotch and water, Daryl, easy on the water. Okay?"

And Zachary said, "Here, make me another," and thrust his glass at the bartender.

They were silent while the bartender made the drinks.

For one undisciplined moment Robbie thought: to hell with Z, this is my house and my party and I don't have to play up to him, the shit, even if he does think he's God. But this momentary independence terrified him. Zachary *was* God, after all.

"I'm sorry, Zack," he said, and added, "about what happened at the airport yesterday."

Zachary sniffed and made a hocking noise in his throat.

Robbie clucked sympathetically. Zack was in a foul mood. He must be having one of his famous headaches.

Robbie clucked again but his sympathy was drowned out by shouts of delight from the foyer. Eleanora Tuke had arrived, huge and vibrant in a pink satin dress, her meager little physicist by her side. The physicist had invented something to do with bombs and so he was immensely rich, but he was vain and dull and self-important and nobody could stand him except Eleanora who was well paid for it. Way behind, unnoticed in the flurry of greetings and laughter, was Maddy Barker.

Zachary snapped to attention. "The Tuke has dressed down, I see," he said to nobody in particular. At that moment Eleanora spotted him and Zachary gave her the big smile he reserved for academic stars.

Robbie noted the smile, as he was supposed to, and realized that Zachary would be shedding his special grace on Eleanora tonight.

Heartbroken, Robbie put down his glass, edged past the crowd in the foyer and trotted on up the stairs to his bedroom and his dog. He would lie down until he got his feelings under control. He would not let this destroy him. He would not let it depress him. He would rise triumphant, like the goddam phoenix. No fool he.

~

"Well, how're you, Zack?" Gil Rudin said, joining him at the drinks table. "I hear you got stood up at the airport." He laughed soundlessly, another smug and infuriating habit of his. Soundless or snorting: there was no intermediate state with Gil.

"She was in disguise," Zachary said. "I spent the whole fucking day at the airport."

"We, on the other hand, spent the day—pardon, the whole fucking day—at the beach house," Gil said. "The rain was very light, very steady, there was no sun. Very sexy." He twitched back his flopping blond hair.

"Bully for you," Zachary said, not much of a riposte.

"Well, where is she?" Eleanora said, rustling in her pink satin. "I hear she wasn't at the airport. I want to know everything. *Everything.* But hold on, I've got to get a drink." She grasped Zachary's shoulder, as if that would keep him from speaking, and she turned to the bartender. "Daryl, a spritzer? White wine? Daryl's doing a paper for me on *Minima Moralia*," she said, speaking for Daryl's benefit but addressing the others. "I don't think there's anything new there. Adorno's a dead issue. But Daryl's a sweetie. Thanks, Daryl." She took the drink and turned back to Zachary and Gil. "Now tell me everything," she said.

"There's nothing to tell," Zachary said.

"What's the matter, Zack?" Eleanora asked. "Have you got one of your headaches?"

"Olga stood him up at the airport," Gil said, laughing soundlessly. "He waited for her—and I quote—the whole fucking day."

"That was *yesterday*," Zachary said.

"So he's got a headache," Gil said. "Anyhow, *we* spent the day at the beach house. With the rain."

"*We* were in the city," Eleanora said. "It was perfect. No panhandlers in the street. No homeless. Just perfect. That's what a little rain can do—wash away every last trace of the wretched. And no headaches either, nudge, nudge."

Zachary looked at them, blankly.

Eleanora whooped with laughter and Gil snorted.

"Poor Zachary," Eleanora said. "Never mind, no more about headaches. Do you like the dress?" and she turned slowly to give them the full effect. Up close, Eleanora was larger than life and the effect was stunning.

Gil snorted once again.

"Jesus Christ," Zachary said, and left them to join Maddy Barker who was lurking in the dining room pretending to study a picture over the buffet.

~

Maddy Barker had been here for only a year, but she was known in the department and throughout the university as a true genius and a viper. Her dark beauty was disguised this evening in the electrified hair and bulky pantsuit of the humorless academic. She was a puzzle. She had a breathy voice and huge breasts and no intimates, and yet there were stories, all of them unconfirmed, of passionate alliances and violent sex. Rumor had it that she was married and divorced, the mother of two boys, but nobody had ever seen the boys or the ex-husband, and her attitude toward men seemed in general to be contempt. Everybody presumed she was a lesbian.

She was brilliant. She was reticent. Expert in several languages and fluent in all the specialized tongues of literary discourse, Maddy rarely talked at all, except in seminar, of course, or when directly challenged. Challenged, she became ferocious, her small face contracting like a fist, her little teeth moving forward for the attack. Her eyes glistened and her breathiness gave way to a strong, harsh, denunciatory voice. She was terrifying then. But mostly she was a reserved and ambitious woman, badly dressed, willfully plain, eager only to promote her career.

At the moment she was studying a picture that hung above the buffet, a reproduction of "The Scream" blown up to three times actual size.

"Maddy," Zachary said, "can I get you a drink?" He was on his fourth, or his fifth, and was himself a little high.

"Maddy?"

Maddy turned from the picture and shook her head.

He could think of no way to begin artfully, so he just launched in. "This place has got to change, Maddy. It's in the hands of dinosaurs. No standards. No values. Nepotism has just about destroyed the place. We're in the last stages of calcification. Am I right?"

"The patriarchy," she said.

"Right," he said.

"Dead white males," she said.

"Right, right," he said.

"The old boy network," she said.

"Okay, all right," he said, beginning to get annoyed. "What we need, really," he said, "is a chairman. A living one—right?—not one of the fools. A new *kind* of chairman."

"You," Maddy said.

"Not me. Robbie. They'll accept Robbie. Besides I have no ambitions to be a figurehead."

"You want to be Secretary of State, not President."

"You got it."

Maddy thought about this.

"And then we've got to get rid of these fools. They're dog shit.

They're *old*." In fact, he had memorized each of their birth dates and could say within a week or so when each of them would retire, or *should* retire. He began to recite some of these dates to Maddy.

"I just want to get on with my work," Maddy said.

"We've got to cut them off, we've got to put an end to them."

"Murder?" Maddy said. Her face tightened a little.

He moved into more delicate territory. "And Francis Xavier Tortorisi, it goes without saying, has to *go* without saying . . . if you'll forgive the *mot*. He writes those shitty novels, for Christ's sake. We shoot him down at tenure."

Tortorisi was fat, with a gray complexion and bad skin, inappropriate to California, and he was very probably a *fegelah*, but Maddy often went over to his place for Sunday breakfasts. It had been noted.

"He gets tenure over my dead body," Zachary said. "Right?"

"Look," Maddy said, and her face got dangerously small, "my work comes first. My career."

Eleanora's little physicist came by, saying, "Have you seen my wife? Have you seen Eleanora?" but they ignored him and he went away.

"So don't push too hard," Maddy said and headed for the bathroom.

Zachary stood there, thinking. He'd like to mess around with those great big breasts of hers. He'd like to screw her back into heterosexuality. He'd like to lay her out flat and drill her till her little teeth rattled.

He shook his head to clear it. He needed a drink, he realized, and some fresh air.

～

The fools began to arrive just as Robbie Richter made his second descent. He had been lying on his bed, saying to himself over and over "A calm mind in a calm body," and when he felt he had achieved both, he gave Ozzie pats and kisses and, fortified, descended the stairs once again.

Cynthia was at the door, the model hostess, greeting the fools.

Some twenty years earlier when they'd first come to the university, Cynthia had been thought a supreme ironist. She had a glassy look to her eyes and an exaggerated warmth to her voice and she exhibited such concern and admiration for everybody, even for people who didn't matter, that the faculty thought she was making fun of them. Later, they came to suspect that she was not an ironist at all, she was just out of it. And there had always been a few who thought she was dumb as a post.

The fools were all milling around, shaking each others' hands and kissing each others' wives, shouting, carrying on. From his vantage point on the stairs, Robbie could see how they had looked twenty years ago—before they'd become fools—when they were all newly tenured and idealistic and convinced their future held only good things for them: books and booze and a little extracurricular romance here and there. He had been one of them then. He had felt the way they did. But he had changed with the times, and they hadn't. They were failures and flops. They were ridiculous. Still, he couldn't help liking them a little, for old times' sake.

"Robbie Richter, you old bore, how ya doing?" Toby said. "Come down here," and he gave Robbie a sort of hug. Catherine, Toby's wife, gave Robbie a kiss.

Robbie was strangely moved.

And then Kenneth greeted him, and Nora. Then Stephanie and Mike, Sheila and Dave, Michelle and Graham, Allan and Sweet Jesus—the old gay couple—and Spencer, who was still not married but was nice anyhow. And Ron, who had found God. Leslee was standing behind them all, trying to get through. They were wonderful people, fools or not, and he liked them. If only they had kept up. But they hadn't kept up. They were still lost in literature.

Robbie hardened his heart against them. Zachary was right. It was too late. He could not save them.

Tears came to his eyes. He didn't know what was happening to him, but he knew he didn't want it to happen here in front of everybody. He turned around and trotted upstairs to get control of himself. Then he'd start all over again.

~

With the arrival of the fools, the entire party had moved outside. There was a food table and a drinks table and lanterns were hung from the trees, and bug zappers gave off little flashes of blue as they electrocuted random bits of insect life. The party was beginning to get noisy.

The pregnant women, Betz Rudin and Rosalie Kurtz, were seated on either side of a little table loaded with canapés and they were eating their way toward the middle. They had eaten all the tiny sausages wrapped in bacon and had started on the crackers and brie. There were also little circular sandwiches with some kind of fish paste.

Like all the faculty wives, the pregnant women had Ph.D.'s and they had teaching jobs. But only part-time, and at lesser universities and at lower academic rank. They were rivals, of course, and there were husbands involved, but Rosalie Kurtz and Betz Rudin had a grudging respect for each other. In particular Betz admired Rosalie's sexy body and her wiry red hair that never needed curling. Rosalie admired Betz's ruthlessness.

"This Olga stuff is a trip," Rosalie Kurtz said. "Have you read her books?"

"Just *Medea's Daughters*," Betz Rudin said. "That was enough for me. All those descriptions of tables and chairs, and that eternal present tense. And the bed that converts into a dining table. And the bookcase. God, I felt like I was fucking the furniture."

Rosalie Kurtz pondered this. The tables and chairs, she had thought, were meant as satire. And the convertible bed.

She decided to risk it. "Things are merely as we perceive them to be. Isn't that the point?" she said. So she was one up.

"One book was enough for me," Betz Rudin said.

"I've also read the one on Foucault." Rosalie Kurtz thought for a minute. "This Olga hates Foucault, I think, or maybe she just hates men. Try one of these little round jobs, Betz. It's shrimp paste . . . maybe."

Betz Rudin tried one. "*Very* good."

They ate the circular sandwiches for a while.

"But of course everybody hates men," Betz Rudin said, gaining on her.

"Everybody hates some men," Rosalie Kurtz said.

"Olga's on to something different."

"Like what?"

"Like hatred as some modern replacement for faith. You know those books *Comic Faith* and *Erotic Faith* by Whosiewhatzis? Well, this is more like deconstructive faith. Or hatred as faith."

Rosalie Kurtz thought about this. "What *is* this stuff we're eating?" she said. "God, I just can't stop."

"Or maybe hatred as power." Betz Rudin was pulling ahead. "Or hatred as deconstruction."

"It's all dog shit, of course, as Zacky would say."

"Which? The sandwiches or the book?"

Rosalie Kurtz laughed.

Betz Rudin laughed too and pushed aside the empty tray of food. "God, don't you hate these parties?" she said.

"No," Rosalie Kurtz said, regaining the upper hand, "I sort of like them."

~

Rosalie went inside to look for her husband and found him, alone, on the back deck chugging a drink. He was well on his way to being drunk.

"Party, party," Rosalie said, only mildly sarcastic.

"I'm getting some air," Zachary said. "That lesbian gives me a pain in the ass."

"Which lesbian?" Rosalie said.

"Oh, for Christ's sake. Maddy Barker! Who else!"

"Concepcion, for one. And maybe Betz Rudin for another. And maybe a good half of the Women's Collective."

"Concepcion never comes to these things."

"*Is* Maddy a lesbian?" Rosalie frowned. "I don't think she is."

"She's a ballbuster, whatever she is."

"We're all ballbusters according to you," she said. "Mistah Kurtz! He busted!" Zachary winced. "Poor Zacky, you've got a headache. That's why you're cranky."

"I'm not cranky."

"Of course you are. You've got a headache."

"I *haven't* got a headache."

"Everybody gets headaches, and when they do, they get cranky."

Zachary tried to remain calm. He tried to think pleasant thoughts. But all he could think was: this is why—some day—I will kill her.

"I haven't got a headache, Rosalie, and I am not cranky." He spoke very slowly. "Do you understand?"

"Of course I understand. Anyway, it's not your fault."

He waited and she waited.

"I get headaches myself," she said.

"WHERE IS THAT FUCKING OLGA!" he shouted, and his voice carried out over the neighborhood and returned to him only slightly diminished.

~

At that moment, at the front of the house, Olga pushed the door gently open and came inside. Behind her was Francis Xavier Tortorisi, her neighbor in Faculty Terrace. They made an odd couple: tubby Tortorisi and Olga, tall and mysterious. She wore a black dress, long and unfashionably severe, and granny shoes that laced up the front. Her hair was folded back in a French twist. She wore no jewelry. She didn't look any age in particular and it was hard to say if she looked attractive or not.

"What she looks like is trouble," Gil Rudin said. He had come inside to take a look and went back outside at once. But the fools crowded around, welcoming her and saying how much they liked her books and how lucky they all felt to have her here even for just a while. It was nice, an honor, it was terrific.

Cynthia Richter gave up hoping for Robbie to come downstairs and began to make the introductions.

Someone went to get her a drink—white wine, please, Olga said—and the others asked about her flight and was the apartment okay and where did she get that marvelous dress? They were sincere. They were warm. The fools, at their very best.

Finally Cynthia asked Olga, had she known Francis Tortorisi before? In Paris? At Yale? Since, after all, they did arrive together.

Tortorisi was not a friend, Olga reassured her, just a neighbor in Faculty Terrace, but she hoped they'd become friends, she and Tortorisi and, for that matter, she and Cynthia too. It seemed a friendly place.

It seemed a very friendly place, she said, and Robbie, descending the stairs, heard her low, rich voice and wondered who this peculiar woman could be. And then he realized with a jolt that this must be Olga—good God, it *must* be Olga—and she was surrounded, trapped, by fools. Zachary would kill him.

"Professor Kominska!" he shouted, and fairly danced into the foyer. "I'm your host. I'm Robbie Richter."

Olga smiled and put out her hand.

A doggie whimper from above made Robbie turn away from Olga and look up the stairs. Ozzie was on the top step, wagging his tail.

"Oh! And this is my dog, Ozzie."

"How do you do, Ozzie," Olga said.

The fools drew back, just a little, and Tortorisi was heard to snicker. Someone handed Olga her drink.

"I mustn't have closed the door tight," Robbie said. "Ozzie hates parties. He hates it when we have guests. He pees."

Olga was taking him in, and in. He would be very useful.

"He peed on my trousers, just as you all were arriving—my brown twills—and I had to change, and poor Ozzie didn't know what to make of it. He's not good with company." He was desperate to explain. "Ozzie has a scholar's disposition . . . "

One of the fools, unable to endure another minute of this, suddenly shouted, "White wine? Something? Please, let me get you a drink!"

"She already has a drink," someone said.

Cynthia Richter stood silent, wringing her hands.

Robbie turned to go upstairs with the dog.

Olga smiled generally at the fools and particularly at the retreating Robbie, and then she took the arm of the man who offered her white wine and they strolled together out of the foyer and down the lawn toward the drinks table.

"And your name?" Olga said.

"Oh, I'm just the Chairman," he said. "Sorry about that, back there."

"The Chairman," she said.

"Well, yeah," he said. "Until they close us down, I guess. Two white wines, Daryl? Please?" He turned back to her and noticed she was staring at Daryl. "This is Daryl," he said, "fifth year, comp lit, very gifted. And this is Professor Kominska, our guest of honor." He saw they were assessing one another. "You've met? No?"

"The cab," Daryl said, and Olga, at the same time, said, "Hmmm."

She put aside her glass of white wine and accepted a new one from Daryl's hand and smiled a little smile, collusive.

Daryl, nervous, fingered his bushy red beard.

Then Zachary Kurtz descended and Olga was whisked away, the property, at last, of the young and the Turkish.

∼

Zachary led her over behind the drinks table where everybody could see they were having a private conversation. It was a safe zone, universally understood as forbidding approach. Nobody would dare to interrupt them here.

"Just ignore him," Zachary said, "he's a fool. Good-hearted and well-intentioned but, I'm sorry to say, utterly without vision. A fool."

"The Chairman?"

"He can't help it," Zachary said. "It's a generational thing. You'll understand once you're here for a while. Let me give you a brief rundown."

Olga put her mind on hold and summoned up her subconscious.

"The faculty breaks down into two camps, along generational lines, but not totally. I mean, there's Eleanora Tuke—she's the great big one over there in pink—and she's old . . . oldish . . . mid-fifties, but she knows what's going on in the discipline and she recognizes that English departments are a thing of the past. She's good. A pain in the ass sometimes, but good. The pretty one she's with, Gil Rudin, is good too if you can forget his Hollywood background. You probably know his work: *Metaphilosophy and Dissonance*, *The Hypothetical Unconscious*, et cetera, et cetera. He's big. He's good. He's working on sexuality now, from Freud to Foucault and beyond. He's good. And the one joining them, the butch one, that's Maddy Barker. A star theorist. Gynocritic of nunneries in the Fourteenth Century. Appropriate, if you ask me, but she's good. Very big career, very touchy. Gay, of course. And then there's Concepcion. She's gay too, but they don't get along. Concepcion teaches Chicana Lit—please note, Chica*na*, not Chica*no*—and Barthes and gender stuff. And Leroy O'Shea, he's the Black, he teaches African American and African Anglophone, but he's okay. He's pretty good and tending toward really good. So the Chicanos and the Blacks are good. And we'll be hiring an Indian next year and maybe an Eskimo. We've got the multicultural bag sewed up. So, you see, it pretty much does divide along generational lines, except for the Tuke. Oh, and Robbie, of course. Robbie seems like an asshole a lot of the time, and he's hung up on theory—he thinks theory is what's in question here, rather than the larger picture, which, needless to say, he just doesn't get—but he's okay, Robbie. He's good." He took a breath. He was a little drunk, a little dizzy. "You follow?"

"We must talk," Olga said, her voice low, her accent pronounced. "But not now."

Abruptly she turned and walked to the other side of the drinks table, out among the people, so to speak, a movement that was generally interpreted as permission to approach. Zachary pursued her, but he was not quick enough, and by the time he caught up to her Olga was already the property of Gil Rudin and the very pregnant Betz.

"What ho!" Gil Rudin said, and snorted at them.

"I'm Betz," Betz Rudin said, and shook Olga's hand.

"And I'm Rosalie," Rosalie Kurtz said, coming up from behind. "We're pregnant."

"But I'll deliver first," Betz said.

"And I'll deliver better," Rosalie said.

Everyone laughed to make it seem like a joke.

Cynthia Richter approached, moving solemnly across the grass. She was escorting a black man and a white woman, both splendid to look at, and she was trailed by a delicious young woman in a dress of chartreuse spandex.

"Cynthia!" Zachary said. "You've brought us Moo and Leroy! I was just talking about you Leroy. And Concepcion! Quite a dress! What is that made of, rubber? Lookit," he said to Cynthia, "where the hell is Robbie, anyhow? Isn't he coming to his own party? We've got the whole group here now, if Robbie was here. Shee-it." He had begun to slur his words.

"The dog!" someone shouted, laughing, and then Robbie's high, nervous voice rang out, "Here, Ozzie. Come on, sweetie. Ozzie! OZZIE!" and his voice ascended, slipping more out of control as he pursued Ozzie wildly through the crowd, the dog yipping and dodging between legs and behind chairs. All across the lawn people stepped aside, jostling one another, spilling drinks, amused or annoyed. "What the hell's going on?" Zachary said, and as he said it Ozzie appeared in the middle of their small circle, cornered suddenly and frightened. He crouched back on his haunches, growled, and looked around at them. Then, without warning, he hurled himself at Zachary Kurtz. Zachary screamed, a high feminine scream, and tried to break away from the dog. But Ozzie wrenched his trouser leg back and forth, tugging and jerking, a dog possessed, until the material gave way with a comic ripping sound and Ozzie took off toward the house, a large chunk of Zachary's trouser leg hanging from his jaws. Zachary stood where he was, disbelieving, shaken, and looked down at his thin white leg, exposed to the knee.

Robbie appeared, out of breath, and saw what had happened. "Oh

God," he said and made a despairing sound, a whimper. He turned and ran back to the house.

~

The party had gone on and on and the fools had continued to laugh and drink while the young Turks had continued to compete for time with Olga. They all stood outside on the grass, drinking and carrying on. The noise was terrific.

Olga longed to be alone with her thoughts so she put on her dark glasses. By an act of the will she closed herself off from the talk and laughter and, encased in this invisible shell of privacy, made her way through the little knots of conversation to the comforting silence of the house. She went up the stairs to the bathroom and closed the door behind her. She turned the lock.

There was this Kurtz to consider, and his little conspiracy. A small man. An ambitious man. He wanted to be at the center of things, she could see that, and thus far he seemed to be destined for that role. Still, she felt she could not care for him. He did not appeal to her; worse, he did not even interest her, at least as he was now. She would have to find something more challenging in him—some wit, some irony, perhaps even criminal intent—if he were to be at the center.

Then there was Daryl, the cabdriver/bartender. He was a fifth year student in comp lit and therefore very likely unbalanced. Poor Daryl. He wanted to fit in, whatever the cost. Her mind raced ahead and she could see, dimly, that the cost for Daryl would be high indeed, extreme. Mentally she crossed him out. She did not write that kind of book. She shifted uncomfortably on the bathtub rim.

And all those women, quiet and powerful and full of life. Who were they and what did they want? They would be next.

She breathed in deeply, closed her eyes, and let the air out slowly, slowly, between pursed lips. She rolled her head to one side, then to the other, and let it hang limp, her chin on her chest. She stayed this way for several minutes.

Then it came to her. The book, despite the intentions of Kurtz and

Company, must in fact be about power. Who could care about English departments and Theory departments and the petty ambitions of petty academics? She would not write that kind of book. She would not even read that kind of book.

Her book would be about power.

She thought about this: academics would provide the occasion. But at issue would be power. Power . . . and the folly of answered prayers.

Things would move faster now. She had the sense of an ending and the questions that would lead her there and soon she would be given a plot. This was, invariably, how things worked. Her heart began to beat fast with the pleasure of the chase.

She rose from her uncomfortable seat on the rim of the tub. She unlocked the door and went out. And at once she stumbled over Robbie Richter who was crouched there, as if he had been peeping in at the keyhole.

He stood up quickly, then gasped and grabbed at his thigh.

"Cramp," he said.

Olga looked at him.

"I wasn't spying," he said. "I just didn't know if there was anyone in there."

She continued to look at him.

"So I was just checking. At the keyhole."

"And that's not spying," Olga said.

"No. Well, yes, in a sense. Oh my God!" He scurried down the corridor to the bedroom.

Olga heard him lock the door and she heard Ozzie's joyous snuffling and then what sounded like crying. Robbie, it appeared, was having a nervous breakdown.

"It can't be helped," Olga said softly to herself. "It's happening." And she went slowly down the stairs to engage the women.

~

Cynthia Richter stood alone in the foyer, smiling, composed. She could have been greeting invisible guests.

Olga watched her for a moment and then said, "He's having a breakdown, your husband is." She pointed up the stairs.

"No," Cynthia said. "I don't think so."

"Nevertheless, he is."

Cynthia looked at her for a long moment. "You don't know what it's like," she said. "Nobody knows. I love him and I care for him. I try to keep up for him. I even read those terrible books. I read one of yours." Her eyes filled with tears. "It was horrible. I could barely stand it."

Olga took the woman into her arms and held her close. She said nothing. Cynthia began to cry, silently, and then she stopped.

"Sometimes," Cynthia said, "sometimes I think that all I really want is endless quiet, no sound at all, no Robbie talking, talking, talking. But then . . . I love him."

Olga nodded, accepting contradictions as behovely, and moved on, resolute, to the other women.

~

"The funny thing," Rosalie Kurtz said, "and you'll find this out for yourself, the funny thing is that poor Zachary is not what he seems. In a way, he's really only a fool in multicultural clothing. He despises them, and he wants to crush them out of existence because of what they stand for, but the truth is that Zachary reads novels in secret. For pleasure."

"We all have our vices," Olga said.

"He tells people what they want to hear, anything they want to hear. He manipulates people."

Olga noticed the slightly simian quality of Rosalie's pretty face. In a few years, if she did not soften, she would turn into a monkey. Olga smiled to herself. Rosalie Kurtz would be useful.

"You want to destroy him," Olga said. "This Zachary."

"He's ruthless. It's not a quality I admire.

"It's not a pretty quality," Olga said.

"The thing I'm saying is, my Zachary is not what he seems."

"That's good," Olga said.

Rosalie paused over this. "By which you mean?"

"It complicates the equation," Olga said. "Complexity is good, both in life and in books, is this not true?" Her accent was positively Hungarian.

~

"I don't trust you, you know," Betz Rudin said. "None of us does, if you want the truth."

"The truth is good," Olga said, "but dangerous."

"It's that accent of yours that comes and goes. It bothers people."

"Yes."

"It bothers me."

"You're wise not to trust me. I'll write it all down, you know."

"I know that," Betz Rudin said. "I don't think Gil knows it. Or Zachary Kurtz."

"They don't know it. They don't even suspect it."

The two women smiled, a kind of collusion.

There was a moment of silence, weighted.

"I married Gil for his money," Betz Rudin said. "And for his big dick. I'm one of those women who likes them big."

"And now you're pregnant."

"For the money. Or rather for the marriage. He's like Henry the Eighth, he wants an heir. I'm the third wife. And I'll be the last."

"Hmm," Olga said.

Betz leaned close and kissed Olga on the mouth.

"We understand each other," Betz Rudin said.

"Up to a point," Olga said.

~

And so they were opening up to her, completely, unwisely, in the course of this long and trying evening. She was exhausted, or nearly. But she had to go on. She approached Maddy Barker, who had drifted away from the party and was once again standing alone in the dining room studying "The Scream."

"It's an enlargement," Olga said.

"A gross enlargement," Maddy said.

They stared for a while at the picture and then Olga stared for a while at Maddy. Maddy had dark circles under her eyes now, and her electrified hair seemed to fly out from her head, wilder, straighter, more frightening than before. Maddy let herself be stared at.

At last, when the time seemed right, Maddy turned to Olga and said, "Do you know what I want?" Maddy knew that women were in every way superior to men and she wanted to want them. And yet her lesbian affairs were often more political than emotional and, shamefully, she had secret heterosexual urges for which she hated herself. Deep down she suspected that sex was not what she wanted at all. What she wanted was perfection. She wanted to be perfect and she wanted the world to acknowledge it. At once.

"Do you know what I want?" she said again.

"Yes," Olga said.

"I want a little stranger in my bed," Maddy murmured intending it to sound provocative. Indeed, intending it to sound like the proposition it was. But something went wrong, and it came out sounding lonely, wistful, and she as innocent as a child.

Olga kissed her lightly on the cheek and said, "There will be many strangers. Many, many little strangers in your bed." And then she drifted off in her long, severe dress and her granny shoes, seeking whom she might devour.

She was, in fact, seeking Eleanora Tuke.

~

Eleanora was eager to converse.

"I've read all your books," she said. "I've read everybody's books."

Olga didn't say anything.

"And I follow pop culture too. Painting, sculpture, poetry—the scatology poets, even—and the music industry, top to bottom. And I know all the sit-coms. And the trash at the supermarket check out: "*The Enquirer*, *The Star*, *People*, you name it."

Olga wasn't expected to say anything.

"I *know* everything," she said. "I'm cultural history in a woman's body. I just want to teach it all, all at once, to everybody."

"This is what you want," Olga said, and added, "this is a problem."

"It is *the* problem," Eleanora said. "To be so vast, to want so much, to have so much to give."

"Yes," Olga said, "but it can be done." And she wondered, how, but how?

~

"A lovely evening," Olga said to Cynthia and Robbie.

Cynthia was at the door, saying goodbye to her guests, and Robbie had come downstairs to stand by her side. He had been up and down many times in the course of his party, getting hold of himself and starting over, but always something new and awful had happened, and now he was making his final appearance of the evening without ever really having been there at all. His smile was frozen in some kind of terrible grimace.

Zachary Kurtz, who had sent Rosalie on ahead with the Rudins and had lingered at the bar in hopes of driving Olga home, suddenly announced his presence as if he were a surprise. "I'm here!" he said, a bit astonished himself. His little mustache glistened with sweat. He was quite drunk now and had ceased to notice that one leg, thanks to Ozzie, was bare to the knee.

"Listen," he said to Olga, "I'll drive you home. I want to whisper in your ear." He left them and wobbled down the front walk, a rare sight indeed, and with some difficulty he wrenched open his car door and fell into the driver's seat. He straightened up, alert for a moment, and sped off crazily into the dark, having forgotten all about Olga. The group on the steps stared after him.

"What a skinny leg," Tortorisi said.

"How indelicate to notice," Olga said.

"How hard not to," Tortorisi said.

She smiled at him, and he at her, and his heart gave way. He was witty and she appreciated him, even though he was fat and untenured. An understanding, he felt, could not be very far away.

Everyone was gone. That left Olga and Tortorisi to walk back to Faculty Terrace by themselves. They seemed pleased with this arrangement.

Olga thanked Cynthia and Robbie, then Robbie and Cynthia. She went down the path and waved. Fat Tortorisi waddled along behind her.

At the bend in the road Olga turned to wave goodnight. She was just in time to see Robbie Richter sink to his knees and Cynthia crouch down to support and comfort him. Not altogether unlike the Pieta.

Irony, Olga told herself, was the stuff of life.

4

"Does this mean I'm accepted to your Foucault seminar?"

"Of course not."

"But, I mean, we're friends now and everything. And I really want to be in it."

"Wanting things is good. Getting them is not always good."

He began to pout.

Peter Peeks and Olga were lying side by side in her bed. They had just engaged in highly athletic sex for the second time in an hour and, what with jet lag and the drain on her patience caused by last night's reception, Olga was not in a mood to placate the very young.

"Don't pout," she said, "it's unattractive."

"I don't think you're being fair," he said.

And he said, "I lost my job because of you."

"Why *can't* I be in it?" he said. "I *want* to."

Olga turned to look at him, nude and splendid in his firm young body. He was truly an innocent. Expert in the crafts of sex and personal politics—he would always get what he wanted—he was completely innocent of fear and feeling, of evil without and within. His innocence moved her. With her index finger she traced invisible lines across his brow She tried to see him as he might be one day, if he were ever touched by experience.

"Don't," he said, brushing her hand from his brow.

"Poor puppy," she said and nibbled at his ear.

"Don't," he said. And then, pitiably, "I love Foucault. To me Foucault is a god."

"Up to a point," she said.

"Well then, why can't I be in your seminar?"

She propped herself on her elbow and gazed into his blue and empty eyes. What could be done with him? After a moment she decided to indulge him simply because he was such a beautiful thing.

"You're beautiful," she said and breathed into his ear.

"Don't," he said.

She let her hand explore his nipples.

"Don't," he said.

Her hand moved down to his waist, and a little lower, and a little lower. Then she stopped.

"Lower," he said.

And after a minute he said, "Don't stop."

She mounted him then and rode him and for a long time they thrashed around on the sheets and eventually he screamed, a jubilant sound, a kind of innocent alleluia, and they fell away from each other.

They rested silently for quite a while.

"*Now* am I accepted to your seminar?" he said.

"I have other plans for you," she said, inventing, since she had no idea what those plans might be.

And at once it came to her, this time more clear in its implications: power, she thought, and the folly of answered prayers.

"You'll be my spy," she said darkly, "Peter Peeks."

5

The doorbell was ringing as Olga stepped out of the shower. She threw on her silk kimono and tied a towel around her hair and, very like an apparition, materialized at the door.

Zachary Kurtz stepped back at the sight of her. The silk robe clung to her body and the white towel gave her an exotic air, but it was her feet that troubled him most. They were long and thin and naked. They were very exciting.

"I was expecting you," she said, "but not so soon."

He was staring at her feet.

"Leave off the feet," she said, with a vaguely Slavic accent.

She sat him down in the living room and went off to dress.

The feet!

Zachary was very disturbed by her feet. He was a young—youngish—man of considerable gifts. He was acknowledged as a brilliant teacher and a first-rate scholar. He had great plans for his career and great plans for the university, and was everything to founder now on the rocks of a foot fetish? He moved a hand tentatively to his crotch. He didn't care about feet. He never had. And yet he was overwhelmed by this desire to lick her long thin toes, to lap at her ankles and her heels, to worship quite literally at her feet. He felt his blood pressure shoot dangerously upward.

When Olga returned she had on jeans and a sweatshirt and her hair was pulled behind, held by a rubber band. She wore no makeup. On her feet, Zachary saw, she was wearing sneakers.

"Would you like some tea?" she said.

"I could do with a beer," he said. "After a big night I find that a beer really helps."

"Or coffee?"

"No beer?"

"And I have some very bad cookies."

"Jesus," he said.

She watched him as he floundered around for a place to begin, and then she took pity on him.

"About your plans," she said. "Let's get down to it."

"Really?"

"That's why I'm here," she said. "And that's why you're here."

He had a filthy hangover, and he was still upset about her feet, and he worried, frankly, about the wisdom of laying everything out in front of her, but he called to mind his own good sense and his talent and his ambitions, and he said, "What the hell," and let rip.

His plans were in two parts.

The first part was to elect a new chairman, the second part was to dissolve the department and form a new and different one.

"Now let me explain," he said.

The first part was beautiful in its simplicity. At the end of winter quarter there would be a faculty meeting to choose a new chairman. Everybody had tacitly agreed it would be Robbie Richter. Robbie was next in line by seniority, but more important than that, he was a bridge between the theorists and the fools and he was the only one who could command votes from both sides. But—and it was a major but—he'd be only a figurehead chairman.

"And behind the figurehead chairman will be . . . . ?"

Zachary smiled, modest and wicked both.

"Now here's the second part," he said.

At the beginning of spring quarter, as soon as Robbie was installed as chairman, they would hold another faculty meeting and would vote to dissolve the English department. That is, they would vote to create a new department—he made capital letters in the air—The Department of Theory and Discourse.

"Mmm," she said.

"Listen, listen," he said.

This department was his dream; it would revolutionize university studies. It would include Comp Lit, Mod Thought, and all the little language departments—French, Russian, Spanish, you name it. It would take on all written documents, equally and with absolute indifference to the author's reputation or the western canon or the nature of the writing itself—whether it was Flaubert's *Bovary* or a 1950 tax form or the label on a Campbell's soup can; are you following me?—and subject them all to the probing, thrusting, hard-breathing analysis of the latest developments in metaphilosophical transliterary theory. Whatever those theories might be. Wherever they might lead.

His face began to grow very red.

He would found this department, he said, and he would run it. At first with Robbie Richter as figurehead chair, and then with a complete takeover, once the fools' voting capacity had been dimmed by retirement or by his actively driving them out.

"It will be wonderful. It will be great," he said.

His face was crimson and he was gasping for breath.

"And what about the people who want to teach literature?" Olga asked. "What happens to them?"

He made a T sign. Time out. He sat there, purplish, trying to breathe into his cupped hands. After a while he got his wind back and went on.

That was the beauty part, he explained. They could just remain behind and teach in a program of Eng Lit. A program, not a department. A program is answerable to a department. But we'll let them have a little autonomy and they can teach their Chaucer and their Shakespeare, whatever.

"They'll be separate," Olga said, "but not quite equal."

"You got it," he said, and rushed ahead. This second part, that looked so difficult, was actually easy. He had the votes of all the new people; they'd been hand-chosen with this in mind. He had already softened up the Deans and the faculty senate. And the President too, of course.

Olga smiled openly, but he did not seem to notice.

What he had in mind was this, he said. She would make the weight of contemporary theory *felt*. She would serve as a wedge between the new, advanced Department of Theory and Discourse and the laggards, the lost fools who would make up the tiny, diminished Program in English Studies. She would be the lever to overturn the department as it now stood.

"A weight," she said. "A wedge. A lever."

"Well, you know what I mean," he said, and he was sincere.

"And I'm to effect this revolution all by myself?"

"Because you're an outsider. Because you'll count with the Deans. Because you're *other*."

She raised an eyebrow. He had no idea how other she was.

"Lookit," he said. "The Deans will believe anything if it's dramatic enough. The most, the first, the best, that's all they want to hear. I've told them all about you. You're the leading woman theorist in the world, I told them. You turned down Yale and Cornell and Irvine to come here. You've been in *Time* magazine, for Christ's sake."

"I've never been in *Time* magazine."

"Really? It doesn't matter. Nobody ever checks anything. They just believe what they're told. You've gotta understand: they're very ignorant, they're very insecure. I tell them you're the leading theorist in the world and, voila, you're the leading theorist in the world."

She listened.

"Besides, you're a woman, for Christ's sake."

She listened to him strategizing, and she cut away to her own sense of strategy, and then she continued listening to him once again.

He went on and on.

The odd word here, he was saying, the odd denunciation there. She could do it. No problem. He *knew* a single person could do it and he *knew* that she was the person. He was convinced of this, he said.

There was something, however, he did not say.

He was convinced of this because he had nearly pulled it off all by himself at Cornell. He would have succeeded, too, if only he hadn't made himself so visible. In this kind of revolution, the leader always got sacrificed, and this time the leader would not be old Zack. It would be Olga. And maybe Robbie Richter. But not yours truly.

He did not say that she was his point man. Nor did he say that she would get the flack and he would get the glory. No did he say—in the military imagery he tended to favor—that this was Armageddon, and that when the dust settled and the blood dried and the bodies of the fools had been cleared from the battlefield, Olga would be long gone, a happy memory, a nervy European theorist who had served her time here and served it well. And he would be in charge.

He did say, "You can make it work."

He did say, "It's all for the best, of course. It's a *good* thing."

He did say, "It's not for myself. No way."

He paused. "So what do you think?" he said.

What she thought was this: nobody could care about such silliness, not even academics. Zachary was offering her a plot, trivial in origins and awful in its consequences, and if she were to use it, she would have to work miracles to overcome its dullness, its pettiness. She could perk it up with irony and wit. Satire, of course. But in the end she would have to make it matter. She would have to give it some kind of moral resonance. And how, working with such flimsy material, could she accomplish *that*?

"Well?" he said.

"I'll have to think," she said.

She said, "I have certain gifts."

"And I'm here to put them to use," she said, sounding rather French.

And then she stumbled onto it. She said, almost flirting, "You're obsessed by power, aren't you."

"By rank," and he felt himself grow hard. "I like to be on top."

"And you have needs, prayers you want answered."

"Well, I'd hardly put it that way."

"It would be foolish to put it that way?"

"You got it."

"Let me think," she said.

She had the occasion, the sense of an ending, a rickety and boring plot. None of this interested her much. At issue, however, was power and the special ruin achieved by answered prayers, and this interested her very much, and more, as she thought about it. And more.

"I'll do my best," she said.

"You'll help? You will? Then I'm home free," he said.

"In a sense," she said.

They shook hands and parted.

They were uncertain, a little distrustful, but both of them felt better now they had set the plot in motion.

6

It was noon on Sunday, the anachronistic church bells had bonged their twelve leaden bongs, and there was discontent throughout the campus. Discontent was a permanent presence here, of course, but today, less than twenty-four hours after the arrival of the new person—the divine Olga, the harbinger of bright change—discontent had taken on a new dimension. Only chez Olga was there peace.

~

At the edge of campus, chez Richter, discontent was rapidly moving toward disaster. Robbie had not slept much of the night, and when he did sleep, he whimpered so continually that Cynthia had had no sleep at all. She wanted to bat him one—she had struck him early in their marriage, and it had got him under control for the moment, and it had been satisfying too—but she realized that, in a state like this, batting him would do no good. By dawn Robbie's whimpering had turned to tears.

It was noon now, the caterers' clean-up crew had come and gone, and Robbie was crying in longer and longer sieges. Earlier on, he had cried and stopped, cried and stopped, but as noon approached he seemed to give himself over to it as a permanent way of life. It crossed her mind that he might very well—single minded as he was about everything—simply cry his way from here to the grave.

"What, Robbie? What is it? Tell Cyn-Cyn."

But he only blubbered the more, muttering "Zachary" from time to time and, like a stab of pain, "Olga! Olga!"

She gave him his Equanil, a double dose, and sped off to the bakery for donuts. She was exhausted and she was frantic. Was Robbie losing it? Or was he just experiencing change of life?

And then, as she drove, a terrible thought came to her: he *is* becoming one of the fools.

It was a warm day, sunny, but she felt cold in her fingertips and cold in her heart. She was alone, with nobody to turn to for help. The children were useless. Megan was in New York becoming an actress and Robbie Jr. was still in jail for selling drugs. Ozzie was the only one who cared and Ozzie was a dog.

Poor Robbie. Poor crazy sweet old boring Robbie. Nobody knew him the way she knew him. And nobody realized what all this theory shit had cost him. She ached with her helpless love for him.

~

Maddy Barker was distressed. Small lines pinched the center of her forehead, and her mouth was grim, but as the church bells sounded twelve times, their leaden echo hanging in the warm air, she turned and smiled at Francis Xavier Tortorisi. He smiled back at her and took her hand.

It was their custom to have Sunday brunch together—a few eggs thrown on the frying pan, a little toast, some cut-up fruit, and lots of coffee, gossip, and more coffee. Then sometimes, if the mood was right, they would lie together, chastely, on Tortorisi's bed, fully clothed of course, and he would pleasure her. He did this by lying flat on his back while Maddy, lying flat on her back beside him, reached over with her left hand and gently played with his breasts. Tortorisi reminded her very much of her first lover, a matronly woman some thirty years her senior, who had taught her classics in freshman year college and who liked to be played with in just this way. After college Maddy had gone straight, so to speak, and she still had moments of terrible weakness for—ugh!—the penis, but since the days of her classics professor, sex had never been the same again.

With Tortorisi, who was scarcely a man at all, the issue was not sex but pleasure.

Today was not one of their days for pleasure because Maddy was in love with someone new and she was distressed. They were sitting on his sofa, Mozart playing in the background, and they were silent. When the church bells tolled, however, she turned and smiled at him and he smiled back. He took her hand.

"I want her," Maddy said, "I've got to have her." She kicked off her shoes and sat with her feet tucked under her.

"She's not French," Tortorisi said.

"What's that got to do with it?"

"I think she might be Austrian. Or Swiss. Somewhere in between languages."

Maddy looked at him fiercely, her eyes growing smaller and more intense.

"Not that it matters," he said.

"Do you suppose she's in on Kurtz's plot?" Maddy said. "Do you think she knows about it?"

"Against me, you mean?"

She squeezed his hand. "Not you," she said.

"Kurtz won't rest till I'm out of here. He won't rest till I'm dead."

"Kurtz doesn't care about you," Maddy said, lying. "You're small beer to him."

"Small beer. I feel better already."

"You'll get tenure, stop worrying. Just write your novel. That's what you're *supposed* to be doing."

They were silent again for a while.

"If she wanted something," Maddy said, "if I knew something she wanted, and could get it for her . . ."

"I want something. I want tenure."

"Do you think she likes women? Or just men? Her books make you think she hates men, but I wonder."

"She's very attractive. She's sexy."

Maddy disentangled her hand from his and turned to stare at him. "What do you mean?" she said.

"She is. Sexy."

"Are you attracted to her? Francis? Do you want to do the dirty thing with her?" Her face took on that fierce, inquisitorial look that had terrified so many of the fools. "Tell me, I want to know, and I want to know right now. Do you want to have sex with that woman?"

"I've never had sex with *any* woman, so how would I know? Or anybody at all, for that matter. I've never thought about it. It's just too scary."

"Well, think now, dammit."

He smiled to himself and looked away from her. He had an unusual, dreamy look on his face and it turned to a look of surprise. "I suppose I could try it," he said, "if she wanted. I mean, if she really wanted." He raised his eyebrows playfully.

At once Maddy snatched up her shoes and put them on. She shouldered her backpack.

"Do you want to go lie down and let me pleasure you?" he asked, apologetic.

"You're disgusting," she said. "A hetero disgust." And she left.

~

As the noon bells rang out there was disquiet too among the fools. But it was their ordinary disquiet of a Sunday: the quarter would begin tomorrow, classes to prepare, the syllabi, the book lists, and, for many of them, children visiting with their eternal problems—money and jobs and failing marriages. For the fools it was an academic disquiet, with little real desire to kill and a pleasant sense of busyness beneath it all. Life was tough, life was a bitch, but it was a good life, it was the best life. They had seen Kurtzes come and go. In their time they had had their own lesbians and gays—Allan and Sweet Jesus had the best marriage on the west coast—and they had had their own young Turks and they had had affairs, some of them, with each other's spouses. But decently, they would say, without rancor and without the vulgarity of raw ambition. The sexual romps of these new young Turks were passionless, political things, and always with an agendum. What about romance? What about fun, for God's sake? Still, they knew that Kurtz would pass, and Rudin, and all their kind. They would not last. They could not last. They would disappear, as the fools themselves had disappeared, into the great leveling compost heap of the department. Ripeness was all.

~

Things were overripe, decaying, up on Presidential Hill.

The President lay in bed listening to the noon bells. He felt abandoned, naked unto his enemies in his old age. What was that quote? And who had said it? His mind tended to wander these days.

He felt deserted by his supporters, by the university trustees, by the faculty he had nourished over all these years. Why were they all such rats? Except Missy, of course. She was not a rat. Missy was his only consolation. A woman of strength and principle. She had enough energy for both of them, as well she might, since she was thirty to his sixty. Missy was a union organizer for computer firms and she had been up since dawn working on a position paper. What a tigress. What a girl.

Poor Missy had suffered in this marriage. People said ghastly things about her when actually all she had done was marry him. He had been a bachelor for fifty-five years and then he had married a younger woman. A lot younger. Was that so bad? So what if she'd been twenty-five at the time? So what if she'd been his graduate student? Didn't everybody marry their graduate students? And why blame Missy? Why not blame him?

But of course they did blame him, that was one of the problems. He'd married her, a quiet dignified serious marriage, and then, bango, there was an earthquake. Literally. It didn't seem like much at the time, a whole lot of shaking going on—who said that, he wondered, a whole lot of shaking going on?—but when the shaking stopped, the damage was incredible. A hundred million, it looked like. And when the engineers were done their survey, it looked more like two hundred million. Then the scandals began. The government alleged fraudulent billing for research projects, first to the tune of twenty million, then for two hundred million, and most recently for three hundred million. At the same time, female professors began suing for sexual harassment—in the law school, the business school, the medical school—and they were winning, the bitches, and costing the university a fortune. There was a sensational murder, a number of suicides, a rape in the middle of the quad in the middle of the night. These things had nothing to do with him, except that they happened on university grounds, but the university, and therefore the President, took the blame. Finally there were a series of extortion cases—in the gymnasium, in the student center, in the chemistry labs—and if that weren't enough, a messenger boy in the Dean's office was accused and found guilty of pushing crack cocaine, to staff and students both. This was a terrible blow to morale, because the young man was black and cheerful and the secretaries thought he looked adorable skimming around on his blue roller blades.

If only the scandals would stop. If only they would just go away. If only another earthquake would hit and just obliterate the whole fucking mess. If only. If only.

The President cried soundlessly into his pillow.

~

The great had much to bear, and the little had only some. At the foot of Presidential Hill, in tiny cottages built for the college servants of an earlier century, all the little people were at work.

Concepcion snuggled abed with her pink panda and her well-thumbed Barthes. She loved tradition, and so she had lit the vigil light before her shrine of the Virgin, and she had made a cup of cinnamon tea, and now, having smoothed away the wrinkles in the bed, gave herself up to the erotic play of her beloved *Mythologies*. Perfect joy would have meant the addition of plump little Suzie Sweezie cuddled at her backside. But life was not perfect and joy itself was transitory, and so Concepcion settled for Bathes and for cinnamon tea.

Leroy O'Shea, black and quite generally considered beautiful, sat at his desk plunged deep in the close analysis of diction and caesura in the works of Ma Rainey. Across from him at a facing desk, sat Moo Wesley Rudin, white and winsome in her long blond hair. They made a very pretty picture. Leroy and Moo were lovers of long standing, a cause of some agitation to Gil Rudin, Moo's previous husband, but a joy to each other and to their admiring friends. Moo was an illustrator of children's books and she was working now on an interracial theme, a sort of Dick and Jane story with Leroy as a black Dick and herself as a white Jane. They made adorable children. As the noon bells tolled, she looked up at Leroy, and they exchanged a smile, sad and loving, and then returned to their work. It was their great sorrow that, though they never ceased to try, they could not have children of their own.

And all the lecturers scattered about the campus—living in guest rooms, in attics, in converted garages; living, in one instance, in the library and, in another, in the gym—all the lecturers were at their work and all of them were discontent, but only a little, and in an academic way.

～

Chez Kurtz, it was not so, for discontent had turned to misery. Long before the church bells tolled noon, Zachary Kurtz had convinced himself that Olga was mad for him, that she was his sworn ally, that his revolution was already in progress.

He was walking home in the hot sun, and it took real effort to believe these things, particularly now that the euphoria had passed and his headache was in full bloom. He paused in front of his house and looked ruefully at his little car, half on the curb, half off, just as he had left it in his stupor last night. Guilt began to set in on top of the headache and he wanted only to take an Alka Seltzer and lie down and think consoling thoughts about Olga and her long thin feet.

The noon bells tolled just as he was entering the kitchen.

And Rosalie, as if she were possessed by the devil of discontent, looked up from the sink where she was repotting plants, and said, conversationally, "What makes you think Olga is going to take part in your little conspiracy?"

All his confidence was shattered. Rosalie was right: Olga disliked him, she would betray him, she would make him look like the asshole he was. He felt the blood rush to his head and it was all Rosalie's fault.

"Don't you ever listen?" he said. "Are you deaf as well as stupid?"

"I was expressing interest," she said. "I just asked a simple question."

"You've never asked a simple question in your life!"

She stared at him as if he were a lunatic.

"And don't stare at me like that! I'll be glad when you've had the damn baby. I think it's affecting your mind."

This was too much. "Mr. Reason," she said. "Mr. Theory. Blow it out your ass, Shorty!"

"Typical," he said, and fixed himself an Alka Seltzer.

"You've got a headache, that's why you're cranky."

"STOP SAYING THAT!"

Rosalie murmured into the sink: "Mistah Kurtz. He dead."

Limping with rage and frustration, Zachary retired to his study. He downed the Alka Seltzer in one long gulp and then sat at his desk waiting for it to take effect. The quarrel had depressed him with its low level of articulacy. But lately everything depressed him.

He hated the day after official receptions. He hated everything he had said and done, he hated everything he could remember, and most especially he hated the fact that he couldn't remember everything. How, for instance, had the evening ended? He knew he had driven home because he had just seen the car out front. He knew he had come home alone, that is, unaccompanied by some little tootsie to warm his bed. And he knew—well, he *hoped*—he had not detoured for a midnight run on Maddy or Concepcion, the lesbian delights of the department. But these known facts were only marginally reassuring; it was what he didn't know that worried him.

The Alka Seltzer had not yet kicked in, but he was determined to work anyhow. He picked up Olga's *The Death of the Patriarch*, not his favorite book. To be honest, he had never succeeded in getting through it. He read the first page and then the second, searching out the memorable lines, a *mot* even—something to quote to her for a quick dazzle—but by page three he hadn't yet hit anything he liked and he was beginning to feel sleepy. The pain in his head was ghastly, and his mouth tasted like the cat had slept in it, and Rosalie was driving him out of his mind. He flung Olga's book across the room.

In a moment he got up and locked the door. Then he unlocked his desk and took out his worn, beloved copy of *Emma* and stretched out on the couch for a good read.

In time the pain abated somewhat.

~

Beyond the campus, beyond the sound of those tolling bells, all was peace. Except chez Rudin, where Betz had suddenly gone into labor. Except chez Tuke, in the City, where Eleanora was throwing a brunch for twenty at Campton Place. But even they would not remain forever safe, untouched by Olga, untouched by fate.

~

Daryl sat in his cab at Airport Arrivals and waited for his wife. He felt like killing her, truly. She was a beauty and restless, and so her job as a flight attendant was perfect for her, but it was murder for him. He worried about her safety and he worried about her beauty and most of all he worried that she was unfaithful to him. But his best friend, a Thomasite priest in Denver, assured him he had nothing to worry about.

She was a good woman, Father Owen said and above reproach.

She was Caesar's wife, Father Owen said.

Father Owen said she was a lesson to us all.

Daryl waited, and had been waiting for two hours now, and still his beautiful wife had not arrived. The bitch. The whore. He knew she was cheating on him, he was sure of it. Where, for example, did she get that turquoise ring?

The airport clock struck twelve and, for no reason at all, Daryl thought: I'll tell Olga. She'll know what to do.

~

Olga herself sat, cosy, at her desk. It had been a busy morning, what with Peter Peeks and then Zachary Kurtz, and she was glad for this stretch of time by herself. She had finished her syllabi and she had finished preparing her classes. She was engaged now in doing her thoughts.

Her apartment was on the second floor, and the big window in the study looked out on the street and, at an angle, on the garden and the swimming pool beyond. At any moment she cared to look, she could see this little world go by: her colleagues walking the dog, taking out the trash, entering or leaving the apartments of friends. Or of enemies. Or of lovers. And she could see who was swimming and what they wore, and, since voices carried clearly from the pool, she could sometimes even hear what they said—especially at night, especially in the dark. She could hear and she could see without being seen herself. This was an aerie ideally suited to her needs.

In a short while she finished doing her thoughts.

She got out her notebook and made cryptic little jottings on the reception of the night before, on Zachary Kurtz and big Eleanora Tuke, on Robbie Richter and Gil Rudin, and on all the exciting women, and on Peter Peeks. She didn't bother with the ridiculous plot.

Satisfied, exhilarated, she closed the notebook and sat back, waiting for the doorbell to ring.

A moment later the doorbell rang.

7

Francis Xavier Tortorisi stood at the door, grinning nervously.

"I've brought you my novels," he said. "And the new manuscript." He handed her two very thin books but held on to the manuscript.

"Come in," Olga said.

"The manuscript isn't finished," Tortorisi said. "I'm blocked, actually."

"Come in," she said.

"The novels aren't very interesting. And the manuscript is dead on the vine."

"Come in here," she said. She grabbed his arm and led the way to the living room.

"They're all about sex," he said. "As an obsession."

She went into the kitchen to put on the tea. "I'm making tea," she said through the passway.

He sat down for a second and then got up and came over and leaned against the wall, looking in. They were face to face, with the passway between them. He was still clutching the manuscript.

"Constant Comment," she said. "It's my favorite tea."

"Just between you and me, I don't even know anything about sex," he said. "But everybody thinks I do."

"You must be a good writer," she said.

"I'm a fake," he said.

"That's what I mean," she said.

He laughed nervously.

She smiled at him.

"Usually I alienate everybody," he said.

"How?" she said. "Why?"

"I just do it. I find myself saying the wrong thing, something snide or superior, when really what I want is for them to like me, and they take offense of course, and I go right on and make it worse and worse until they can't wait to get away." He thought for a minute. "That's how I do it. I don't know why I do it."

"Yes."

"And I'm fat, of course."

"Yes."

"I don't know why I'm talking to you like this. You're practically a stranger, and you're new here besides, and I'm telling you things I've never told anybody except Maddy Barker. About myself, I mean."

"Yes."

"Maddy . . . " but he stopped himself.

"Yes?"

He looked into her deep brown eyes and fell silent. Did she hate men? Did she like women? Did she like *him*? He wanted to tell her every secret thing about himself.

"I pleasure Maddy," he said, reckless. "I don't care if you know."

He said, "Sex is an absolute mystery to me."

And he said, "I want to get tenure. I've got to. If I don't get tenure, I'll kill myself."

"And it depends on the new book?" She pointed to the manuscript he held clutched to his chest.

"Kurtz wants me out of here."

"Then what difference will the new book make?"

He looked puzzled.

"If he wants you out, surely he'll get you out. With the book or without it."

He saw her point.

"Come sit down," she said, and carried a tray into the living room.

On it were teacups and the teapot and a saucer of cookies she had found in the cupboard.

"Try one of these," she said. "They're bad, I think."

He ate a cookie and nodded. "Not so bad," he said. He reached for another.

She picked up one of his little novels, *Love Hostage*, and read the first paragraph. She looked up at him, surprised.

"Oh, you're quote unquote experimental," she said.

He nodded, glum.

"It's Joyce revisited. Anybody else?" she asked, flipping through the pages. "*At Swim-Two-Birds?*"

He nodded.

"Any Proust? Gide? Ronald Firbank?"

He nodded.

"I should have known," she said.

"But there's a lot of sex," he said, hopeful.

She tossed the book aside as if there were no point in looking at it further.

"It's sex as *obsession*," he said. "It's *symbolic*."

"Let me read the new thing," she said, and made him give her the manuscript. "Maybe you're approaching sex all wrong."

Did she mean actually or in his books?

"In your books," she said, knowing his thought, and she began to read his manuscript.

As if on cue, he fell asleep.

An hour passed and she put the manuscript down, both troubled and amused. It was not unlike one of her own early books, except that Tortorisi lacked irony and wit. And economy and daring. And energy. His characters were abstracted from earlier works of fiction, but he made nothing of them, not satire, not illumination. What his work proclaimed—and quite intentionally at that—was the death of the imagination.

She could see no way to save any of this.

She poured herself another cup of tea, cold now but no matter, and took it to her study to do her thoughts.

The phone rang and she snatched it up at once. It was Daryl, the cabdriver/bartender, and he was disturbed. No, he could not come and see her, she said. No, he could not come and talk. No, he could not be in her Foucault seminar. She had to go now, she said, and she hung up. That was that. She would not take responsibility for the Daryls of this world. She had seen enough of chaos.

With a conscious effort, she forced him out of her mind, and, she presumed, out of her life.

She sat at her desk and looked at the wall. She turned and looked out the window. At the pool somebody was swimming laps despite the coolness of the afternoon and there was a bunch of old-timers in the Jacuzzi. She didn't know any of them. But as she looked, a familiar figure—Zachary Kurtz—came barreling through the bushes intent on some mission. He disappeared up one of the walks on the far side of the complex. She made a mental note to find out who lived there. Maddy Barker? She smiled. Her subconscious was working double-time.

Peter Peeks appeared at the foot of her stairs. She glanced at her watch—5 o'clock—and then glanced back at him. He saw her. He was just standing there looking up toward the window.

He raised his eyebrows, offered himself with his hands out, palms up. He tempted her with a slow smile.

She thought of Tortorisi asleep in the living room and Peter Peeks desperate for experience and she nodded, yes, to Peter Peeks, and moved to the door to let him in. Peeks was, after all, a protégé of Zachary Kurtz and Kurtz was a determined enemy of Tortorisi. A little conflict would move the plot along nicely.

"Wow, cool," Peter Peeks said, as she stood aside and showed him into the living room.

Tortorisi woke up as they came in. He had been dreaming and there was a little bulge at his crotch. He moved his hand to cover it.

Nobody said anything.

Then the two men talked at once.

"I should go," Tortorisi said.

"Should I go?" Peeks said.

"I'll make a pot of tea," Olga said, and carried the tea tray back out to the kitchen, where she ran the water loudly and banged the kettle around. In her mind she was continuing to compose. "She ran the water loudly and banged the kettle around," she wrote, mentally, "while in the living room . . ." She smiled and banged the kettle some more.

In the living room Peter Peeks fell into awkward silence and Tortorisi into rage.

"These books are by you!" Peter Peeks said, just to say something.

"She's *reading* my books, unlike some people."

"I didn't know you had written any," Peter said.

"No, of course not. You presumed, I suppose, that they hired me to teach creative writing because they saw me clerking at K-Mart and felt bad for me."

"No, I . . ."

"Or, like your friend, Kurtz, that all real books are written by dead Europeans."

"No."

"Or that people like me aren't worth consideration. Because I'm fat and I don't look like a Californian and I don't belong to the theory set. Is that what you thought? You might be surprised, Peter Peeks, if you ever took the trouble to read one of my books and find out who I really am. I *am* somebody, you know. I'm not nobody."

Olga stopped rattling in the kitchen. "I'll be just a minute," she said.

"Can I read one?" Peter said, ready always to say the necessary thing. "When she's done, can I?"

"Why should I care if you read one? Read one if you want, or don't, what do I care?"

"I'll ask Olga if I can take it when she's done."

"They're in the library, you know. They're in the bookstore."

"I'll get one," Peter said. "I'll buy one."

They sat there looking at one another.

Olga came in carrying the tea tray. "I have some lovely tea," she said, "and a saucer of bad cookies."

There was silence.

"A little conflict?" she said, cheery about it.

"I'm sorry," Tortorisi said.

"Geez, Mr. Tortorisi," Peter said.

"I overreacted," Tortorisi said.

Tortorisi said, "I'm a little too sensitive."

And Tortorisi said, "Call me Tortorisi, okay? Never mind the Mister."

Peter smiled at him tentatively.

"Look at that smile," Olga said.

Tortorisi looked at it, and then he crossed his legs, and there was silence in the room once more.

"These cookies are very bad," Olga said, nibbling at one.

The two men reached for the cookies. Tortorisi pulled back. "You first," he said. Peter smiled and took the cookie.

"They're stale," Peter said.

"I found them in the cupboard," Olga said. "God knows how old they are."

"They're kind of nice," Tortorisi said, swallowing hard.

Everybody took another cookie.

"Tell me about this place," Olga said. "I want to know everything. About everybody."

They told her everything, some of it truthful, some of it fabricated, and they made no distinction between the two. They talked about everybody but Zachary Kurtz, since at least tacitly he was off limits, and they had a very good time.

～

The two men had just left to pick up a pizza when Zachary Kurtz appeared at the door.

"There's been a tragedy," Zachary said. "Can I come in?"

Olga smiled at the turn the evening was about to take and said, "Do you like pizza?"

Zachary was sweating despite the chill in the air. "What?" he said.

"Sure. Oh sure. Listen, there's been a tragedy—well, sort of. Can I sit down?"

She gestured toward the couch.

"Robbie Richter," he said, "seems to have had a nervous breakdown. Talk about wonderful timing!" And before she could respond, he said, "What's this?" and indicated Tortorisi's two thin novels lying on the coffee table. "You reading this stuff?"

"A breakdown?"

"Well, he can't stop crying. He keeps saying my name and your name and then he starts crying again." He tapped Tortorisi's books with a dirty fingernail. "This stuff's crap, you know."

"Poor Cynthia."

"Anyway, it looks like he's *hors de combat* for a little while anyhow. Classes begin tomorrow. Tuesday, really, but there are office hours and, you know, it all starts tomorrow."

"Perhaps he'll stop crying by tomorrow."

Zachary looked at her.

"Or by Tuesday."

"He's a mess," Zachary said. "It's been coming for a long time and now it's here. He's a mess."

"Poor Ozzie."

"Anyhow, this is the deal. He's got this course he always teaches, 'The Problem of Evil,' and it's very popular, lots of undergraduates sign up, and we wonder if you'd be willing to take it over for him this quarter? Now let me explain. I just saw the Chairman and I talked to Maddy Barker and to Concepcion and they're all agreed if you're agreed. But you're the pivotal signatory here. You'd postpone your feminist drama course until spring—which would be better anyhow because both Maddy and Concepcion are teaching their feminist courses this quarter and we don't have *any* feminist course in spring— and you could take over Robbie's 'Evil' course and you'd have a nice light spring quarter, same salary, that goes without saying, and you could really be a help around here as we clean up the department, restructure it, et cetera, et cetera."

Olga stood, listening.

"So what do you think?" Zachary said.

"You expect him to be sick all quarter? Is he very bad?"

"No, no. Oh Christ, no. He's *gotta* get better. And quick. I've got plans for him, as you know."

"This changes the equation," she said.

"Jesus," he said, "let's stick to the point. So what do you say about the 'Evil' course, for starters?"

"I don't know about staying for the spring," she said. "It depends on how the plot unfolds. But I'll do the course."

"Oh good," he said. "Oh great," he said.

"I'll change the title, though, for the sake of accuracy."

"It's always been called 'The Problem of Evil,'" he said. "With a subtitle: 'Hitler, Stalin, the Holocaust, Ecology'—it's *very* popular."

"I'll call it 'The Problem of Good.' Evil is finally not very interesting."

He was looking at her feet. "What size shoe do you wear?" he said. "You've got fantastic feet," he said.

"With no subtitle," she said.

There was laughter, then, outside the door. Someone rang the bell at the same time someone else knocked, and there was more laughter. Olga opened the door.

"Shit," Zachary said, and looked for some way of escape.

"We got beer, too," Tortorisi said, "I hope that's okay."

"And two pizzas," Peter Peeks said. "Medium. You get a lot more in two mediums than you get in a large."

They saw Zachary Kurtz scrunched up on the couch.

"Zack!" Peter Peeks said, guilty at being seen with the enemy.

"Kurtz!" Tortorisi said, instantly nasty.

Zachary stuck his legs out and sprawled. He belonged here. They didn't.

"You all know one another, I think," Olga said. "I'll see to things."

Effortlessly she steered Tortorisi into the living room with Zachary, set down the pizzas on the kitchen counter, dispensed with Peter Peeks who had followed her, trying to hide, and she had the kitchen to herself and her surprise and amusement. If conflict was what she wanted, she could not have planned it better.

But at once Peter Peeks reappeared, a knowing look on his face.
"What?" she said.

"They hate each other," he said. "They're talking about books."

"Take out these beers," she said.

As she spoke, Zachary loomed in the kitchen passway, his face crimson. He snarled at Tortorisi: "That's it, that does it," and his voice was furious, though he wore a maniacal grin. And to Olga he said, "I'll tell them you're all set for the course, okay?" A second later he plunged out the door.

"I told him that you're reading my books," Tortorisi said. "I told him you were crazy about them."

"Crazy, up to a point," she said.

They ate the pizza and drank the beer and after a while their good spirits returned. Tortorisi proposed going out for more beer, and Peter Peeks seconded the motion, but Olga said no, they had to leave now so she could do her thoughts.

And so they went, and Olga did her thoughts.

Late in the night, despite the cold that had settled around the campus, she woke to the sound of laughter from the pool and recognized the voices of Peter Peeks and Francis Xavier Tortorisi at play.

How strange, she thought, how useful. And though she was very tired, she reached for her notebook, wrote for a while, and, grateful as always, drifted off to sleep.

She had had a busy two days.

Part II
~

8

Olga had intended, of course, to bring fire and the sword—it was her job—but not with such dispatch, not with such lunatic thoroughness. Within two days of her arrival many horrible things had happened and many more were in progress.

It is time, therefore, to speak of Olga.

Asked about herself, she would probably say, "But there are so many *nice* things to talk about" or "I teach and I try to write" or "There's nothing to say." This would not have been modesty; in fact, there was little to say. Like all writers Olga existed more truly in her books than outside of them. She felt that she was dull and desperate, and for the most part she was right, having no life to speak of except the one she created.

Or rather the *ones* she created, because even though she had written only two novels—and, quite properly, regarded them both as failures—she had discovered the peculiar process by which she could make her characters live. No matter how closely they were based on real people, no matter how precisely she had caught their looks and gestures and speech, they failed to come truly alive until she gave them something of herself—some dimly perceived moral laxity, some lurking vice, some unsuspected criminal tendency of her own. With each book she was forced to search deep inside herself for new possibilities of the self and, indeed, in each book there appeared new Olgas, radically modified in sex and temperament and desire. These characters were alarming to her, all the more so because she recognized in them what she might become, given their awful circumstances and a little more or less grace. She lived in these characters, sometimes painfully, as she created them, and then forgot them as soon as she moved on to the next book. Meanwhile she sympathized with their limitations and encouraged their often touching aspirations, but she never sentimentalized them nor did she keep them from the disasters their actions or their fate brought upon them. And, remarkably, she loved them all in a way she could not love herself. She had the dark suspicion that in the end she would have become so many characters that she herself would cease to exist altogether. This did not seem to bother her at all.

Her books were few and thin: two works on theory and two puzzling works of fiction. Her life depended on her work.

Olga's first book *Truth and Methodology* had been widely misunderstood, much to her advantage. She had begun it as a kind of parody of Husserl, rejecting, as he did, the commonsensical belief that things exist in the world independent of ourselves and of our knowing them. With Husserl, she reduced reality to the contents of our consciousness alone. That was orthodox enough, conventional even, but then she proceeded to overleap Husserl and his scientific subjectivity and posited in place of his deep structures of the mind what she called "intuitive essences of the feminine." She discoursed lengthily on this new and provocative term, citing ancient literatures and Gnostic texts and women writers from Hroswitha to Aphra Behn and down to Carolyn Keene. Then she pulled in a whole lot of terminology from Heidegger and Lacan, from Jakobson and Todorov, and redefined it all in feminist terms, and had a very good time doing it. The book was well received indeed, though a few nay-sayers felt she had failed to define her semi-mystical term "intuited essences of the feminine." Her defenders insisted that the whole point of the book was that "intuited essences of the feminine" could not *be* defined, and that she had nonetheless managed to illuminate the term without destroying the mystery. The matter was left there.

She wrote a novel next, *Medea's Daughters*. She wrote for fun and out of wickedness and with the desire to tell a story. She knew, as everybody knew, that the novel was dead and that the story was a base and atavistic form, and so she exploited for her own purposes the ancient *nouveau roman* of the Fifties and Sixties. Though everything within her yearned toward the future, she cheerfully embraced the present tense narrative, the constant and repetitive presentation of events. Drama disappeared. Character may or may not have existed. She was quite a successful mimic and critics congratulated her on a *nouveau nouveau roman* that explored anew, for our age, the boredom and despair and meaninglessness of society at the turn of the century. They overlooked completely that she had chosen this sterile form of writing to explore and assess the sterility of her characters, who lived out their lives surrounded by an abundance, material and spiritual, that left them staggered. Characters who, in their blindness, could not see abundance, and, in their egoism, could not want it. She had succeeded in creating a tightly woven parable of possibility and redemption. It was a nasty little story full of wit and irony and, quite incidentally, it indicted the lives of the very people who admired it.

Her next two books, now that she had discovered her method, followed quickly and easily. She wrote *The Archeology of Text*, working out of Foucault and into her own inspired sense of feminism. Having recognized that literature is, in essence, an illusion, she took it as her task to establish that Foucault too is an illusion, and thus his theories, and thus his minions. Discursive practices, as she began calling literature, pointed unequivocally to the irrelevance of both Foucault and his authorial intentions. Whatever the rich resources of his historical excavations, it was nonetheless obvious even without them that sex has been, is, and will be. Period. And that sex is a consolation and a weapon. We did not need Foucault, she said, to understand the tyranny of patriarchy, the dominance of sex, the need for female emancipation. She said other things. She said, "Foucault is the great conspiratorial epistemologist." She said, "Power is the norm by which Foucault interprets human interaction." And she said, unforgivably, "A little Foucault goes a long way." She was chastised for this, and though there were some among the theorists who began to compare her to Julia Kristeva, there were others in and out of the feminist establishment who said she was a nut, an Eastern European hippie, an anti-theory maniac who ought to be put in a rowboat with Camille Paglia and abandoned on the open sea. Nevertheless, her reputation grew.

She wrote a second novel, *The Death of the Patriarch*, once again out of fun but also as a kind of homage to Foucault, who had provided her so much good material, and with a nod at Harold Bloom, just for the hell of it. This novel too was a tidy little parable, with much to say about the connections between writing and death, and a little ridicule to poke at the anxiety of influence. It did not seem at all absurdist or *nouveau*. It did not offer another squint at the abyss. It seemed to be merely about good and evil at work in the similar acts of dying and writing. There were a lot of unhappy, self-centered men in it, writers all, addled in the attempt to defeat death by living on in their works, and it was a relief to their respective wives when these vain and tiresome men finally died. The wives themselves never seemed to die at all. None of the critics much liked the book, but Olga had become a figure now, and *The Death of the Patriarch* was translated into seven languages and, in France at least, sold well.

These were the books that had first impressed Paris and The Hague and, in turn, New Haven and Ithaca and Irvine, and so finally and at length the rest of the civilized parts of the United States. They were the books that had troubled Betz Rudin and Rosalie Kurtz, large with child and impatient by nature, as they went belly to belly at the reception for Olga Kominska. And they were the books that had inspired Zachary Kurtz to bring their author to the university for an academic quarter, to do his will, to seduce the Deans, to create irremediable change.

Economy and daring were the basic principles of her work and Olga had gratefully allowed these principles to spill over into her life. And so it did not surprise her that so much had happened so swiftly and that everything was proceeding tidily toward the as yet unforeseen but nonetheless inevitable end.

9

Peter Peeks was working out very well in his career as a spy. He reported everything to her, early and late, and on the morning after his swimming party with Tortorisi, he was careful to report his personal news first.

"I went to bed with him," Peter Peeks said. "I mean, like I had sex with him, you know?"

Olga tried to process this news.

"It was cool. It's not like I've turned gay or anything, it was just an experience."

Silence.

"It seemed like the right thing to do, I mean, in the circumstances." He was puzzled by her silence. "Now how about us? Can we hit the sack?"

Olga recovered enough to say thank you, no, and to send him on his way. She was shocked, and embarrassed that she was shocked. She would have to give further thought to Peter Peeks. Right now, however, she had office hours to keep, and orientation meetings, and she had to investigate the library. It was the first day of winter quarter.

The next day Peter Peeks reported with fresh news.

"Maddy Barker isn't speaking to Tortorisi any more. Do you know why? Because he's a friend of yours."

"Hmmm," Olga murmured.

"And because Maddy's in love with you, she says."

"Hmmm."

"Also—and this might really interest you—Zack has tried to jump her bones . . . twice. Zack! Can you dig it? He's anti-lesbian, Maddy says, but he tried to jump her bones anyhow."

Olga sent him on his way.

She gave her first lecture on the problem of good, and many people came to look at her, this odd feminist, this critic *cum* novelist. She was part Susan Sontag, part Meryl Streep, if you could believe what you heard, but they knew you couldn't, and so they had come to see La Kominska for themselves. She concealed her nervousness beneath a brittle voice and rapid speech and what seemed that day to be a British accent. The Christian Coalition for Decency and the Jews for Justice taped everything she said.

Later that same day, after classes, Peter Peeks returned with his report on her lecture. Good enough so far, he said, though everybody was upset that the course had no subtitle. The problem of good: what was that supposed to mean? Nobody could figure it out. About her Foucault seminar, he had nothing to report, since the seminar was not open to the public and—he barely concealed how hurt he was— *he* was not allowed to attend.

He had lots of other news. Robbie Richter had suffered a breakdown, for real, not just a crying fit. Betz Rudin's baby was born with something wrong with it—an oxygen deficiency or something like that—and so it might be retarded. And there was talk that the Christian Coalition for Decency and the Jews for Justice might picket Olga's class on the problem of good because they were opposed to it.

"Opposed to the class? Or to the problem of good?"

"They think it's a cover-up. Of evil."

She made a mental note to find a subtitle.

"They want you to talk about Stalin and the Holocaust and air pollution the way Robbie Richter used to."

"They want their evil to look like snakes and toads," Olga said.

He thought about this.

"Something easy to recognize, easy to feel superior to," she said.

"Well, it's just that they think St. Thomas Aquinas is biased," Peter Peeks said and added, apologetically, "because he's Catholic."

"All this," Olga said, "over a subtitle."

He could restrain himself no longer. "*Why* can't I be in the Foucault seminar?"

As she so often did, she sent him on his way.

It was time to get on with it, and the first order of business was Zachary Kurtz. He had been calling every few hours, leaving messages on the answering machine. He had come to her office and was surprised that she would not interrupt students in order to talk to him. He left notes in her mailbox and he left notes at her door. She always had reasons for not seeing him.

"Zachary Kurtz," she said aloud, just to get used to the sound.

He was impossible, unlikable, unredeemable. He was crude and vulgar. He was ambitious and conniving and underhanded and a manipulator of people—he was a shit of hell. Zachary Kurtz was without redeeming social value and it was her task, Olga knew, to find something in him which would allow her to care. Which would *convince* her to care.

She must care. Her mind raced ahead to a Zachary Kurtz so endowed with saving graces that her care for him had turned to love and her love to infatuation. She saw herself in bed with Zachary, green and slimy, and she saw herself padding around the campus after him, desperate for his glance, his smile, his lingering pat on the behind.

"Zachary Kurtz," she said, and shook her head.

It was too awful.

Zachary could not be the first order of business. She would leave him for later—she needed a few days, a week maybe—and she would begin at the beginning, with poor demented Robbie Richter. Just to get the plot moving.

The problem of good. Subtitle: Frustration and Desire at the End of the Twentieth Century.

~

Robbie Richter was not allowed to have visitors and so Olga went to visit Cynthia, whom she found plunged in near-Eastern gloom, in a shawl and sunglasses. Cynthia roused herself to fill Olga in on the details.

Robbie had stopped crying, Cynthia said, and was laughing all the time now, and frankly she found this even more disturbing. Had Olga ever heard Robbie laugh? The sound could pierce your brain. And the dog, Ozzie, was howling through the night since he couldn't sleep without Robbie at his side. Cynthia sobbed a little here. She was lonely, she was frantic, she felt like killing herself. Or the dog. But not Robbie. She felt bad for Robbie. It's this place, she said, and mopped her nose with a tissue, it's this university. They've driven him out of his mind.

Perhaps, Olga suggested, he just didn't have the nerves for the life of theory.

Cynthia agreed. He had brought it on himself. He should have been content with just books.

Nonetheless, she wanted him back. "The way he used to be," Cynthia said.

He used to be half-crazy, a silly ass, an egomaniac—Cynthia knew all that—but she had got used to him that way and she loved him.

"The way he used to be," Olga said, seeing the route she must take. "Perhaps I can help."

Cynthia began to feel hopeful almost at once.

And so Olga went to the hospital, severe in a dark suit, her hair pulled back tight. She was brisk and official, nobody would dare question her presence there. Despite the ban on visitors, the ward nurse directed her at once to Robbie Richter. "Just follow the laughter," the nurse said. "You can't miss him."

Robbie was laughing at full throttle when Olga entered the room. He paused, choking a little, when he saw who it was.

"That's enough," she said. "Stop it."

He stopped altogether.

"Your wife is concerned about you," she said. "So is Zachary Kurtz." He began to laugh again.

She raised her hand as if to strike him and he fell silent.

"This will be a start," she said, reaching into her carry-all.

She had brought him four novels by Barbara Pym. She had wrapped paper jackets from Foucault's multi-volume *History of Sexuality* around the more innocent Pym bindings and she had slipped the books into a bag from The Gap. She placed the bag on his night table.

"We'll start with these," she said.

She said, "The book jackets will attract the nurses. Be warned."

"The books themselves are not dangerous," she said.

Robbie's eyes moved from Olga to the Gap bag and then aimlessly about the room. He seemed unsure what to do now that he had stopped laughing.

"You've got to get better," she said. "There are plans for you." She leaned close to him, confidentially. "They need not involve theory."

He began to giggle and she gave him a sharp look. She could see he was really far gone. He might well require a more drastic remedy than Barbara Pym.

~

"Why can't I come in?" Peter Peeks said. "Why can't we go to bed?"

"I'm on my way out," Olga said.

"Where to?"

"Out."

"Why can't I be in your seminar on Foucault?"

Involuntarily, she laughed. He was so perfectly made, with his big shoulders and his hard little behind and that empty empty brow. She had given him much thought but it had all come to nothing. Innocent Peter Peeks. Sweet Peter Peeks.

"Come back tonight," she said. "We'll swim."

~

Olga went to visit Betz Rudin. The Rudins lived in a rustic mansion high in the hills above the university. The main house had eleven rooms and three garages and a fully equipped gym. Separate from the house, but connected to it by a cloistered walk, was a small guest cottage and a huge hexagonal library containing many thousands of books. There was also a pool and a tennis court and, therefore, a grounds man, a cleaning woman, and a cook. Gil Rudin didn't like live-in help and so there was no maid or butler. They let the cleaning woman answer the door.

This vast spread was made possible by Gil's inheritance. His father had been a Hollywood producer of rip-off films, campy and crazy versions of whatever the big hits of the season happened to be. He could churn out a film in three weeks, writing the script himself and filming it with his little repertory group of B actors, recycling sets and improvising lighting, and editing it with as much care for art and chronology as was consistent with the two days allotted for the process. They were hilarious films, satire verging on plagiarism, and they had touches of genius. He cleaned up on the foreign market and he invested every dime. He died in a car crash, drugged out of his mind, and the several million dollars he left to his ditzy wife she invested in breakfast cereals, cosmetics, and, of course, oil. When she died in her own car crash, drunk—she hated drugs— she left the ten year old Gil with a considerable fortune which grew and grew as he wandered, lonely, from St. Paul's to Harvard to Oxford and on to the chilly fame he currently enjoyed at the university.

His values were not the values of his parents nor of the film industry, he was emphatic about that. As his weighty books testified, he was concerned with matters of the intellect and spirit, with the life of the mind, and—for himself—with the creation of a true family. His Hollywood wealth had facilitated his three marriages and two divorces, but it had done nothing to provide him an heir. He wanted a family and that meant an heir and that meant a son. And a wife too, of course.

At the time of Olga's visit, Betz Rudin had been home from the hospital for two long days. She was filled with anti-depressants and she had also drunk a little vodka for breakfast, but nothing seemed to improve her mood. She had not really cared about this baby until its mismanaged birth, and the idea of motherhood meant only restrictions on her freedom, so why should she feel so down? It was, after all, just a baby, and a defective one at that. Gil wanted to put it away and have another one, a good one, as quickly as possible, but now that the baby was here, a real thing, Betz couldn't help feeling a little sorry for it. Still, Gil wanted to get rid of it and so they would.

Betz lay on a chaise longue among the tropical plants in the orangerie. She remained heavy, but her sunken cheeks and the dark circles beneath her eyes gave her face a starved look and intensified her pallor. She was staring out into the garden and would not look directly at Olga.

"You want to know about the baby, I suppose," Betz said, accusing. "You want to write about it, don't you."

"I've brought you these," Olga said, and held out a small bouquet of violets.

Betz looked at them and turned away.

"You look pale," Olga said. "You look tired." Her voice was soft, caressing almost, and there was no trace of an accent. She smoothed Betz's forehead and touched her soft hair.

"What have they told you about the baby?" Betz said.

"You tell me about the baby, if you want. Or tell me about you. Or just get some rest."

Betz took the violets and began, unconsciously, to crush them. "Gil wants me to get rid of it. He wants to put it in a . . . place for babies like her."

"Yes?"

"So I guess we will."

"Is her name Susanna?"

Betz looked at her, startled. "I was going to name her Susanna. How did you know? I didn't tell anybody, not even Gil. How did you know?"

Olga smiled at her.

"Susanna was my first girlfriend's name," Betz said. "I was in love with her."

"When will you bring her home, the baby?"

"We won't," Betz said, "we can't," and she pressed her lips together hard. And then she went on: "Oxygen just didn't get to her brain, they don't know why, and it affected her heart too. We're not bringing her home. Period. How did you know I was going to name her Susanna?"

"Susanna is a nice name."

"We're not going to keep her. Susanna."

"You'll keep her," Olga said. "If you keep her, she'll make you very rich," and she bent over and kissed Betz on the forehead.

Betz pulled away from the kiss. She was already rich and the baby had nothing to do with it. She had married Gil for his money and, by God, she intended to hang onto it. What she had not considered was hanging on to the baby. And yet, why shouldn't she? What could Gil do about it? Her mind began to move into unfamiliar territory. She felt an awful swelling in her chest, as if she were having a heart attack. This wasn't about Gil. Gil was irrelevant.

She was filled suddenly with a great longing for the baby. For Susanna. She wanted to hold her and press her against her breast. She wanted to feed her, she wanted to say she was sorry, she wanted to give her—it must be possible, somehow—her own good brain and her own good heart. She lunged forward then, her arms clutched to her belly, and a long wailing sound was torn from her, primitive, the sound of despair.

"I want my baby," she said, and the tears began to come. "I want her. I want to keep her." But the words were lost in her choking sobs and in time the sobs gave way to silence.

After a long while Olga leaned forward and took the single whole violet from the crushed blossoms that had fallen to the floor. She turned it back and forth between her fingers. She placed it finally in Betz's trembling hand.

"Susanna is a good name," Olga said.

Betz Rudin lay on the chaise longue, exhausted. She felt empty, bitterly deprived. She hated her life and she hated her luck and she hated everything except Susanna, the one thing that was hers only. She would never give Susanna up.

~

"No," Olga said, "you can't be in it."

Daryl had come to see her during her office hours.

"I'm fifth year," he said. "I'm comp lit. I should have some rights," he said.

He said, "I drive a cab and I tend bar just so I can get an education. A little Ph.D. is all I'm after here."

He said, "Is it too much to ask you for a little help? You could help me. You should, you know."

He fiddled with his bushy red beard, deliberating.

"It's about my wife," he said, broken.

"No," Olga said, "you can't be in it."

~

Olga put on her severe suit and pulled her hair back in a knot and went off to the hospital to check on Robbie Richter's dissolution. He was still laughing—indeed, he seemed worse than ever—and she could see the Pym books had failed to work their anticipated magic. She looked at him and shook her head, which caused him to shriek more wildly and laugh more loudly, and she determined on more desperate measures.

She returned the next day with Sendak's *Higgledy Piggledy Pop*, an important children's book which had the additional merit of being about a dog. She brought an armful of *The Lone Ranger* and *The Hardy Boys* series and, in the event that these were successful, a copy of *Robinson Crusoe*.

There would be time enough for Pym, and then some day for *Pride and Prejudice*, for *Emma* and *Middlemarch*, and—who knows?—perhaps at last for *Lady Chatterly's Lover*. Lawrence, she concluded, was Robbie's final destination.

~

Late that afternoon Olga met Tortorisi at the swimming pool and said
to him, "I've read your manuscript, Tortorisi. It's a dead end. Forget
it." He maundered and sorrowed and twitched his fat until she felt
obliged to say more. "You have a gift for mockery," she said, "a small
gift but it can carry you far. Give up this silliness—it's pretentious, it's
obscurantist—and write what you were meant to write. Do a best-
seller. Less sex and a little more action."

"I've tried that," he said, babbling, defensive. "I've tried
everything."

"You haven't tried that. You're trying to be deep," she said, and
waited till he got control of his emotions.

He said, "I have to be faithful to my vision. I have to."

"I'm an artist," he said.

He said, crumbling, "I don't know what to write about. I don't have
a subject."

"Scandal is your subject," she said. "It always sells."

"But . . ."

"Proust wrote about scandal," she said.

She said, "So did Flaubert."

"Look around you," she said. "You're not Proust and you're certainly not Flaubert, but you've got it in you to write a scandalous best-
seller, so do it. It's your vocation. It's your calling. You've got the
gift."

For just a second Tortorisi opened his mind to her words, and in
that second something went ping in his psyche, and he caught a
glimpse of a very funny, very scandalous book about the university.
He could write it, he knew he could. Why should Kitty Kelly have all
the fun and make all the money? Here was a book that opened the
way to vengeance. He could send up Kurtz or Maddy Barker or anybody just for the fucking hell of it. He'd call it *Scandal* or *Exposed* or
something grabby like that. Maybe there'd be big bucks in it. He

laughed aloud. Maybe there'd even be—accidentally almost—a chance at tenure.

"The book would get you tenure," Olga said. "I guarantee it."

Tortorisi, filled with hope and malice, went home and began writing at once.

~

To Concepcion she said, "Tortorisi was just telling me about you. He says you're brilliant. He says he worships you."

"Tortorisi?" They were at the produce section in Safeway and Concepcion was fondling melons.

"Not sexually, of course," Olga said. "He's no threat sexually," and she let a little smile play at her lips, for Concepcion personally.

"Look at these melons," Concepcion said.

"You must come to tea," Olga said.

~

"We must have tea," Olga said to Maddy Barker. "Come to tea."

And to Leroy O'Shea, she said, "Come to tea and bring your darling Moo."

And she invited the Chairman even though he was a fool.

She did not invite Eleanora Tuke, on the grounds that Eleanora lived in the City and led such a busy life, but Eleanora got wind of the tea and came along anyway, figuring reasonably that if there was a party she must have been invited.

Olga served Constant Comment. She plied Eleanora with cakes and little sandwiches, purchasing her silence with food, while she led each of the others out of themselves and into the world of public conversation.

Eleanora scarfed up the goodies, and more goodies and more, while Maddy Barker swooned with politically correct love for Olga, and Concepcion spoke of her admiration for Francis Xavier Tortorisi, and Leroy O'Shea charmed the Chairman with his account of the career of Ma Rainey, and Moo Wesley Rudin blurted out suddenly, to Olga in particular, that she wanted a baby, she needed a baby, and Concepcion mentioned that she liked men who were chubby, and chubby girls of course, and Maddy Barker said Francis Xavier Tortorisi wasn't chubby, he was fat, plain fat, and the Chairman said he couldn't wait until this year was over and there was a new Chairman at last, somebody younger perhaps, not an old fart—and what did they think of Zachary Kurtz's secret plan to enthrone poor Robbie Richter? Everybody fell silent at that, and Eleanora stopped chewing, and Olga, realizing at last that everyone knew, leaned forward, smiling, and said, "Tea?"

In a while they began to talk again, more formal now, more cautious, but their caution was too late. Olga had listened and she had taken it all in and stored it all up. The fools were not altogether foolish and Zachary was not at all the danger he seemed, which was interesting, which was useful.

And so, before her guests departed, Olga dropped into their ears an enticing mention of Betz Rudin's new independence, of Robbie Richter and his growing taste for *The Hardy Boys*, and, in a lower voice, of Tortorisi and his astonishing new novel. Astonishing? Tortorisi? They were surprised and curious but she would tell them, alas, almost nothing about it, except that it was funny and perhaps even scandalous. And—she laughed in the most beguiling way—perhaps it was about them.

For their professional delight, she let fall a *mot* or two from the greater worlds of Paris and The Hague.

She had nothing to say about Zachary Kurtz.

~

Peter Peeks had made his spy report and was about to go.

"And Zachary?" Olga asked.

"He's really pissed off. He thinks you're avoiding him."

"I am avoiding him."

"You don't answer his calls, he says. He says you don't come to see him."

"I'll go to see him."

"He says you're ungrateful."

"You're a good spy, Peter Peeks."

"And I'm good in bed." He wiggled his eyebrows at her.

"Go away," she said.

"We could swim together tonight," he said. "We could do it underwater."

Olga smiled enigmatically and sent him on his way.

~

Olga felt much better about Zachary Kurtz now that she realized his secret plans were public knowledge. He seemed less Machiavellian. He seemed almost tame. Suddenly she saw him as just another young academic, angry and indignant because it was almost midnight and he was not famous yet.

Poor Zachary. They all saw through him. He was no threat at all.

And, poor thing, he was short besides.

She put on pea-green slacks and sneakers and a raincoat—she had never looked more unattractive—and went out in search of Zachary Kurtz.

10

Zachary Kurtz was in the library stacks, despondent. It was raining outside and, for Zachary, it was raining inside. Everything was as awful as it could be.

He was leafing idly through *Rage and Madness: a Primer*, hoping to find something helpful about Robbie Richter's craziness and, since the book was a primer, perhaps some early warning signs that might be helpful in his own case. Because he had begun to fear he couldn't go on.

All his plans had fallen apart. He had confided in Olga, foolishly presuming she'd be on his side, and he had invested his hopes in Robbie who promptly had a mental collapse, and now Olga was telling her class that a little Foucault went a long way and Robbie was in the hospital laughing his ass off at *Higgledy Piggledy Pop* and on top of everything he himself was about to become a father. A father! Of what? A baby with brain damage? A porcupine? Who knew? It was all hopeless.

"Psychology?"

He was caught off guard. He looked up, confused, and there before him was Olga.

"I didn't expect to find you in psychology."

"Dog shit," he said. He closed the book and hid it behind his back.

"I hear wonderful things about your classes," she said.

"Well, I don't hear wonderful things about yours. I hear that you're deconstructing Foucault. I hear that you refer to him as a terrorist."

1

87

"An epistemological terrorist," she said. "And a paranoid."

He had no response for this.

"You've read my books," she said.

"Yes, but I didn't think you'd *say* things like that. It's one thing to write them and another thing to *say* them. Holy Christ!"

She fixed him with wide eyes and a taunting smile, and her voice dropped a full octave. "What is it you want?" she said.

Once again he was caught off guard. But this time he gave her his full attention and was astonished to see how unattractive she looked. She had on a ratty old raincoat the color of vomit and her hair was all in knots and she wore dirty-looking sneakers on her feet. He stared at the feet but they did nothing for him at all.

"You look terrible," he said. "What's the matter with you?"

She laughed softly.

"I mean . . . " he gestured at the coat, the sneakers, the hair, ". . . you look like hell."

She continued laughing.

"What?" he said. "I'm missing something here." And he wondered how he could ever have found her attractive. Or what could have made him think she might be useful to him. Her course on the problem of good—even with the subtitle added—was losing enrollments every day, and the kids had begun to suspect she was a closet Catholic or something, and she was saying all those shitty things about Foucault.

"What do you want?" Olga said.

He looked at her. What he wanted was a drink, and for Rosalie to get the damned baby born and done with, and . . .

"I can get it for you," she said, "whatever it is."

Suddenly, for no reason he could identify, he felt a movement of hope in his heart and a small answering movement in his crotch.

"What I want," he said, "is for Robbie Richter to get back on his feet."

"I'll take care of it," she said.

"And get back into the department."

"Done," she said.

"*Before* we elect a new Chairman."

"Done. And done," she said. "Think of me as the answer to your prayers."

When she had gone, Zachary slipped *Rage and Madness: a Primer* back onto the shelf. He put his hand to his heart, but it was beating normally, and then to his crotch where there was nothing much going on. But there had been, undeniably, a moment when things had looked up.

Oh, if only, if only, if only Olga could make these things happen!

He thought of her again in her vomit raincoat and her bilious slacks and, good God, those sneakers. When had she gotten to be such a bow-wow? Even her feet were a turn-off.

Nonetheless she gave him hope. Nonetheless she gave him, so to speak, a lift. He would force himself to believe that it would all turn out well: Robbie would be Chairman, his Department of Theory and Discourse would be rescued, and Rosalie, maddening Rosalie, would give birth to a baby, not a porcupine.

He stroked his nifty little mustache, for luck.

With his spirits lifted, he moved from the books on madness to the more ample shelves on sex and sex problems. He was in search of a book on fetishes. On feet, to be exact.

11

Tortorisi had pitched out the old novel and begun a new one, but he was having a lot of trouble with it. He worked all day, he worked late into the night, but still it wasn't coming out right.

He had taken Olga's advice to write a novel about the university scandals, but he was determined to do it disjunctively, deconstructively, from the most contemporary point of view. That, of course, would mean post-post-modernism, a tradition that hadn't really been defined yet, which made the enterprise even more attractive. He had long since discarded the conventions of plot and character and he was determined now to get rid of theme and, if possible, subject matter as well. No Oulipo crap for him, no more retread Joyce, no torture games like writing a novel without the letter *e*. What he wanted to produce was a novel that approximated sculpture: a meditation on text in its essence.

The trouble he was having was new to him. Characters kept intruding into his narrative, they were always saying things and doing things, and so the novel slipped out from under his careful, artful, post-post-modernist control. It was as if—in the old cliché of novelists—these characters were taking on an imaginative life of their own. He didn't want this. He wanted to render them static, freeze them in time, make them into sculpture.

He had a vision of the novel as sculpture garden, with an eerie wind blowing through it from the abyss.

With great effort he finished the first chapter, seven pages blessedly free of dialogue. He spent the next week polishing it, and he would have spent another, but he just couldn't wait any longer.

Flushed and exultant, he brought the chapter next door to Olga. He read it aloud to her in that ritual voice the poets use: a kind of incantatory monotone that caressed each word, lingered lovingly over commas, and surrendered to periods only with regret. It was reading as an act of adoration, which was right, since like God he had created this work from nothing.

Olga sat in silence until he was done. Then she leaned close to him and fixed him with her look.

"Dog shit," she said.

He was speechless.

"It's terrible," she said.

She said, "Tortorisi, listen to me. It's boring."

"This isn't fiction," she said. "It's self-abuse under the guise of love."

He was furious, naturally, and he cried and carried on, but when he calmed down, she gave him further advice.

"Get a story," she said.

She said, "Get a character."

"Just begin anywhere," she said, "so long as it's true." And then she amended her advice. "So long as it's fictionally true. Do you know the difference?"

He sulked. He was aiming at a deeper truth, he said, a truth that had nothing to do with character and action. He was trying to do something in fiction that had never been done before.

"Dog shit," she said. And then, more reasonably, "Look, it's *all* been done before, all the plots have been used, all the combinations and permutations of human character have been worked out, but *people* are still a mystery and their actions are still problematic and even Chekhov thought it was a good idea to ask who we are and why we're here and where we're going . . . even though it's all been done before."

He sulked a while longer.

"It's your vision that makes it all new."

"But I'm not Chekhov."

"Exactly. So write about Maddy Barker," she said, looking at him with big eyes, as if she knew all his secrets. She smiled, cryptically, "Write about your pleasuring her. Write about Peter Peeks. Write about the things that make you wake in the night and cover your face in shame."

These words opened a chasm into which Tortorisi felt he might fall, and continue falling, forever. Write about personal stuff? Secrets? The unspeakable Sunday scenes between him and Maddy Barker? Not to mention what he'd done with Peter Peeks. Never. He'd rather not write at all. Out of the question.

~

That afternoon in Safeway, as he was pawing through the beet greens and the iceberg lettuce and the Swiss chard in hopes that something healthful might appeal to him, Tortorisi heard a woman's voice call out and he knew without looking that she was addressing him.

"Hey, fatty," she said.

He froze. He felt for a moment that he was back in high school. His face began to burn.

And then, incredibly, a hand reached from behind him and squeezed the little roll of fat around his middle. He yelped, violated, and turned to face Concepcion.

She gave him a big wave although she was standing only inches away. He could tell at once she had been drinking.

"That's nice," Concepcion said, patting his belly, and her hand lingered there. "That feels so nice."

Tortorisi shook himself like a wet dog and moved back from her.

She moved forward, laughing, and patted him again.

"What are you doing?" he said, in a high voice. "People will see you!"

In fact two people had already stopped to stare—at a distance, of course, for safety.

"Are you going to scream, 'Rape'?" Concepcion said. "In the Safe-way?" She hugged herself, and then she reached out to pat his belly again. Tortorisi moved away. She made a lunge at him. "Rape!" she said, in a hoarse whisper. "Rape!" She made another lunge at him.

"Stop!" he screamed. "Stop it!"

A small crowd began to gather.

Concepcion leaned over her grocery cart, laughing uncontrollably. She could barely get her breath.

"Are you all right?" a woman asked.

Concepcion pushed herself up from the cart, shaking her head, her face wet with tears. "It's just so funny," she said, and seeing Tortorisi's stricken face, she could not help herself. "Rape!" she croaked, and made another lunge at him.

Tortorisi fled, leaving his grocery cart behind.

~

Olga was amused, and then she laughed outright.

"It's not funny," Tortorisi said, "it was humiliating."

"It *sounds* funny," Olga said, "and that's all that matters, really, to a writer."

"And what's that supposed to mean?"

"It's great material," she said. "Use it."

He thought again of that demented Concepcion doubled up in laughter as her black hair tumbled about her face and she lunged at him, patting his fat, stage whispering "Rape!" loud enough for the whole world to hear. And everybody looking.

In that instant he was indeed back in high school, a freshman in a corridor full of upperclassmen, and he was reaching up to the shelf in his locker when somebody grabbed his arms and pinned them against the wall and somebody else yanked his pants down hard, and then his underpants, and they all began to whistle at him as he squirmed to get away, crossing his legs to hide his thingy, and he could hear the girls laughing and then suddenly he was free and nobody was there except Mr. Hemond, the chemistry teacher, who stared right at his penis and said, "Put your pants on, Tortorisi, nobody wants to look at that thing."

Olga was waiting for a response. Tortorisi was very red in the face and he felt tears spring to his eyes. Olga nodded, in agreement with whatever he was thinking.

"That's right," she said. "Use it. It can be fun, actually."

He said he couldn't. Ever.

He wouldn't.

And that was that.

Later, however, he gave it a try, changing names, changing ages, stopping long enough to cover his face in momentary shame, and then going right on, spilling it all out, the unsayable, the unthinkable, the inadmissible truth. In no time at all, he had created a horrifying little scene that starred not himself but Zachary Kurtz, set not in high school but in the university library stacks, and his own depantsing had become Zachary's impotence, his pitiful organ flaccid and useless before the panting, craven Concepcion.

He reread the scene. It was too explicit, too amateurish in its attempt to make an effect, and the character was too clearly Kurtz. Still the emotion had an undeniable authenticity. He had captured the feeling of humiliation and he had made Kurtz ridiculous and pitiful at the same time.

He reread the scene once again. He had discovered a way of making things up, sort of, and it was really very exciting. Was this how everybody wrote fiction? It needed work, a good bit of work, but once you gave up trying to be deep, writing was a lot easier and a lot more fun. And what a relief to blame your fantasies and your nightmares on fictional characters.

No wonder Olga liked writing novels.

There was the sound of laughter from the pool and something about it caught his attention. It was a laugh he recognized. It was Peter Peeks' laugh. He felt a twinge of envy and then a twinge of embarrassment. The things they had done together! His face got red again.

"Write about the things that make you wake in the night and cover your face in shame," Olga had said, but he couldn't. He simply couldn't. Ever.

Unless . . . unless he made Zachary into a bisexual and tossed him in the pool with Peter Peeks. Or with Gil Rudin. Or with, let me see, the Chairman? Robbie Richter? Leroy O'Shea? Yes, Leroy. Zachary and Leroy. Ebony and Ivory. Of course, he could attribute his fling with Peter Peeks to somebody other than Zachary. Who? Whom would it absolutely kill? The President! Of course. And give Missy President a fling with Maddy Barker. Mix it all up. Mix and Match. Bisexuality was very trendy.

He paused for a moment in his excitement. Could he be sued? Could he be ruined?

But then he saw the President and Peter Peeks climbing all over each other, the President gasping and grabbing at Peter Peeks, bewildered and ecstatic as he himself had been, and it was just too good *not* to write it down.

There was more laughter from the pool, but he ignored it and leaned into the computer, eager, absorbed, inventing his fiction out of a new humility and a little wickedness and the godlike urge to create something where before there had been nothing at all. Except the truth. And that was unknowable anyhow.

After her confession there was silence except for the tinkle of tea cups and the occasional sputter of a defective candle.

There were, she insisted, extenuating circumstances.

She had gone to Kurtz's house to see Rosalie's baby, and to bring a present, and—nobody could blame her for this—to earn the requisite brownie points toward tenure. So she saw Rosalie Kurtz and the baby, who was a boy but nice anyway, with Rosalie's blue eyes and pretty mouth and a smile that was kind of sinister, actually, and she oohed and ahhed over the baby, and she meant it, more or less. When it was time to go, Zachary showed her out the back way, but he stopped in the kitchen and said he wanted to talk to her for a couple minutes about her tenure because the vote was only a month or two away, and he said have a little sherry, it's harmless, and she told him no, and he said, oh come on, come on, and anyway she took a sip and it seemed okay so she took another sip and then another sip and eventually, of course, he made a pass at her. He was talking about teaching reports and whether or not they should request a few more letters from Chicano/Chicana students to keep the recommendations from looking too Anglo, and then he put his hand on her waist, just lightly, to pat it, and the next thing she knew he was nudging her breast from the underside with his fat thumb, and she wanted to kick him in the crotch and scramble his eggs for good. She could sue him for sexual harassment, of course, but get real, we're talking tenure here, so she pushed his hand away and said, "Honestly!" And then she took off. She paused, reflective. Nothing would have happened if she had driven straight home, but she stopped at the Safeway for some of their nice melons, and that was when she saw fat Tortorisi bending over the lettuce, and she said to herself—before she realized she was high from the glass of sherry—"How would *you* like to be groped, fat boy?"—and the next thing she knew, she had reached around him from behind and grabbed a little roll of fat. And, this was the surprising part—it really felt nice. It was like grabbing a woman. Really.

They all leaned forward, surprised at this, and interested.

Well, anyway, that was when she realized she was high as a kite and was grabbing fat in the middle of the supermarket and it struck her so funny that she couldn't stop laughing, and—this was the worst part—she couldn't stop *doing* it! If you could have seen his face.

But they didn't want to see his face, or even to know about it. What they wanted to know was how touching him felt—Tortorisi, yikes!—and did he really feel like a woman, and what was her personal reaction to this as a feminist and a lesbian?

Concepcion got very serious here. The truth is I liked it, she said. It was like grabbing Suzie—she smiled over at Suzie Sweezie—only a little tiny bit firmer, a little more resistance to the flesh, probably because of the fat-to-muscle ratio, even though Tortorisi didn't seem to have any muscle at all.

They pondered this. Suzie Sweezie touched the flesh at her waist and then reached over and touched the flesh at Concepcion's waist, which was just perfect, and she tried the flesh of the other women, one by one, but it was clear from her expression that she was unable to reach any conclusion.

Nobody said anything. They were appalled to discover their leader had been tempted and had fallen. After a while Suzie Sweezie put this into words: she was truly grieved.

"I've fallen," Concepcion said, "but with your prayers I know I can rise again."

She assumed the position, a kind of yoga squat, and the four others stood around her in a circle, their arms intertwined. They closed their eyes and prayed for a moment in silence. Then one of the graduate students led them in a recitation of the Hail Mary, after which the other graduate student led them in song, the "Regina Coeli," on which they harmonized. Each of the undergraduates took a try at improvised prayer; Suzie Sweezie prayed for female chastity and her friend Patti prayed for an increase in woman-love. Finally it was Concepcion's turn and she repeated her confession, ritually, omitting nothing.

She concluded: "I have strayed from the path of female righteousness, but I am lifted up in my sisterhood and made whole once again. Deliver us all from the curse of the penis and the arrow that flies by night."

"Amen," they said, and placed their hands, two at a time, on Concepcion's head.

She rose and they embraced each other and then, silently, as from a church, they all took their leave.

Concepcion was alone, cleansed, revirginized. She did a little dance of joy, and then she put out the five candles and lay down on the couch to watch TV.

She hit the button for the VCR. She would treat her new self to a half-hour of the soaps she had recorded that afternoon. Just a half-hour.

She watched the first part of "Days of Our Lives" and it was terrific, so she watched the second part, and then she said "What the hell" and watched the rest of them.

~

It was late that night. Concepcion was drugged from all the soaps she had watched, and she was newly-cleansed, but her heart was full of romance. She couldn't stop thinking of Tortorisi.

He liked her—she knew that from Olga—and he had expressed his admiration for her work and, the poor fat thing, he was probably crazy about her. Because she was, to be honest about it, a great-looking feminist lesbian and he was just a heterosexual white male who wrote boring books full of abstract sex. He was probably pining away for her. He was probably standing out in front of her house right now, staring up at her lighted window like that asshole Freddie in My Fair Lady.

She went to the window and looked out.

Well, he was probably pining away somewhere else, at home maybe, in Faculty Terrace.

She'd like to go see him, have a nice little chat, take away some of his longing. She understood how it was. When you were dizzy with love, sometimes you just wanted to *be with* the beloved. You didn't have to be grabbing at them all the time like that pig Kurtz. Just be with. Maybe she could do Tortorisi a good turn, a big favor even, by showing up at his place and letting him look at her, talk to her, tell her about his feelings. They could be friends. No sex—yuck!—no matter how much he wanted it. Just a mature, intellectual, caring friendship. After all they were both up for tenure at the same time, they were both insecure about it, they had a lot in common. And it was only broadminded for a feminist and and a lesbian to have a male friend. It showed you didn't hate the whole sex, even if you did, pretty much.

She decided to get dressed and take a stroll over by Faculty Terrace. She could see if Tortorisi's windows were lit, and if she ran into him by accident, she could always say she was on her way to see Olga, and, by the way, she hoped she hadn't embarrassed him this afternoon at the Safeway. That was good, the Safeway was good. Then he'd say, come on in for a drink or something, and she'd say, no I can't, I really can't, and he'd say, just for a minute, please, *please*, and he'd look at her with heterosexual longing, and she'd say, listen Francis, there can never be sex between us, not of *any kind*, and he'd say, yes, yes, anything you want, only come in and let's talk, and she would go in and they would talk and talk and talk about Roland Barthes and relationships and true intimacy. It would be just like her lesbian friendships except without the sex.

She put on her black fishnet stockings and her black leather miniskirt and her Mexican peasant blouse, worn low on the shoulders. All her clothes were tight and set off her plumpness to advantage. She would knock him dead.

It was nearly midnight, a lovely clear sky with no sign of rain, and except for her spike heels and décolletage and the time of night, she might be any English professor out for a stroll. As she entered Faculty Terrace she ran into the Chairman who had come out with Hamlet, his bulldog, who was old and mostly incontinent and took forever to pee and poo. The Chairman looked at how she was dressed and said, bug-eyed, "Good God, what are you *doing?*" She replied nonchalantly, "Just out for a stroll," and swung her handbag on its chain to emphasize the casualness of this stroll. She gave him a big smile and walked on by. He remained where he was, staring after her, as Hamlet trotted back and forth on the grass looking for the perfect spot to pee.

She strolled on past Tortorisi's place and past Olga's and continued on to the end of the Terrace. She turned then, twirled her handbag for the casual effect, and started back toward Tortorisi's.

She paused in the drive outside his windows. There was a light in his study where he was probably working on a new boring book, unable to write anything because his mind and imagination were preoccupied with her. The thought made her brave, and, tugging her peasant blouse a little lower on her shoulders, she went briskly up the stairs and knocked on his door. The sound was very loud in the clear night air. She listened at the door but could hear nothing. She waited a moment and then knocked again, harder. There was some noise from inside now, and she moved away from the door, ready with her smile.

The door opened. Tortorisi saw who it was and gave a little scream and jumped back.

Concepcion stepped through the doorway, advancing on him.

Tortorisi shrieked. "Get away from me! Get away!" He was clutching his middle.

At that moment Olga appeared behind him, coming from the living room. She held a sheaf of papers in her hand.

Concepcion stood, confused, staring from one to the other.

Olga thrust the papers at Tortorisi and smiled, saying, "Triangular desire. More good material." And to Concepcion she said, "The night is young." Olga pushed past Concepcion and skipped down the stairs in her dirty sneakers and then, for her own practical purposes, disappeared.

Concepcion looked at Tortorisi and he, still clutching his middle, looked back at her. It was a moment of illumination. There had been some terrible mistake, she suddenly realized, some failure in basic understanding. She had been misled by language; she, a disciple of Barthes! Truly, it was the end of the twentieth century and human communication was no longer possible.

She turned and—as fast as she could in her three-inch heels—she clattered down the stairs and out of Tortorisi's life, forever.

But as she rounded the corner she ran smack into the Chairman who stood patiently while Hamlet crouched, undecided to pee or to poo. Concepcion choked back her sobs and gave her handbag a little insouciant twirl and tip-tapped her way past the old fool and his dog.

"Have a good one," the Chairman said, and the church clock began to toll midnight.

Hamlet continued his search for the still point of the turning world, found it at last, and peed.

13

"Franklin W. Dixon has a very interesting mind," Robbie Richter said to the attendant, "not altogether unlike Conrad's." He paused for effect. "I've written on Conrad, of course. It was my first book, but in some ways my best, because the intellectual life was still new to me and I was bursting with ideas. I didn't have one of those privileged educations—St. Paul's, Harvard, Oxford, you know—I went to a public high school, Glendale, and to U. C. San Diego, and they said I'd never get into a first rate grad school, but I got into Virginia and I *stayed*. Very few do—stay, I mean—they wash out left and right, but I stayed and I did exceptional work. Exceptional! Nobody could believe it! I could have done my dissertation on Conrad or Lawrence, either one, or I could have written novels or plays—I was encouraged to do both, but I felt my greatest strengths were in criticism, and they were, are—but in the end I decided on Conrad. And that was my first book. There's a passage in *Heart of Darkness* where Conrad says of Marlow, and I quote, 'to him the meaning of an episode was not inside like a kernel, but outside enveloping the tale which brought it out only as a glow brings out a haze.' Well, that *is* Conrad's aesthetic. Or, to be precise, it's the aesthetic that informs *Heart of Darkness*. You see? Allusive, not realistic. Suggestive, not explicit. Do you get my point?"

The attendant nodded, afraid to say anything, since the patient was so clearly off his head.

"Well, the same is true of Franklin W. Dixon in *The Hardy Boys!*"

There was no response, but Robbie went right on. "Now, my second book was on Hudson, W. H., *Green Mansions* et cetera, and there are some critics who think my Hudson is even better than my Conrad, but I don't agree. It's good, of course. It's really superb, but I think my insights there were limited by the limitations of Hudson himself, who was certainly no Conrad, but who *is*? Where was I? Oh yes, in my book on Hudson . . . ."

But the attendant, concerned about the patient's extreme over-excitement, had slipped away to the dispensary and Robbie Richter was talking to the empty air. After a while the attendant returned with the nurse, who led Robbie off to bed and put him on a drip Valium that would have felled a man twice his size. Robbie slowed down, but he continued talking.

The attendant made a note to phone the Richter family: the books the professor read seemed to be destroying what was left of his mind.

Late that afternoon Olga appeared, tugging behind her a suitcase full of D. H. Lawrence. Things were moving very rapidly.

14

Betz Rudin was nursing the baby. The tug at her nipples was both sensuous and soothing, and the warmth and weight of the baby reassured her. Everything was fine, everything was good so long as she had her baby at her breast. Betz found herself humming Brahms' "Lullaby."

Her left nipple began to feel sore and so she eased it from the baby's lips. Susanna opened her gray eyes wide and looked up at her mother, surprised, trusting. Betz caught her breath because once again she was assailed by the crazy hope that there had been a mistake, that Susanna was the good and perfect baby they had hoped for. She held her at arm's length, carefully examining those gray eyes for surprise, for trust, for the light of intelligence that would reassure her. But Susanna's eyes remained blank and her mouth moved hungrily, and Betz, defeated, lifted her to the other breast.

The doctor, who was the gynecologist of choice for all Gil's wives, had advised against any contact with the baby. The break should be immediate and total, he said. These things happen. There are places for such babies, good places, and why put yourself through unnecessary grief? Start a new one, later, when you're yourself again. Take a month in Puerto Vallarta. Forget about it. Life has to go on.

Betz had not cried at the news. She'd gotten sullen and angry—why did these things always happen to *her*?—and then she demanded to see the baby with her own eyes. She expected something horrible-looking, but it looked like any other baby, with these tiny fingers and hands and squinched up eyes. When she took it in her arms, she couldn't help feeling a little sorry for it, poor thing. It *looked* all right. Still, there was no point in starting out with something defective, and she saw the wisdom of letting them put the baby away. Gil insisted on it, however, and wanted her to sign papers right there in the hospital, so out of spite she refused. Why should she be the only disappointed one? She went home and the baby stayed in the hospital.

In her mind, though, it was all over. Gil was right. She told him she would sign the papers.

But then Olga had visited her and asked if the baby was going to be named Susanna. Susanna, Olga said, would make her very rich. Betz had been insulted, naturally, and infuriated too, but suddenly all other emotions were swept away by an irresistible rush of desire. She would keep the baby. It was hers. And so that afternoon she brought the baby—Susanna—home to stay.

Now, nursing the baby, she knew she had done the right thing. Susanna needed her. She needed Susanna.

She heard a door slam downstairs and she heard Gil banging around in the kitchen, drinking juice and chatting up Luz, the cook. Gil was wonderful with the help. They loved him.

He had just come in from jogging, so he'd be full of energy and most probably full of sex. In the old days he would always come straight up to her bed, rip off his jogging shorts, and say, "Let's do it." And after that—after a regulation screw that gave him a chance for an heir and namesake—he'd position himself in front of the mirror and watch their reflection while they did the kinky things he really got off on. Once, on his last birthday, he had gone too far. After they finished with the mirror, he asked her to lie down in the bathtub— "Trust me," he kept saying, "just trust me"—and then he had pissed on her. She was so stunned she didn't try to stop him, but she decided at that moment that there were some things she would not do for any amount of money. There was such a thing as human decency.

What a shit he was, Gil Rudin, with his Hollywood sex habits. He had pissed on her, a man who couldn't bring himself to say the word fuck. Let's do it, you wanna get done, do my big dick. He was unnatural. He was some kind of pervert.

And then he was standing in the doorway, drenched with sweat, just looking at her. He had not spoken to her since she brought the baby home.

"I've made up my mind," he said. "We're getting rid of it."

"And I've made up my mind," she said. "We're not."

He came over and stood in front of her, his hands on his hips. He tilted his crotch toward her face.

"Think of the good times," he said. "We'd have them again."

"I've been thinking of them," she said.

"We'll go down to the beach. Or anywhere you want. Only just get rid of it. What do you say?"

"She's not an *it*. Her name is Susanna and I'm keeping her. There is such a thing as human decency, you know."

He left her then, and when he returned he was wearing his cashmere sweatshirt and designer jeans and the scuffed Bruno Maglis that he wore on teaching days, the reverse snobbery of Hollywood. He stood by the door watching her as she cradled the baby against her breast.

"Are you listening?" he said.

Betz looked up at him.

"Are you?"

"Yes," she said.

"It goes," he said, deliberately. "Or you go."

Betz sat there staring after him, the baby in her arms. She did not move, even when she heard the back door slam and a moment later the sound of his Lexus tearing out of the gravel drive. She told herself he did not matter, she was not afraid of him, she did not care. But she did care. And she was afraid of him. He had money and power and he always got his way. Just look at the other two wives, that pathetic first one and then Moo Wesley Rudin who went whimpering through life by the side of that Negro . . . Black . . . African American . . . whatever the hell they were called this year. She was a broken woman, Moo was, because she had not produced the required child. Gil crushed anybody who got in his way. He could be sweet when he liked you—or rather, when he wanted you to like him—and he could be charming and thoughtful and romantic when he wanted to seduce you, but once he got angry, he turned vicious and implacable. He just wouldn't stop until he'd won. He had a killer instinct. And not just an instinct. He could do it, she was sure of that, he could kill someone. She realized suddenly that he could kill *her*—my God, he could kill the baby—he was crazy enough sometimes. No, she was exaggerating. This was just lunacy.

There was a car on the the gravel drive. Had he come back? Was he going to take the baby away by force? Well, just let him try, the bastard. She ran to the window, but the car was parked beneath the porte-cochere and she could see nothing.

The doorbell rang.

She clutched the baby to her chest and went quickly down the stairs. "Luz!" she called from the landing, "Luz! Don't answer that!" But as she descended the last stair she saw that Luz had already answered the bell and was standing aside, holding the door wide open.

Sunlight poured into the foyer. A woman stood in the doorway, a dark shape framed by the light behind her. She was motionless and she looked huge, ancient. She could have been a goddess.

Betz stopped and stared. Her irrational fear had turned to awe and her panic to relief. Her fate was in the hands of the gods.

The goddess stepped forward but it was only Olga. She was just a young woman in an ugly raincoat and as she moved into the shadows of the foyer she returned to her old self. Nonetheless she said in her low, solemn voice, "I came at the right time, I see. The answer to your prayers."

~

On his furious drive down Old Ladera Road Gil Rudin had very nearly slammed into Tortorisi's orange Pinto, but he had wrenched the wheel around quick enough to avoid a crash and do only minimal damage to his own car. He drove through some sage brush and leveled a sapling and just kept on going. It was only as he approached the campus that he realized who had been behind the wheel. It was Olga.

Gil had taken an instant dislike to her when they'd met that night at Robbie Richter's party. There was something about her. He knew at once that she was trouble and he was never wrong about these things. And now she was on her way to talk to Betz? Why? He would have to think about this.

One of the advantages of having always been rich was that the desire for money never clouded your thinking. Not about people. Not about power. He saw things clearly and he saw people for what they were. Shits, most of them, especially women. He had never met one of them who wasn't first of all interested in his money or in Hollywood. And only then in his big dick. Except for the lesbos, who were first and last interested in each other.

What he wanted just once in his life was a woman who was independent, her own person, who would love him for himself and not for his money. Someone intelligent. Someone . . . it struck him then that Olga was the most independent woman he had ever met in his life. He wondered for a moment if Zachary Kurtz had been there yet. Zack loved to be first.

Gil thought about this.

And then he considered doing the job himself.

Maybe that's what she needed, maybe that's what she wanted. He could do her right this minute. He was up for it.

Inspired, though not by Olga, Gil pulled into the parking lot and drove around until he found Zachary's car. It was parked illegally in a handicapped space. Which meant, he presumed, that Rosalie was home alone . . . with her puffy little boobs and her body squirming like a weasel. Rosalie ranked right up there with the best he'd ever done, and he had done plenty. He'd have married the bitch except she was already married to Zachary, so he had stayed with Betz, who was better-looking but not as sexy. Oh, do it, he thought, do them all.

He pulled out of the parking lot and drove downtown to the florist for a dozen yellow roses and then on up the hill to Zachary's house.

Rosalie was on the back patio, the baby beside her in a bassinet.

She was getting her body back already, he noticed. She was ripe for the doing.

"Gil!" she said, genuinely pleased to see him. "And look at those beautiful roses!"

He bowed and, looking at the ground, held out the roses like an awkward schoolboy. He was being charming.

"Stop that," she said, "you silly, go and put them in a vase."

Gil went inside and reached up to the cabinet above the refrigerator where Rosalie kept the vases. He found an old milk bottle, the kind they didn't make any more, and stuck the roses into it. He went back outside and set the flowers down at her feet.

"Don't you want to see the baby?" Rosalie said. "Look at him."

"I came to see you," he said.

She examined Gil's face closely then. "It's not yours," she said. "Really. It's safe to look."

Gil smiled, awkward, and bent over the baby. It looked exactly like him. He bent closer and examined the face, the shape and set of the eyes, the protruding nose.

"Are you sure it's not mine?" he said.

"We've been through this," she said. "He's not yours. it's not possible—physically or temporally or however you say it. He's Zachary's, I guarantee it."

"But it looks like me."

"That's just your vanity," she said. "Look at the nose, that's pure Zachary, and the rest of him is me."

Gil continued to stare at the baby. He had not really looked at Betz's baby—who wanted to look at a retard?—and he was surprised to see how tiny and perfect Rosalie's baby was. He felt like touching him.

"Can I pick him up?"

"He just got to sleep, Gil. Don't."

"Just let me pick him up."

Gil slipped his hands under the baby and with great care lifted him from the bassinet and held him to his chest. The baby kept on sleeping.

Gil rocked him in his arms. He was light, but with the wonderful weight of a living thing, and Gil, very gently, held him closer.

"He looks just like me," Gil said.

"Well, he's not. Yours. Zachary is the father."

As a matter of fact, Rosalie was not at all sure that Zachary was the father, but she had long since decided to insist he was, knowing that as time passed it would become true even if it wasn't.

"Are you *absolutely* sure?" Gil said.

"Absolutely," she said.

He squeezed the baby, who woke and began to cry.

"Oh Christ," Rosalie said, "give him to me."

"Hush," Gil whispered, "hushaby bye," and he rocked the baby back and forth in his arms until the crying stopped. "See?" he said, and handed the baby over to Rosalie.

He watched them for a while, mother and child, and was surprised to find that all his emotions were pleasant ones. He sat down and continued to look at them. Rosalie, with her halo of dark red curls. The baby, with hair like flax, like spun gold, like his own hair when he'd been a child. He flicked back the floppy gold hair from his brow and smiled to himself. Somewhere, inside, a plan was forming.

He kissed the baby goodbye and, as an afterthought, kissed Rosalie as well.

He drove back to the parking lot, humming. He felt very good. He had driven up there with the intention of getting done, or sucked off at least, and the baby made him forget about it completely. There was more to life than just sex.

~

Gil was still feeling warm and fatherly when he walked in on the scene in the mail room. He looked from Maddy Barker to Concepcion and, seeing that they were otherwise engaged—indeed, seeing that they were likely to start throwing punches—he decided he would pick up his mail later in the day. He stepped outside to read the notices and to eavesdrop.

"Leave him *alone*!" Maddy said.

"What? He's *your* property?"

"You're making a fool of yourself. Dressed like a hooker. Going to his place at midnight."

"I happened to be returning a book."

"At midnight?"

Outside the mail room, Zachary Kurtz joined Gil at the bulletin board. "What's all this?" Zachary said and jerked his thumb toward the mail room. The women's voices were rising.

"Foreplay," Gil said.

Zachary patted down his little mustache and prepared to listen. From inside the room there was silence, and then Maddy was heard saying, "I don't know which is more disgusting—your pursuit of him or of her."

"Him?" Zachary said to Gil. "Her?"

Gil shrugged and said, "Shhh."

But the women had lowered their voices and the men, outside, could hear only angry murmurs.

Olga approached them from behind. "Gentlemen," she said.

Zachary spun around. Gil, caught eavesdropping, let out a snort.

Olga looked at them, her brows raised.

Concepcion and Maddy Barker appeared at the door. Maddy's eyes were narrowed dangerously and Concepcion was flushed a violent red.

"Were you *listening* to us?" Maddy said. "Eavesdropping?"

At that moment the Chairman came out of his office, saw the group at the bulletin board, blanched, and hurried back inside. He locked the door behind him.

"Well?" Maddy said. "Were you?" Her eyes were narrowed on Gil.

Gil looked around, stricken, and snorted once again.

The main door slammed open and there stood Eleanora Tuke. "Hi-yo!" she called, and did a large pirouette so they could see her outfit. She wore a red plaid skirt, pleated, with a matching jacket, and a white blouse with ruffles at the collar and cuffs, and ruffles all down the front. She looked like a perfectly enormous third-grader.

"What do you think?" she said. But before anyone could respond, she said to Zachary and Gil, "Oh, look, everybody here has just had babies, I want to know everything about them, how much they weigh, and how smart they are, and if they're of either sex," and to Maddy she said, "I hear you've moved to Faculty Terrace, but never mind that, have you seen the *New York Review of Books*? My God, wait till you see it, what they do to Paglia," and to Concepcion she said nothing because she didn't like Barthes and she had never been able to see the point of Chicano literature but she gave her a big smile, and to Olga she said, "What? What's going on? I want to know. I hear your course in the problem of good is a disaster. Tell me. Tell me everything."

Gil fled as soon as she mentioned babies, but as he entered his office—around the corner and down the hall—he could still hear her babbling. "Tell me. Tell me everything," she was saying.

Gil had done Eleanora once, just for the hell of it, when she and her little physicist had come down to the beach house. Gil had been married to Moo at the time, and had decided to annoy her by taking on Eleanora while Moo and the physicist sat downstairs playing tiddlywinks. Also, frankly, he felt like it. Though Eleanora had never stopped talking the whole time, she had turned in an impressive performance. She seemed to be able to bring all that psychic energy into physical play and still continue rattling on about Nietzsche or "I love Lucy" reruns or whatever happened to be on her mind at the moment.

He wondered for a second if Eleanora, chatter aside, might be the woman he'd been looking for. No, he decided, because the chatter was not aside. The chatter was here to stay. Besides, she didn't need him since her little physicist, thanks to his bombs, had more money than God.

Women were a disaster. His first marriage was poison right from the beginning, forget it, and Moo had been hopeless—not to mention sterile—and Betz . . . he hated to write off the marriage to Betz, but he could see he might have to. Betz was great-looking, she was a trophy, and she was tough. Like a man, almost. And she liked the kinky stuff, at least she had at the beginning.

The baby was the problem. They had to get rid of the baby, and now. He thought of Rosalie and *her* baby, and the nice feeling of warmth and fatherliness he had experienced just a short while ago. Why should he be deprived of that? Why should he be the only one without a son? Or even a daughter? Though he preferred a son.

He decided to call and give Betz one more chance. He'd offer her money. A half mil, cash in hand, and she'd get rid of the baby. Hell, he'd go up to a full mil. They'd take a trip, start over, do it right this time.

The phone rang just as he was reaching for it.

"Betz?" he said.

But it was not Betz on the phone. It was Huddle, of Huddle and Pilbrick, Attorneys at Law.

Huddle drawled in that annoying Texas voice he assumed when-ever he had bad news. He had just received a call, Huddle said, from Betz's law-yuh? Did Gil know she had a law-yuh? Her own law-yuh? Well, he'd called this morning.

"It just may beee," Huddle said, leaning on the vowel, "that we should get together tooo? Y'all and me? At four?"

15

Olga sat at her desk with her chair swiveled slightly toward the window. This way she could continue her work—at the moment she was making notes in her journal on possible futures for Zachary Kurtz and Robbie Richter and Betz Rudin—and still be aware of any slight movement below her window, across the driveway, and for some distance on either side of the pool. Thus, unaided by the spy reports of Peter Peeks, Olga had learned a very great deal. She knew that Maddy Barker was house-sitting a condo diagonally across from Francis Xavier Tortorisi's. She knew that Maddy and Concepcion had—separately—laid siege to Tortorisi. She knew of his comings and goings and who his visitors were and how long they stayed, and she knew too that Tortorisi was not above playing one against the other. From this marvelous aerie, this contemporary lime-tree bower, she could observe without being seen observing. She took her notes, she made her plans, she intervened in the lives of the great and the little, and, rejoicing, she wrote it all down. Human nature was a movable feast and a perpetual one.

~

"You're worried that you want a man," Olga said. "Isn't that what you've been saying, really?"

"Yes," Concepcion said, "I'm so embarrassed."

Concepcion had been telling Olga about her sufferings. No one else understood, she insisted, no one else cared. Not even her prayer cell. Not even Suzy Sweezie, her undergraduate beloved. They all wanted to simplify the problem and accuse her of coarse heterosexual desires. But it was not that at all. It was just that Tortorisi brought out in her something—some desire, some need—that her girlfriends did not understand. Nor did she herself understand it. And nothing in Roland Barthes seemed to help.

She began to cry. Was she really different from a normal gay woman? Why, suddenly, was she not content with her life? It was all terrible. Terrible. She put her hands to her face and wept.

Olga let some time pass and then she explained, calmly, patiently, that though it was true that not everyone is called to be gay, Concepcion had nothing to worry about. It was clear she was a true and loving lesbian. You can put away all doubts, Olga said. This heterosexual dalliance has been vain and delusory, a momentary fit, a temptation perhaps, a testing. What must be faced now is who we are and *what we want*, Olga said. And, once again, "You're worried that you want a man. Isn't that what you've been saying, really?"

Concepcion nodded. Her mascara had run badly and her lovely round face was marked with crooked black lines.

"Put your mind at rest," Olga said. "You don't want a man. You just want a baby."

Concepcion looked at her, startled.

"Consider it," Olga said. "Just think about it."

Olga said, "Motherhood is natural."

"Motherhood is good," Olga said.

"Do you think it could be that?" Concepcion said.

"Many women want babies. That doesn't mean they're not gay. Clearly, you are one of those."

"A baby," Concepcion said, letting it sink in. "Maybe it's the Chicana in me."

"A permanent relationship," Olga said, "and a baby." She saw that Concepcion was receptive to this line of thinking and so she continued, with examples from contemporary life and from the lives of friends in Paris and The Hague, and—thanks to her ingenious new exegesis of old familiar texts—from literature as well. She finished finally and waited for the reaction.

"A baby," Concepcion said. "A permanent relationship?"

"Exactly."

Concepcion hesitated and her mind wandered. "Tortorisi is so soft and plump," she said.

Olga said nothing.

"But what I want is a baby. And lots of plump girlfriends."

"Babies don't flourish in a house with lots of plump girlfriends. Babies need a permanent relationship."

"Well, I don't know about *that*," Concepcion said.

Again Olga was silent. And stern.

"Variety is nice," Concepcion said, and smiled at Olga suggestively. "Don't you find that you crave a little variety? Now and then?"

"Maybe you *do* want to marry Tortorisi," Olga said, getting tough. "Or maybe it's sex you want . . . with a male . . . with a penis."

This startled Concepcion back into reality to such an extent that she took out her compact and began making repairs on her face. She was a liberated lesbian who believed, passionately, in the advantages of make-up. A touch of cleansing cream to remove the mascara streaks, a little pancake base, some powder, rouge, eye shadow, eyeliner, mascara, a touch of mahogany lipstick, and voila: the old Concepcion was back.

During all this time Olga said nothing.

"Perhaps a baby," Concepcion said. "And perhaps—someday—a permanent relationship."

She thanked Olga and left.

~

Concepcion had barely disappeared down the drive when Maddy Barker appeared. Maddy's black hair stood out in tangles around her head and her farmer's overalls hung upon her shapelessly. She wore her thick glasses because today was one of her teaching days.

Maddy was distraught over the marauding Concepcion.

"She's after Tortorisi, isn't she!" Maddy said. "What is she up to?"

"How about some tea?" Olga said. "Come in and have some tea."

"I saw her from my window. Are you on her side?"

But Olga merely held up her hand, palm out, indicating silence, and Maddy fell silent.

She leaned against the kitchen door while Olga made tea, waiting impatiently.

Maddy was impatient about everything—her work, her life, her love affairs—but particularly about her love affairs. She was no good at flirtation and had no desire to be. Flirtation was a waste of time and energy. Consequently, no sooner was she smitten with Olga, than she had approached her—in the library, nearly a month ago now—and said, "Are you special? I have to know." Before Olga could respond, Maddy had said, "Because I'd like to go to bed with you."

"Special?" Olga said.

"Gay," Maddy said, "lesbian. You know. Do you like women? Have you ever been to bed with a woman?"

"Yes," Olga said, "in my young youth I thought it was essential to try everything at least once."

"And?" Maddy's eyes narrowed critically.

"And nice as it was, I decided I was not special."

"Do you want to give it another try?"

"If I were to give it another try, it would certainly be with you," Olga had said. "But I think, for the moment at least, I shall retain my status as non-special."

Maddy had accepted this intellectually, though on an emotional level she continued to hope. She felt she owed it to feminism and to her personal independence to sleep with Olga. She resolved, however, to be patient in the matter of sex. But then Concepcion had made a move on Tortorisi, attacking him in the supermarket, knocking him up at midnight, and Maddy had decided this was too much. She would have to take action. Tortorisi was hers, after all, mess though he was, and she was not about to share him with that idiotic Concepcion. By the next day she had arranged to house-sit in Faculty

Terrace where she could keep one eye on Tortorisi's comings and goings and the other eye, as it were, on Olga.

Maddy was troubled now as Olga went about the business of making tea.

"She's after Tortorisi, I know it," Maddy said again, but again there was no response.

Olga carried the tea tray into the living room, poured each of them a cup, and curled up in the corner of the couch.

"Have a cookie," Olga said. "They're only a little stale."

"Well?" Maddy said.

Olga sipped her tea, Constant Comment, and smiled with approval. She reached for a stale cookie.

"What is she after?" Maddy said. "That bitch."

"She's after a baby," Olga said.

"A baby? What do you mean, a baby?"

"A baby. A small person, newborn, sweet and cuddly, with lots of poo inside."

"But, I mean, whose? Why does she want a baby and where is she going to get it? You can't just *have* a baby because you think you want one. Some random velleity."

And then it struck her.

"Oh no, not Tortorisi! He wouldn't do that. He couldn't." She thought for a second. "He wouldn't know *how*."

Olga sipped her tea.

"Would he?" Maddy said, suspicious suddenly.

"He's a lovely man."

Maddy narrowed her eyes.

"I'm interested only in his writing," Olga said. "He wants tenure and I'm going to help him get it."

Maddy relaxed a little.

"His new book will help," Olga said.

"Kurtz wants him out, you know." Maddy frowned. "Kurtz is determined."

"I'll handle Kurtz."

Maddy thought for a moment and decided the direct approach was the best approach. "And will you handle Concepcion too?" she asked.

Olga stared into her teacup.

"Keep her away from Tortorisi, I mean?"

"People do what they feel they must," Olga said.

"He's mine." There, she had said it. "He's mine and I won't share him with anybody. Besides, it's interfering with my work. I have to think of my career."

"Leave it to me," Olga said.

"My career comes first. Always."

Olga smiled and nodded agreement.

Maddy sat back in her chair to study this Olga. She wrote novels. She was the last person on earth anybody should trust. Why, then, did everyone come to her with their problems, their secrets? Who was she? Who did she think she was?

"We treat you like a goddess," Maddy said.

Olga sipped her tea.

"Do you think you're a goddess?"

Olga smiled.

"*Are* you?"

"No," Olga said, and put down her tea cup. "Jessye Norman is a goddess. And Muriel Spark . . . up to a point."

"Muriel Spark?"

"Up to a point."

As she saw Maddy out, Olga leaned close and said confidentially, "You make an interesting couple, you and Tortorisi."

She watched from her window as Maddy Barker descended the stairs, paused in thought, and then, having made her decision, went up the adjacent stairs to Francis Xavier Tortorisi's.

Satisfied, Olga turned to her desk to do her thoughts.

~

Olga tried to return to Robbie Richter and Zachary Kurtz, those lost souls, but her concentration was scattered and her mind wandered

freely over the battlefield, disposing of none of the bodies but mar-
veling merely at the quality and nature of the various participants.
The enormity of Eleanora Tuke. The timorous fidelity of Cynthia
Richter. Rosalie Kurtz, as yet unknown, but ripe with promise and
with a new baby into the bargain. Leroy O'Shea and Moo Wesley
Rudin, who would have to have a baby, but how, but how? And the
Chairman, stepping off into a dark that was not visible to her.

Daryl flickered in her mind's eye, but she blinked him away with
firmness and dispatch. He did not belong in this story, she would not
accommodate him. If he persisted, she would not take responsibility.
She could not.

And poor horny, beautiful Peter Peeks, perfect in his firm young
flesh, eager for love. Was there anything, anything at all, she might
give him?

Finally, exhausted, she returned to the present: to Maddy Barker
and Tortorisi and Concepcion. Done. And Betz Rudin and her baby
Susanna. Done. And Gil Rudin? More or less done, whether he knew
it or not.

From them, of necessity, she passed on to Kurtz, the eternal
Zachary Kurtz, who must be dealt with firmly, now . . . but once again
she was seized by indecision. She could not deal with him yet. She
would not deal with him yet.

Zachary Kurtz would have to wait.

Robbie Richter was next. He had begun on Lawrence.

16

"You don't understand," Cynthia said, "this is how he *is*!"

"But he's hysterical," the doctor said, "he's in a frenzy."

"That's his normal state!"

"But . . . " the doctor said.

"He's his old self! He's cured!"

The doctor thought for a minute. He was a young doctor, eager to learn and willing to consider all possibilities. Perhaps, as the patient's wife claimed, this was his normal behavior. Professor Richter was, by all reports, a prodigious scholar and a unique personality. Perhaps his metabolism—perhaps even his *brain*—required him to behave in this way, jabbering incessantly, making cryptic references to his first book and to his latest book and to his first student's book on *his* book. Perhaps this is what scholars did these days. But what was he talking *about*? And why? And how could his nervous system withstand the ravages of such constant activity?

"But how can he stand it?" the doctor said. And then he blurted out: "How can *you* stand it?"

Cynthia cried with relief. They understood at last, they believed her, they would release her little Robbie and let her take him home. It was a miracle. Thanks, let it be said, to Olga.

~

Olga would drive the Richters' car so that Cynthia could have her hands free to deal with Robbie, who, naturally, was excited to be going home. He gibbered and twitched and carried on. He giggled. He was a mess. He managed nonetheless to supervise the packing of the books, to offer his voluble thanks to the doctors and nurses, and at the same time to explain to everyone the nuances of his proposed book on D. H. Lawrence. Finally he was ready to go.

An orderly stacked the book boxes on a hand truck and wheeled them out to the car where he and Olga packed them away in the trunk. There were an awful lot of books. Robbie followed in a wheelchair pushed by the confused attendant and trailed, glowingly, by Cynthia.

Robbie was lecturing the attendant on the follies of post-structuralism.

"It's a held truth," Robbie was saying, "that, because language *constructs* the reality of a text, all texts are fiction. Whether we like it or not. Whether the author intended it or not. Quote, unquote: all texts are fiction. That's a post-structuralist given, you see, a *point du depart*. Argal—therefore—all biography is fiction."

He twisted around in the wheelchair to make sure the attendant was listening. The attendant nodded agreement.

"But I've rediscovered in Franklin W. Dixon and most recently in Lawrence that fiction is fiction, and biography is sometimes not fiction. There are fictional facts and there are empirical facts and they are not the same. Or shouldn't be. There's a distinction between— *comment on dit?*—the 'factualness' of each, and you've got to preserve the distinction if you're going to have biography. And you're *going* to have biography whether you like it or not, because I'm going to write it. Do you know why?"

"Why?" the attendant said.

"Because my life is not coterminous with the Hardy Boys."

He twisted around again, grinning madly.

"It's coterminous with Lawrence!" He shrieked, or perhaps it was a laugh, and he beat his fist on the arm of the wheelchair. "I *am* Lawrence, or rather, I'm going to *become* Lawrence and write my biography . . . which of course is his autobiography, or vice versa, whichever applies. Do you see?"

"Yes," the attendant said.

"Why, you ask? I'll tell you why." Robbie began to declaim:

'I am the origin of my texts,

I am the captain of my soul.'

He laughed a lot more than seemed necessary and he jiggled about in his seat. He pumped his arms in a victory sign.

They reached the car, and with a groan of relief the attendant unhooked the safety belts and helped Robbie out of the wheelchair. Robbie stood and breathed deeply, looking around him. Cynthia was at his side and Olga was holding open the car door when Robbie suddenly assumed his role as master of the situation.

"You have been most kind," he said to the attendant, "and I should like to present you with a signed copy of my very first book, *The Glow And The Haze: Conrad's Aesthetic Strategies*." He extended his hand to Cynthia, who looked puzzled for a moment and then reached under the car seat where Robbie kept his traveling *Foucault Reader*. She brought it out and handed it over. Olga gave him a pen.

He saw at once that it was not *The Glow And The Haze* but he shrugged and signed it anyway.

'To the attendant,' he wrote, 'from the biographer of D. H. Lawrence.' and with a flourish: 'Robbie Richter, Ph. D. (U. of V.)'

He gave the attendant a distant smile. "Not at all," he said, "not at all," and climbed into the back seat where he held hands with Cynthia.

Olga roared out of the hospital drive.

The attendant, grateful, watched them go. He could see Robbie leaning forward, talking excitedly.

~

At first, when Robbie was taken away, Ozzie had lain at the front door waiting for him to return. Days went by and Ozzie would not eat his kibble nor would he leave the door. Cynthia bought him special dog treats. He would not touch them. She left him little saucers of hamburger, steak bones with succulent bits of meat clinging to them, lamb chops raw and cooked. Ozzie ate them grudgingly and lapsed into a funk. He left his vigil at the front door and went up to Robbie's study where he lay curled up on a purple cushion as if he were dead or wanted to be. He began to gnaw at his legs and hind quarters. He pulled patches of hair out by the roots. There were little orange chunks of Ozzie all over the study. Cynthia experimented with meats and grains, with condiments and spices, and had taken finally to cooking him chicken dijonnaise since that seemed to make him less self-destructive. But Ozzie entered a new, silent stage and Cynthia's haute cuisine served only to keep him alive. His coat was dull and patchy and there was no luster to his eyes. He was pining away. He made a soft mewing sound, desolate.

But now as Olga pulled up to the house they could hear Ozzie barking. Instinct had asserted itself and love had triumphed. Ozzie was his old self, and so was Robbie, and Cynthia trembled with relief. From the sheer happiness of it all, Robbie began to cry. They leaned close together, Cynthia and Robbie, crying, trembling. They kissed.

Olga, ever discreet, left them at the curb.

Inside the house all was jubilation. Robbie and Ozzie rolled on the floor and barked at each other until Cynthia could stand it no longer and rolled on the floor with them. Robbie squeezed too hard and Ozzie peed on the carpet, but nobody cared, and they all just barked some more. Cynthia was the first to give out. She lay, breathless, watching them play. And then Ozzie gave out. Robbie nuzzled him one more time, but the dog just lay there, panting, unable to go on. Robbie crept over to Cynthia and nuzzled her. She nuzzled him back. He began to giggle. He nuzzled her neck and he nuzzled her breasts and he began to nuzzle between her legs.

Ozzie, still panting, raised his head to look.

Propriety descended on them all.

Robbie rose and, proudly erect, went into the kitchen. He searched the refrigerator for a suitable treat. He wanted to keep Ozzie happy and occupied for as long as it would take them, and he guessed it would take them a good long time.

Ozzie stood in the doorway looking quizzical.

Cynthia waited, trembling, at the foot of the stairs.

Filled with pride, swollen with ambition, Robbie reached deep into the refrigerator, pushed past the hamburger and the chicken, and grasped the roast of beef. He tore off the wrapper and flung the meat to the floor. The dog fell upon it, slavering.

With no backward look, Robbie snatched Cynthia's hand and they fled, giggling, up the stairs.

Robbie slammed the bedroom door, and locked it behind him. There was a long silence in which the thud of their heartbeats could be heard. And then, suddenly, Robbie began to cry. The trip upstairs had been too much for him and he had lost all potency. He stood there, flaccid, ruined.

So much for D. H. Lawrence.

But Cynthia, operating from animal instinct, from purest inspiration, transformed herself for love's sake into Frieda von Richthofen. She wound up for the pitch and batted him one on the side of the head.

Robbie was stunned for the moment and then he began to breathe heavily.

She batted him again, determined.

He let out a scream of triumph, the ape man, erect.

And then, fully clothed, they fell together on the bed, gasping, clawing, abandoning themselves to a Lawrentian frenzy.

17

Robbie Richter was home, his old self once again, and everybody was glad about it.

The Chairman came by with a bottle of champagne. A good number of the fools brought presents, discreetly, for Cynthia or Ozzie. Zachary Kurtz showed up. Nobody stayed very long because Robbie was still recovering and because, frankly, he talked more compulsively than ever—some new lunacy about the Hardy Boys and D. H. Lawrence and his own true life story. But they didn't mind his carrying on. They were pleased to see him back. They cared about him because they knew that beneath the jabber and the silliness and the monstrous ego there lay the heart of a very good man.

~

The big news was that Robbie's recovery had been engineered, somehow, by Olga. The Chairman had taken note of this and he had sent a memo to the Dean. There were things to be said for having this Olga here. She was smart. She was useful. She might be more useful still. Critic, novelist, a female voice from the front line of theory: let us give some thought to Olga, he said.

Perhaps she could be prevailed upon to stay?

Perhaps she could be an opportunity appointment?

Perhaps she could be considered—not now, maybe, but soon—for the Chairmanship?

Perhaps, just perhaps, she was the answer to their prayers?

~

Meanwhile Olga paced the floor, and paced. She was a fraud, a fake. She could no longer think and she could no longer write and she was a failure as a human being as well.

Zachary Kurtz came and rang the bell and went away.

Tortorisi came.

The Chairman came.

A sizable portion of Olga's world here on the west coast, here at the university, came and rang the bell and went away.

And Olga, the failure, paced. She drank tea and paced. In desperation, she prayed, and went back to pacing.

This was always the way before a breakthrough, but how many times and for how long could she survive these acts of faith?

She paced, waiting.

~

Olga had reached a turning point in her life, or at least in her life here at the university. She could not write. Worse, she could not contrive. Her mind was at a standstill and her unconscious remained stubbornly inaccessible to her. Who were these people and what did they want, what did they fear? If she knew what they wanted, she could give it to them. If she knew what they feared—well, there was only so much she could do about that, given her limitations as a semi-divine being and their limitations as the possessors of free will. She was blocked and therefore frenzied and therefore dangerous.

She gave herself up to teaching.

"The problem of good," she said, "is rooted in the problem of love and desire. Aquinas defines love thus: *velle bonum alicui*, to wish the good of another, to desire good for another. It's not a bad definition."

'Aquinas,' they all wrote in their notebooks. 'Good = love plus desire, etc.'

"We want evil to be hard," she said, ironic and apparently conciliatory, "we want evil to wear a uniform with a swastika on the arm. We want evil to *look* evil. It seems a reasonable request. Evil, however, is as natural as the air we breathe. It looks good because it looks convenient. It looks, in fact, reasonable. It is the most natural thing in the world. Good, on the other hand, is above nature."

And on she went, and on. Responsibility, discrimination, and more responsibility.

Good was pretty much a downer.

Her students were divided on just what she was talking about. "It's the environment," some of them said, "she's anti-pollution," and they cited her frequent comment about the air we breathe. Others felt she wanted people to take responsibility for moral discrimination, whatever that was supposed to mean. But there were others, quite a few in fact, who pressed her on the point and who decided that her lectures implied the existence of an absolute standard of right and wrong, which they found disturbing. Absolutes, by definition, were not democratic. They were not multicultural. They were unfair. Why couldn't she just talk about Hitler and the Holocaust? But no, she kept invoking words like mystery and mysterious, grace and aspiration, the unknowable, the supra-rational, the purely metaphysical: abstractions that she used in a way different from Derrida and Lacan and all the neat people way back in the '80s.

Enrollments in the problem of good dropped off severely.

Her seminar on Foucault fared rather better. You couldn't really destroy the history of sexuality, after all, and it was kind of fun—at least Daryl thought so—to hear her being iconoclastic about somebody as great as Foucault, even though she must be kidding. Or why else would she be teaching it, right? Peter Peeks disagreed. Foucault was a god, he said, and you just didn't make funny cracks about a god. Olga had no right to say some of the things she said. Especially about Foucault and sex. Daryl and Peter Peeks were not in the seminar, of course, but people talked about it and they all knew everything she said as if they'd been there themselves.

"In the end," Olga said, "you find that sex has almost nothing to do with anything."

Everybody laughed. Because this *had* to be a joke.

"Greed makes the world go round," she said. "And power," she said. "And in this sense Foucault is absolutely on target. Indeed, if you stop thinking of him as a historian or a philosopher and think of him instead as a kind of inverted poet, you'll find that he's very often on target. He works from metaphor. He operates out of instinct. Insight is his procedural method—not science, not history—and he shapes history to his insight. And very often he's right."

She leaned into the podium, determined.

"He knows the enemy, does Foucault. He recognizes danger and the danger is power. We talk about freedom. We talk about free will. All very well, Foucault says, but talking is irrelevant and so is free will. All our energies, all our emotions, our impulses toward good or evil, even our sexual instincts have been institutionalized by larger social forces. Freedom has surrendered to power and power is all, Foucault says. In power lies the repression and finally the destruction of all human possibility."

She bit off her words.

"Thus far Foucault," she said. And then she went off on a rant about Aristotle and Aquinas and the still small voice, which was a quote from somebody, and she got very boring.

Still, at these moments she had a way of talking that electrified them. They knew it was just drama, and some of them resented it, but in her voice there was a tone of desperate intensity, as if this were her one chance to get the truth across. That tone imposed silence on them, and maintained it, and made them for the moment forget about everything except power and their threatened powerlessness. As if they were guilty of something. A few of them wrote "fuck you" on their books and notebooks, spontaneously, out of an uncomprehended need, and some wrote "fuck religion," and one actually wrote "fuck metaphysics," but nobody said anything aloud and few were willing to discuss her lectures afterward.

There were some—a few—who thought, and doubted, and were troubled by their thoughts and doubts. They were the weak and uncertain who would make messes of their lives, obsessive types, not healthy. They would end up drop-outs or saints or ax-murderers. You couldn't take them seriously.

The general feeling was simpler. "She's just too negative," someone said. She didn't have the right attitude toward life. She was definitely a downer.

Part III

18

For the first time in his life Zachary Kurtz was in love. Moreover, he *felt* in love. He hugged the baby and he kissed the baby and he wanted more than anything to protect the baby. From harm. From everything. From life. Therefore they were going to have the baby circumcised.

At his insistence they named the baby Adam Zachary, A to Z. At his insistence, too, they planned a full-scale ritual bris, with rabbi, mohel, sandak, prayers, the whole *schmeer*. At his insistence they were going to do it right. Never mind that more than eight days had passed since the baby's birth—in fact nearly six weeks had passed—it was never too late to *start* doing things right. At his insistence, therefore, they invited the entire English department, fools included. And finally, in an access of good feeling that bordered on hysteria, they invited the Deans, and the poor addled President and his dreadful Missy.

Zachary had never attended a circumcision before; he had no religious interests or talents. But this was for his son, his firstborn, and so he felt he could swallow a little religion. He was finding it a strange and wonderful ceremony and it filled him, as he stood cradling his son in his arms, with all the feelings of love. He felt generous, he felt selfless, he felt he had lost himself in this incredible, tiny, precious, *living* manifestation of his own creative powers. Next to this, the Department of Theory and Discourse was small beer indeed.

The rabbi was a sophisticated man, an academic himself, and he conducted a very nice bris. He began with a brief explanation of the reason for circumcision. Health, cleanliness, the Law, all that stuff, but then he bore down on his main point: look, Abraham did it to Isaac, Isaac did it to Jacob, that's why we do it. Because they did it. The kids have to understand this: up is up and down is down, there's right and wrong, it's tradition. That's just how it is. Period. Then he did a lot of wailing in Hebrew, instructional reminders and psalms of thanksgiving, meanwhile moving the baby from Zachary's arms to the arms of the honorary mother and then to the honorary father, and after some more prayers, back to Zachary. It was all part of the ritual. The baby held up very well under all this moving around, and Zachary, with the baby once more in his arms, smiled at Rosalie and smiled at the baby. He was still smiling when the rabbi burst again into song, this time in English.

> Praised be Thou, O Lord our God, King of the Universe,
> who has sanctified us with thy commandments and
> commanded us concerning the rite of circumcision.

He stopped smiling, though, when the rabbi lifted the baby from his arms and laid him on the table in front of the godfather, Gil Rudin. The table had a stiff white pad on it and the rabbi took a couple Velcro tabs and taped the baby's arms, cruciform, to the pad. He stepped back to examine his work. Zachary looked at the baby and then at the rabbi and then back to the baby. Could this be right? There must be some mistake. The baby began to whimper. Zachary watched in horror as the mohel, silent and menacing, something out of an old Russian film, stepped forward and pinched the baby's foreskin and with his free hand produced the ritual knife. Zachary's horror turned to disbelief as the mohel, wincing only slightly, cut through the soft pink flesh. The blood spurted a terrible red as the baby let out a piercing wail and Zachary, bug-eyed and white, sank unconscious to the floor.

There was a stir while somebody ran for water and somebody else propped Zachary up, but otherwise the ceremony continued without interruption. The mohel wrapped the baby in the ritual bandages and made an effort to cover up the bloodstains while the rabbi sang another psalm and another cautionary verse, and by the time the rabbi turned to congratulate Zachary, the fallen father had been lifted to his feet and leaned palely against the sofa. And so it was over.

Everyone congratulated Rosalie and Zachary, and smiled at the rabbi, and condoled with the baby. Gil continued cooing to the newly circumcised Adam Zachary, holding him in his arms in a rather proprietary manner. They were all waiting for the next thing to happen.

Missy, the President's wife, raised her hands above her head as she assumed a dancer's pose and, clapping rhythmically, with only a hint of seduction, attempted to lead the males in the Hava Nagila. She looked stunning in her black velvet suit. The President followed her dutifully but without joy, and one of the Deans—in psychology—attempted to follow too, but he was a clunky dancer and almost nobody knew the words and it turned out that very few people at the celebration were Jewish anyhow. There was a tacit agreement to put the Hava Nagila to rest. Missy took a little bow, smiling broadly, but the President, who couldn't figure out what had happened, continued to dance alone until a little burst of applause clued him in. Fortunately the caterers appeared just then with lots of hors d'oeuvres, Daryl set up his bar and began pouring drinks, and Rosalie had the good sense to put on some Barry Manilow, softly, so it was clear this was intended to be a party.

The rabbi and the mohel could see, however, that it wasn't their kind of party—this one was ninety percent *goyishe*—and so they took off.

Everybody clung together in little groups, except Missy who bellied up to the bar. She chugged a scotch on the rocks, standing there, and then extended the glass for a refill.

The people in groups began to chat. At first they were fairly discreet about it, but soon everybody was commenting openly on Zachary's fainting spell. "A sign of humanity," one of the fools said, and the Chairman replied, "And who could have guessed *that?*" The comment was repeated around the room as if it were a *mot*.

"Men," Maddy Barker said to Olga, "they always have to be the center of attention."

"Zachary, you mean?" Olga said. "Or the President dancing? Which?"

"All of them," Maddy said. "They're all the same. Men."

In fact, it was Peter Peeks she was thinking of. Maddy had observed Peter Peeks on his trips in and out of Olga's condo and she was watching him now as he passed hors d'oeuvres among a little crowd of women. He wore a white shirt and black tuxedo pants with splendid red suspenders, decorations merely, since the pants were tight and in no danger of falling down. She slitted her eyes and gazed at him. He was a disgustingly male creature. What on earth did women see in them?

"Look at that," Maddy said, and Olga turned in time to see the President's wife lean into Peter Peeks and hook a finger beneath those red suspenders and snap them hard against his chest. Peeks smiled at her and waited for more. She made a little kissy-face at him, and Peeks moved on to the rest of the women with his sausages and sauce, and they admired his many white teeth and his boyish smile and his hard little behind. Maddy watched all this. "Women," Maddy said, "disgusting."

"Tell me," Olga said. "Tell me about women."

"Tell me about Peter Peeks," Maddy said.

So, it was a stand-off.

Across the room Rosalie Kurtz was doing her best to raise conversation among the three Deans: a tall one, a black one, and a yellow.

"Such a lot of responsibility," Rosalie was saying, "I don't know how you cope, all of you. *Any* of you."

"I teach," one of the Deans said, the tall one, "otherwise I couldn't survive under all the pressure. Teaching is the only thing that makes it bearable."

"Pressure, pressure, pressure," the psychology Dean said. He was Chinese and knew all about pressure.

"Service," the third one said, "knowing you're doing something for the community: the black community, of course, and also the general community. And, quite frankly, for the Prez. He's been through a bad time of it, let me tell you. All those scandals. All that money down the toilet. *He* has suffered."

"Yes, I suppose," Rosalie said. She had just seen Missy belt down her third scotch and rocks. "And then there's Missy, of course."

Silence fell among them.

"Zachary," Rosalie said, mindful of her duty, "Zachary has some splendid ideas for the department. Very . . . you know. Very advanced."

"Yes," the tall Dean said. "I've heard about this Olga Whatzis. The world's foremost, I'm told. Now, *she's* somebody I've got to meet. I've had letters about her. The Chairman—Whatzisname—wrote me a very impressive memo about her. An opportunity appointment or something."

"Pressure, pressure, pressure," the psychology Dean said, keeping an eye on Missy, who was back at the bar.

"I'll introduce you," Rosalie said, and led him across the room to present Olga to him. At that moment the President and Peter Peeks converged on Olga as well.

"This is Olga Kominska," Rosalie said. "Olga, this is the Dean. *The* Dean. The *cognizant* Dean . . . for the department.

"Dean," Olga said, shaking his hand. "And this is Maddy Barker." Maddy nodded and stepped back, distrustful, since he was a Dean and a man. "It's a very interesting department, this," Olga said. She sounded French for the moment.

"Well, hell," the Dean said, "I certainly hope so. It's teaching that makes the whole thing worthwhile, right? I couldn't survive without my teaching."

"Who said that?" the President asked. "Somebody said that."

"Said what?"

" 'I couldn't survive without my teaching.' Somebody said that."

"I just said that."

"No, not you. Yes, of course you, but I mean somebody else." He pondered for a moment. "Well, it's one of those things people say, isn't it."

"Have a sausage, Prez," Peter Peeks said.

The President shook his head. "Cholesterol," he said. "Gotta keep young." He did a couple jumping jacks, his arms flapping. "Fit," he said.

"You old fart," Missy said, approaching. "You're as fit as you're ever gonna be and that's just fine for me." She slipped her left arm around his waist and with her free right hand she began to stroke his chest, up and down, up and down. She had had too much to drink. "Nice," she said, cooing.

The President beamed with pride and vanity. Missy moved her hand down to his waistband and began to tickle him.

"Tickie, tickie, tickie," Missy said and he laughed, making no effort to stop her. She moved her hand a tiny bit lower.

The group watched in silence, horrified, until at last the President came to himself.

"We've gotta go," he said, pulling himself free from Missy's tickling hands. "I want to thank you all for coming. It's been a very special afternoon. Very fine." And he began to circle the room, shaking hands and thanking the guests for coming, and then he bounded up the stairs to the foyer where Missy joined him in a Nixon wave of farewell.

"Thank you," he said, "I thank you all."

And then he was gone.

To kill the silence somebody turned up Barry Manilow, very loud. They all listened for a while to the song about Lola at the Copa, concentrating.

Rosalie stole a quick look at Olga and at the Dean and at Maddy Barker. They all looked at one another. No one could think of anything to say.

"Have a sausage," Peter Peeks said, and each of them took a sausage and ate it.

"Good stuff," the Dean said. "Is this *Jewish* sausage?"

"Yummy."

"Mmm."

"Mmm."

"Have another," Peter Peeks said, though his tray was empty.

"We can go now," the Dean said, and gave a nod to the black and yellow Deans. "You come to see me in my office," he said to Olga, "I've got things to ask you." And quietly, under cover of Barry Manilow, the Deans made their escape.

Rosalie watched them leave—"The Deans," she said, "the President and Missy"—and then in a creditable imitation of the poor afflicted President, she said to the group at large, "I want to go poo-poo. Who said that? Isn't that a quote from someone? Well it's one of those things people say, isn't it." She set off in search of Zachary and the baby.

Everyone smiled. What an afternoon! First they discover Zachary is human, then they discover Rosalie has wit.

Peter Peeks lingered with Olga and Maddy Barker.

"Too bad about Zack fainting, wasn't it," he said. "Usually he's a rock. Mostly."

"The prevailing opinion," Maddy Barker said, nasty, "is that his fainting spell was a demonstration of his hitherto unsuspected humanity."

Peter Peeks looked at her. Language always excited him.

"Well?" she said.

He hinted at something with his eyes.

Maddy blushed and looked to Olga, who said, "I want to circulate," as she moved off, smiling, toward the fools. Maddy was left on her own.

"We've never talked before," Peter Peeks said. "Of course I'm just an undergraduate and all." He was tempted to do more interesting things with his eyes, but he held back. Lesbians interested him, naturally, because he felt that—given time—he could straighten them all out, but this one was scary, if in fact she was a lesbian. He held off on the eyes and just looked expectant.

Maddy decided on a line of attack. "What did you think," she said, "when the President's wife snapped those red suspenders of yours?"

"I was surprised."

"Was it a come-on?"

"I guess so. I wouldn't presume, of course."

They looked at one another. Then, as if neither had control over what they were doing, and knowing they would do it no matter what, Peter Peeks put a thumb beneath his right suspender and held it out—an offering—and Maddy, accepting the offer, took the suspender and pulled, letting it snap back against his chest. All at once her eyes filled with tears and she pressed her palm to his chest and said, "I hate violence."

"I do too."

"I'm sorry."

"It's okay," he said. "It didn't even hurt. Honest."

Her hand remained on his chest.

"I should go," she said. "My career."

"Should I come see you? Not tonight, I mean, but sometime?"

Maddy thought about this. "No, I don't think so," she said.

"It could just be an experiment," he said.

"No. Don't."

"Sure," he said, "I understand."

He left her then and drifted toward the bar.

"Putting the moves on her?" Daryl said. "It won't work, you know, she's a daughter of Lesbos."

"I don't think she is."

"Zack says so."

"I'm pretty sure she's not." Peter Peeks assumed the moral high ground. "Besides," he said, "some relationships are not merely sexual. There are other kinds of relationships."

And they discussed the other kinds of relationships until Maddy Barker approached the bar and asked for more white wine. Peter Peeks, convinced now that she was interested, went off to do his catering. He would call on her tonight.

There were bursts of laughter from the fools. Olga was telling a story about Queer Theory in Spain. The Chairman, who was straight, looked very nervous about it, but Allan and Sweet Jesus were giggling insanely, and that got Toby going with that booming laugh of his, and Catherine joined in because she could never resist old Tob, and then Stephanie and Mike started up, and it was old home week for the fools, with Olga right in the middle. She did a very funny imitation of a Spanish accent, but Sweet Jesus didn't mind, so why should they?

It was turning into a remarkable party, really. Only where, everybody wondered, were Rosalie and Zack? Zack probably had one of his famous headaches, but where was Rosalie? For that matter where was Gil Rudin?

All three of them were in Zachary's study squabbling, in a mild academic way, over Adam Zachary, A to Z.

"I want to hold him," Zachary said.

"I'm holding him," Gil said.

Rosalie came into the room and stood with her back to the door, watching this.

"You've held him plenty," Zachary said.

"He's doing fine," Gil said. "Don't disturb him."

"What's going on?" Rosalie said. She had searched everywhere for Zack and the baby and then gave up and went looking for Gil and was surprised to find them, all three together, in Zachary's study. "What're you doing, you two?"

They ignored her.

"I want to hold him."

"Shh. You'll wake him."

"He's my baby. Give him to me."

"Shh."

"I said give him to me."

"Rock-a-bye, baby."

"Give me the goddam baby." Zachary made a lunge at the baby, but Gil clutched it to his chest and turned away. "Give me it!" Zachary said. "Give it! Give IT." But Gil kept turning away, the baby tight in his arms. Zachary was dangerously red in the face and he beat with his little fists on Gil's shoulders. "You pig!" he shouted, "give me back my baby!"

Rosalie moved away from the door finally and, with a contemptuous look at Zachary, took the baby from Gil's arms and left the room. She shut the door behind her.

At once she was confronted by Eleanora Tuke.

"We came late," Eleanora said, "so we'd be sure to miss the barbarity. Oh, and here's the little victim himself. Kootchy, kootchy, kootchy." The baby began to chortle. "He's cunning, sort of. He looks just like you, Rosalie, except for the blond hair. Kootchy, kootchy." She hovered over the baby. "Did they cut your little thingy? Did you bleed like a piggy-wiggy? I can't believe people still do this, Jewish or not. It's barbaric." The baby laughed. "We can't stay, Rosalie, because we've got a salon tonight. Derek Walcott and therefore all the Trinidaddies on the West Coast, am I right? Am I right? We're serving pineapple chunks and rum. It's the conversation that counts at a salon. Conversation. The latest everything. And in the background a little discreet reggae? What do you think? Am I right?"

The baby cackled with pleasure.

Eleanora stepped out into the foyer and twirled completely around. She wore an Italian wool knit dress, neon orange, with a broad band of magenta around the bosom and another around the hips. She had on orange shoes and, completing the outfit, an ancient Egyptian pendant made of malachite. It was the size of a small tombstone.

Her little physicist watched her with admiration.

"Festive?" Eleanora said.

"Festive," Rosalie said, and then getting back to the point, added, "you missed the barbarity. You also missed the spectacle of Zachary passing out during the circumcision."

"Bummer," the little physicist said.

There were shouts then from Zachary's study and in a moment Zachary himself flung open the door and charged out. He stopped when he saw Eleanora and beamed when he saw the baby.

"You've met A to Z?" he said, making fish mouths at the baby. "Isn't he something? Isn't he the cutest thing in the world? Isn't he Daddy's little pot pie?"

"Cunning," Eleanora said. "He's definitely cunning. He looks just like you, Zack, except for the blond hair. Now listen, I want to talk with you about video-poetics, Zacky. There's a really wonderful mod-thought dissertation in that. It's ephemeral, I admit, but that's part of its magic. It's a fad that's not gonna last and we have to catch it on the wing, so to speak . . . are you listening?"

But Zachary was not listening. He was taking the baby from Ros-alie's arms, and plumping him up comfortably against his shoulder when suddenly the baby clamped its lips hard against Zachary's neck and began to suck. "Look," Zachary said, "like a vampire," but he was moved almost to tears and for a moment he wished he had breasts so he could nurse the baby, his little A to Z, his little chicken pot pie.

"Listen," Eleanora said, but Zachary drifted off in the direction of the fools. Eleanora, still talking video-poetics, followed the fleeing Zachary, and her little physicist trailed behind. They were soon lost to sight in a gaggle of old professors and their wives, cooing and goo-ing and carrying on as if they had never seen a baby in their lives.

Rosalie watched from the foyer, thinking about the baby's blond hair. Her own hair was a perfect uncompromising red. Zachary's, though on the way out, was black and his absurd mustache was black too. Little A to Z was, as she realized, the image of Gil Rudin.

As if her thoughts had conjured him up, she was joined by Gil who came sheepishly out of Zachary's study.

"Fighting over a baby," Gil said. "God almighty."

Rosalie examined him and his blond hair, but she said nothing.

"Why did you allow that circumcision?" Gil said. "It's primitive. It's disgusting."

"Well, you're circumcised. And very nice it is, too."

"Yes, but it was done at birth, not at a frigging party."

"Zachary wanted it. He insisted."

"He wants a lot of things. Too many things."

Rosalie smiled to herself. "Mistah Kurtz," she said softly.

"Are you sure he's not mine?" Gil said. "The baby?"

"Don't start with that, I've warned you."

"He looks just like me," Gil said, "even the blond hair." He flicked the heavy wave back from his forehead.

"It's recessive," Rosalie said, "blond hair is in the family."

"Well, maybe."

"Look at Zack," she said, amusing herself at Gil's expense. "He's positively dizzy with love."

They stood silently for a moment watching Zachary do baby talk, ostensibly for the baby but in reality to charm the audience of fools. Clever Zachary. Always conniving.

"The political animal at work," she said. "He's softening them up. First he passes out during the circumcision and they decide he's human. Now they're discovering he's a father, or fatherly at least. Next thing you know they'll be voting for him to be Chairman."

"For *Robbie Richter* to be Chairman," Gil said. "Let's not lose our heads here."

"Mistah Kurtz," she said, "he Chairman."

"He dead," Gil said.

Rosalie smiled. She rather liked the idea of Gil and Zachary fighting over her, or at least over the baby. It was dangerous, but she liked it. She headed into the kitchen to see how the caterers were doing.

Peter Peeks was there, loading his tray, and when she leaned over him, he kissed her dutifully on the mouth. He had often done this because he knew she liked it and he knew also that Zachary liked it, in some kinky way.

"Yummy," Rosalie said and went out to check on the bar.

Daryl was tidying the table, getting rid of stray chunks of lime and crushed napkins and broken bits of cocktail toothpicks. He finished tidying and began setting the bottles in order, labels facing out, caps on, everything in a straight line.

"You keep a neat bar," Rosalie said.

Daryl smiled sadly. "I wish," he said.

"What?" Rosalie asked, pretending she was Olga. "What do you wish?" She was feeling awfully good. If she could grant wishes, she'd grant the wish of this big lummox with his sexy red beard. He was so serious, so grim. "Tell me what you wish," she said, in one of Olga's accents.

"I wish . . . " He was about to say: I wish I had a marriage like yours, I wish I had a baby like yours, I wish my wife wasn't having an affair

with somebody but I think she is, I know she is, and if I find out that
she is, I'll kill him. Or myself. Or her.

"Yes?"

"I wish I belonged," Daryl said. "I wish I fit in."

It was the saddest thing Rosalie had ever heard. Peter Peeks's kiss
had cheered her up no end, so she decided to pass the good cheer on
to Daryl, the poor thing. She leaned toward him and kissed him gently on the lips and then set off in search of Olga. She must tell Olga
about poor sad Daryl. She didn't know why, but she felt she must.

She found Olga behind a crowd of fools chatting up Leroy O'Shea
and Moo Wesley Rudin. Moo looked woebegone, as she always did
when she was around babies, and Leroy looked guilty. Olga was talking with some animation about Ma Rainey and Bessie Smith and the
Gallic fascination with Blacks who sing the blues, so everyone was relieved, including Olga, when Rosalie showed up with her cute little
smile and her perky breasts.

"Moo," Rosalie said, "and Leroy. How nice. And Olga."

"It's a lovely baby," Olga said.

"It's a beautiful . . ." Moo said and burst into tears. She got hold of
herself at once, stopped crying, and said, with a gulp, "It's a beautiful
baby, Rosalie, and you're a beautiful mother," but at this moment
Leroy put his arm protectively around her shoulders, and Moo gave
way to all the tears she had suppressed for months. She sobbed with
abandon, just standing there, eyes open, staring straight ahead, as
tears poured down her face and onto her dress, and her eyes began to
grow red and puffy. After a while, her sobbing abated enough for her
to say something. Everyone was waiting to hear what it would be.

"I want a baby," she said to Olga. "I've got to have a baby."

And Leroy said to Olga, "We've tried. We're trying."

Leroy led Moo off to the sunroom where she could dry her tears in
privacy. Olga and Rosalie watched them go.

"They want a baby," Rosalie said. "But they can't."

"I'll have to do my thoughts," Olga said.

"She's sterile, Moo is."

"I'll give it thought."

"At least that's what Gil says, that she's sterile."

"Gil?"

"Gil Rudin," Rosalie said. "They were married, Moo and Gil, before he married Betz."

"Ah yes, poor Betz."

Betz had been invited to the circumcision party, but nobody had expected her to come, what with her own baby being retarded and then her filing for divorce from Gil and God only knows what else.

"Don't worry about old Betz," Rosalie said. Then recalling her errand, she said, "It's Daryl you should worry about. He thinks he doesn't fit."

"He doesn't."

"He wants to belong."

"He can't. It would cost him a great deal. He's not in this."

"But he is. He *de facto* is in it," Rosalie said, making a case for Daryl and wondering why she bothered. "And he loves Foucault."

"No," Olga said, and it sounded final.

Zachary appeared before them, the baby in his arms.

"There's your muzzy," Zachary said. "See the pretty muzzy? And Auntie Olga?"

The baby snapped its gums at Olga.

"He has blond hair," Olga said.

"He looks like me," Zachary said and at the same time Rosalie said, "He looks like me."

"Very pretty," Olga said.

Just then Moo and Leroy came out of the sunroom. Moo saw the baby and burst into tears and went back into the sunroom. Leroy shrugged, a kind of apology, and disappeared after her.

"My little A to Z," Zachary said, "my little Adam Zachary," and he gave the baby noisy kisses.

"Sausage?" Peter Peeks said. "Zack?"

Zachary stopped kissing the baby and took a sausage. Rosalie lifted the baby from his arms and left. Peter Peeks moved on with his tray of goodies.

And so it happened that Zachary and Olga were left alone.

"Very interesting," Olga said, her accent German.

Zachary popped the rest of the sausage into his mouth and chewed. He had lots to say to her and he wanted a minute to think about it.

"Very, very interesting."

"What? The baby? Or my fainting?"

"They all think you're human now. They're surprised."

"And what do you think?"

"I think you're in love."

"With?"

"With the baby." She seemed very happy about this. "It's a socially redeeming quality," she said.

Zachary smiled, without a trace of irony.

Oh yes, she thought, oh yes. Fear and pity will be possible after all.

"Tell me," she said. "Tell me about the baby."

The party swirled on around them, with Eleanora Tuke talking video-poetics and Gil Rudin trotting around after whoever was holding the baby and Maddy Barker keeping an eye on Peter Peeks and Moo grieving and the fools drinking and gabbling and having a wonderful time. None of this was lost on Olga, who recognized in this cacophony of egos a high, sustained, academic cry for help. She began to feel a resumption of her gifts, a glow about the brow and a corresponding glow within her breast. She smiled, feeling beautiful and strong. A success. A teacher and a writer. A woman at the height of her creative powers.

"Tell me, Zachary," Olga said. "Tell me everything."

19

The party was over, Peter Peeks said to Daryl, but the night was young. Cliché, Daryl said. Purist, pedant, Peter Peeks said. Fuck you, Daryl said. I bet you'd like to, Peter Peeks said, doing Groucho's eyebrows and cigar. It was all very good-natured: they had in common Olga's refusal to let them attend her seminar on Foucault.

"So I suppose you're gonna go horning around the campus now," Daryl said.

Peter Peeks let the tip of his tongue appear between his lips, just for a second.

"That's obscene," Daryl said. He had never been able to understand promiscuity. He suspected sometimes that his wife—because of her association with other flight attendants—regarded sex as an end in itself, but this was only a suspicion, only a fear, really, and it was unworthy of him. Secretly he felt that love was so rare and wonderful that sex, far from being the fulfillment of love, was rather a contamination of it. What he felt for his wife was love, simply that, and then reverence, and then, because it was inevitable, he felt lust. But lust was the end-point, not the start, and he could not imagine how men like Peter Peeks—or Zachary Kurtz or Gil Rudin—managed to live with themselves. He would kill himself before he'd be unfaithful.

"Adorno says that promiscuity is a kind of suicide," Daryl said.

"Adorno never said that."

"Well, he should have. Because it is."

"Anyhow," Peter Peeks said, as the clean-up crew arrived, "the night is young and the women are ripe and waiting." He snapped his red suspenders and prepared to go.

~

Rosalie and Zachary Kurtz, with the baby cradled between them, had just seen off the last of the guests and were standing now on the front steps taking the evening air. For each of them, though in different ways, the party had been a success. For Rosalie there had been a rediscovery of the excitement she'd once felt for Gil Rudin and his rough urgency, that hint of forbidden romance. For Zachary there had been this dizzying love he felt for A to Z, and on top of that a return of hope and determination. Hope for his department plans. Determination to get what he wanted. With Olga's help. Because Olga seemed to be with the program once again, despite all the stuff he'd heard about her classes. He'd been right about her after all.

The Kurtzes stood on the front step thinking their separate thoughts when suddenly the Richters' car roared into their *cul de sac*, slammed to a halt in front of their house, and out leaped Cynthia and Robbie.

"Ta-daa!" Robbie shouted and gave them the victory sign. Cynthia, not at all her old passive self, grabbed Robbie's hand and led him up the path.

The caterers had left and Daryl had folded up his bar and the cleaning crew had already entered by the back patio, so there was no hope of inviting the Richters in. Besides, the Kurtzes were exhausted after their party. They moved closer together, determined that Robbie and Cynthia should not pass.

"So this is the bloody infant," Robbie said, shrieking a little at the pun.

"Circumcised, not bloody," Zachary said.

"I was a circumcised baby," Robbie said. "And my father was a circumcised baby and so was our son Bobby."

"Bobby," Zachary said, "that's the jailbird, right?"

"We just think of him as our son," Cynthia said. She punched Zachary on the arm, playfully, but the punch was hard. "Besides, it was only for drugs and he's only got ten months to go. Don't be a shit, Zachary."

"But he was circumcised," Robbie said, keeping to the point. "And so was I. It's healthy and it's precautionary."

"And it doesn't affect pleasure," Cynthia said.

Robbie shrieked at her new daring. "We've been reading Lawrence," he said.

"I can see that," Zachary said. "Yes, I can see that."

"We can't ask you in," Rosalie said, "much as we'd love to." She gestured toward the window where they could see the clean-up crew hustling about.

"You could come to our place," Robbie said, and added, "sometime. We're having a hot tub put in."

"You've got a hot tub?"

"We're *getting* a hot tub. They're installing it on Monday. Or Tuesday. It depends."

"A hot tub," Zachary said, trying to absorb this: Cynthia and Robbie in a hot tub.

"We're going to use it nude," Robbie said.

Cynthia punched him in the arm and he gave one of his shrieks.

"I wish we could invite you in," Rosalie said.

"It's okay," Cynthia said. "We just came to be polite."

"Why don't you come in anyway," Rosalie said. "We'll find something to drink."

"Stuff it," Cynthia said. And then in case she had gone too far, she added, "We've gotta go, really. The dog."

"Ozzie," Robbie said. "He's alone."

They turned and, holding hands, went down the path to their car. They were leaving not because of the dog or because they were offended at not being invited in but because, as everyone knew, Robbie was allowed out for only a half-hour at a time. He became too excited. He talked too much and then he couldn't stop and they had to load him up with pills.

He was talking now as they approached their car. In fact, they were quarreling. Robbie wanted to drive. Cynthia did not want to let him. Their voices rose, they were getting violent, things were getting out of hand, when suddenly Cynthia grabbed hold of him and dragged him to the passenger side of the car and threw him in. He landed with a loud thump.

Cynthia ran around to the driver's side, waved furiously at the Kurtzes, and jumped into the car. She peeled away from the curb, laying rubber.

"A hot tub?" Rosalie said.

"Think of it," Zachary said, rubbing his mustache against the grain. They went inside, thinking of it.

Gil Rudin had a hot tub, Rosalie thought, not to mention a tennis court and a swimming pool and a ten-room mansion, or maybe fifteen or twenty. If only he didn't have that big thing. She frowned. It took a pro like Betz to handle that thing of his. What would he do, she wondered, now that Betz had left him? Soak by himself in his hot tub? She let her mind dwell on that as she tucked the baby in. Inspired by her thoughts of Gil, she decided on a good soak in the tub for herself.

Zachary too was thinking of hot tubs. Olga had a hot tub, or at least Faculty Terrace had one, and she probably used it with Peter Peeks. Peeks got into every nook and cranny, he was sure of that. That's why he liked Peeks, frankly. Peter was sort of a surrogate stud, banging away at all the women he himself couldn't get to. Zachary admitted this to himself reluctantly. It was sad when you thought of it this way. He went into his study, locked the door, and read two more chapters of *Emma*.

When he came out, restored, the cleaning people were gone. The place was spotless. He settled in on the couch.

Rosalie returned from putting Adam Zachary to bed. She had bathed and she smelled wonderfully of some kind of perfume. Honeysuckle? Something nice. They sat together on the couch and watched a National Geographic documentary on the mating habits of baboons.

Zachary put his arm around her and pulled her close. Rosalie nuzzled his neck. They relaxed.

Anyone looking in the window would have mistaken them for an old married couple. They could have been a TV advertisement for life insurance. They could have been fools.

~

The night was young for Peter Peeks and he drove directly to Faculty Terrace to begin his evening's rounds. It was a very busy place. There were lights at Maddy Barker's condo and at Olga's and at Tortorisi's. There were splashing sounds from the pool and little shouts of pleasure. The Chairman, visibly drunk, was out walking Hamlet. As Peter Peeks parked his car, he saw somebody dart into the bushes. A woman? But of course he had women on the brain. He thought for a second of what it would be like to do it in the bushes, but rejected the thought at once. Zachary had warned him about this. Early in their relationship, Zachary said, the President and Missy had been caught fucking in the bushes and they'd given outdoor sex a bad name. Still, it was an interesting idea.

Peter Peeks sat in his car for a moment, making hard choices.

There was Olga, the sexiest and smartest and most exciting of the women, but she had not been herself lately. She had—he hated to admit it—lost some of her magnificence. Besides, she had said terrible things about Foucault, in public. No, Olga would have to wait.

There was Maddy Barker, the Mount Everest of faculty women, high, cold, unattainable. Why even try it with her? Because, like Everest, she's there. He laughed aloud. Olga would be delighted by that. Maddy Barker had definitely gone for the suspenders and he *did* look good in them. He liked her reputation for frigidity, it provided a challenge: could he cause a melt-down? He laughed again because Olga would be delighted with that too. She loved a phrase well-put. He began to think once again of Olga, with her tight body and her hard little breasts. He liked to play bobbing for apples with them in the hot tub and perhaps he'd do that before the night was over But first she'd have to apologize for the things she'd said about Foucault.

Who else? There was Tortorisi, of course. He was fat and disgusting in himself, and he was the wrong sex, but there was something very—what?—*humble* about him. He was so grateful. More appreciative than the women, even. So eager to please. But everybody knew that if you did it with a man more than once, you risked becoming gay. Not because you caught gayness like a disease, but doing it a second time told you something about yourself it was better not to know. Once was an experiment, twice was queersville.

Then there was Concepcion. Wouldn't *that* be a triumph!

And a hundred or two hundred undergraduate girls laid end to end, just waiting. But they didn't interest him. They already had too much sexual experience and it wasn't a thrill for them the way it was for faculty. Older women were his calling, he felt.

Peter Peeks sat in his car, planning. The balance seemed to be tipping toward Olga. First. While he was still fresh.

~

Olga, who wanted only a long slow bath, was in the kitchen making tea for Betz Rudin and Concepcion. She was taking the necessary steps to move the plot forward. Her bath would just have to wait.

While Olga was at the circumcision party, Betz had phoned and left a message saying she needed to talk. And Concepcion had phoned and left a message saying exactly the same thing. They only thought they needed her, Olga realized, when what they needed was each other. She phoned them back and invited them to tea. "Bring the baby," she told Betz. She told Concepcion, "Come right away." And now they were in her living room, together, and she was in the kitchen making tea.

"I can't bear him," Betz said.

"He's a pig," Concepcion said.

They were talking about Gil Rudin, of course.

"He hates the baby," Betz said. "He won't look at her. I'm done with him, for good."

"Very smart," Concepcion said. "Let me hold the baby."

"Susanna," Betz said, and Susanna smiled and waggled her fists at Concepcion.

"*Querida. Preziosa.* Look at those little fists." Concepcion took the baby in her arms and kissed each of the little fists. Susanna chortled. Tears flooded Concepcion's eyes and coursed down her cheeks and fell on the baby's chest. Susanna gurgled. "Susanna," Concepcion said.

Betz smiled, happy for a moment.

In the kitchen Olga put some cookies in a saucer and waited for the silence in the living room to come to an end. But it went on and on and finally she put everything on a tray and entered boldly.

"I have some tea," she said, "and some stale cookies."

There was more silence as Concepcion pressed Susanna to her breast, and so Olga, humming the Hava Nagila, set out the cups and saucers and poured the tea.

Finally Concepcion brushed away her tears and leaned forward, enticing in her warmth and her longing, and said in a voice of embarrassing intimacy, "Tell me, Betz. Do you read Roland Barthes?"

"I should," Betz said.

"*Mythologies?*"

"I will."

"I'll loan you my personal copy," Concepcion said. "It's very special."

~

Before the doorbell rang, Olga went to answer it. Peter Peeks stood there, looking anxious but beautiful in red suspenders.

"I didn't ring yet," he said.

"But you were going to."

"Yes."

"You can't come in. There are guests."

"We could swim when they're gone," he said.

"I'm tired," she said.

"I've got spy stuff for you." He waited a bit. "I could tell you in the hot tub."

She began to look interested.

"We could do it in the hot tub," he said.

"Picasso could do it under water, but he's the only one."

"Picasso and me," he said. "Artists."

Olga seemed uncertain.

"I could wait." He thought of Maddy Barker right across the street, also waiting. "Or I could come back later."

Olga stepped back and looked into the living room where Betz and Concepcion were leaning close together in conversation. The baby lay on the couch between them, sleeping.

"They'll never know," Olga said.

She got her pool bag and closed the door behind her and they descended the stairs on tiptoe. There were no sounds from the pool. It was a silent night. For a moment Tortorisi, quite drunk, appeared at his window, and across the street Maddy Barker, spying, appeared at hers, and at the same moment there was a soft scrambling in the bushes. It was, however, the very moment when Olga could no longer resist snapping those sexy red suspenders. She did it, and Peter Peeks yelped. Concealed by his yelp, Tortorisi and Maddy Barker and the person in the bushes went unobserved.

~

Suzie Sweezie crouched in the bushes, crying softly. She knew that Concepcion was inside Olga's place and she feared they had been making love, but now here was Olga going off to the pool with that creep in the suspenders and Concepcion was alone inside. She could go up and tap at the door and whisk Concepcion away. Her heart swelled a little. But what if somebody else was there? What if they had all been making love, three of them, four of them? And left her out. Her heart contracted and she sank lower into the bushes. They were immoral, teachers, the whole pack of them.

Oh Concepcion, Concepcion, how could you do this?

She heard the hot tub motor turn on and she heard loud whispers from the pool and, most maddening of all, the sound of laughter.

But she put aside her despair and prayed for all of them. As a post-Christian feminist lesbian, she was big enough to forgive.

~

The sickle moon rose higher in the sky.

Hamlet had long since peed, and he had finally pooed, and the Chairman went home to his novel and his TV. Peter Peeks said good-night, softly, softly, at Olga's door. Tortorisi maintained his lonely vigil at the window, but much of Faculty Terrace was asleep by now. Suzie Sweezie, in the bushes, was asleep. Concepcion and Betz Rudin were asleep on the couch, their heads gently touching as they lay back arched above the baby. Olga would be asleep soon.

Peter Peeks, adjusting his suspenders, tapped softly at Maddy Barker's door.

"Men," she said. "What pigs you all are." But she invited him in anyway. She was wearing a white satin nightgown that set off her dark skin and her electric black hair and her large loose breasts. Especially her breasts. Peter Peeks was not a breast man, particularly—he preferred them small and hard like Olga's—but here was an experience he hadn't counted on and he felt himself warming to the challenge. Why hadn't Zack told him about these spectacular breasts?

"Have a drink," Maddy Barker said, pushing a glass of scotch his way. She had obviously had several already.

"I don't drink scotch," he said. "Just beer. And sometimes wine."

"God, I hate men," she said.

He looked at her breasts beneath the white satin and her little belly bulging out beneath her breasts, and he saw for the first time how sexy a little extra weight could be. Not fat—Tortorisi was fat—but a little extra weight here and there was really very exciting. It gave dimension and fullness and . . . He had got this far in his thinking when Maddy Barker reached out and snatched him by the suspenders and led him into the bedroom.

"Call me Mommy," she said, and whipped his pants down around his ankles, and then his underpants. "Gimme that ugly thing, yuck," she said, grabbing hold of it and using it as a handle to yank him up onto the bed. "God, it's hideous."

"Let me get my shirt off," Peter Peeks said. "Let me get my tie at least."

But it was too late, because Maddy had stuffed him roughly inside her and was bucking and rearing, now beneath him, now on top, going hell for leather, and there was no question: she was a crazy woman.

"Mommy," he said. "Mommy!" It was a cry for help, but she was far beyond hearing.

"I hate men," she cried, "hate them, hate them, hate them," getting a steady rhythm going, "hate and hate and hate and hate and hate," and on she went, up and down, over and on top, and then all at once she let out a low disgusted groan, a retching sound, and then she bit him on the neck, hard. She held on for a moment with her teeth, quivering, and then she flung him off. She rested, breathing heavily.

Peter Peeks tried to move his legs. He was paralyzed. He would never walk again. What had she done to him? He lay there, afraid to look.

She lay beside him, turned slightly away, making little whimpering sounds like a frightened puppy.

Once more Peter Peeks tried to move. Not a thing. And he had a terrible pain in his neck where she'd bit him. He looked down, prepared for the worst, and saw that his legs were hopelessly tangled in his pants and his underpants, his suspenders were in knots. How had he managed to perform? But then he realized, it was she who had done all the performing. Maddy the Queen of the Ta-Tas. Melon city. He looked over at her and saw that her satin nightgown was rucked up around those huge white breasts, a very nice setting for them. She was slick with sweat and she smelled delicious.

This was the really wonderful thing about sex: every new woman was a fresh surprise. Moved, he placed his hand lightly on the breast closest to him. Instantly, she snatched his hand away and bit it. He yelped in pain.

"Don't be disgusting," she said, and got out of bed and disappeared into the bathroom.

Peter Peeks understood that he was dismissed.

He nursed his hand for a while—the skin was broken only slightly—and then he touched his neck. It was bleeding and his shirt was stained with blood. God, what a woman. He moved his hand down to his crotch, slowly, exploring, and was relieved to find that everything was still there, more or less as it should be. He set about untangling his pants and his underpants, getting the knots out of his miraculous red suspenders. Finally he was dressed. It was time to go. He was uncomfortable with the situation, however: he felt that this was simply not a decorous way for the evening to end. Should he leave a thank-you note? Should he tap at the bathroom door and say, "See ya"? He moped around the kitchen for a while, hoping Maddy would make an appearance. His neck hurt and his crotch burned. He was very, very tired.

And then he heard her shout, low and gravelly, "Leave, god-dammit, get the hell out of here."

He left.

~

As Peter Peeks descended the stairs, he looked across the drive at Tortorisi's where the curtain was drawn slightly aside and Tortorisi's fat, anxious face peered out. Poor Tortorisi. Peter Peeks waved and Tortorisi drew back, but at that moment Olga's door opened and out came Concepcion and—surprise, surprise—Betz Rudin with her baby. As they closed the door behind them, somebody stepped out of the bushes for a quick look and then stepped back in, but not before Peter Peeks saw who it was: Suzie Sweezie, that porky little dyke.

Busy, busy, he said, and in the middle of the night too. He stood at the foot of the stairs to watch.

Betz Rudin gave Concepcion a quick kiss—there was a cry of pain from the bushes—handed her the baby, and they got into the car together. Betz's Mercedes 300SL, Peter Peeks noted, cherry red. As they tooled down the drive, Suzie Sweezie emerged from the bushes, sorrowing, and trailed off in their wake. Her leg was pins and needles and she limped as she went.

Peter Peeks was still looking after her when Tortorisi opened his door and began making loud "psst" noises.

Peeks shook his head no.

"Pssst!" Louder.

"Shh" Peter Peeks said and began walking toward his car. Tortorisi came galumphing down the stairs with a terrible racket and Peter Peeks stopped and turned to him and saw that Tortorisi's face was contorted with grief.

"I don't have anyone," Tortorisi said. He began to cry soundlessly, his head bobbing and his breasts shaking and his fists clutched at his side. He looked like a fat big boy unjustly punished.

Peter Peeks watched this performance for a while and then he patted Tortorisi on the shoulder. "Don't cry," he said, "don't." He patted him some more. "Get a grip," he said.

"I've been drinking," Tortorisi said.

"No shit."

"Because I don't have anyone," Tortorisi said, starting up again. "Everybody has someone and I don't have anyone."

"You do, you do."

"Who?" Tortorisi asked, indignant. "Name one."

"Maddy Barker, for one."

"Ha!" Tortorisi said. "*You've* got Maddy Barker. *Olga's* got Maddy Barker. Anyhow, who *wants* Maddy Barker! I'm done with her. And I don't have anybody. I just want somebody to hold." He tried to look deep into Peter Peeks' eyes, but he was quite drunk and couldn't focus. He put his hand gently on Peeks' neck. "Ooh! You're all wet," he said. "It's blood."

"Oh, that. That's nothing."

"Come on in," he said, "come on, come on, and I'll wash it for you and get you a nice band-aid, and then we'll see."

"I've got to get home. It's practically tomorrow."

"I don't have anybody." He paused, hopefully. "Just a hug? Hmmm? Just a little lie-down for two? I'll read you from my novel."

Peter Peeks thought about this and, given the situation, it seemed the polite thing to do.

"Okay," he said, "but only hugs. Besides"—he was feeling chummy now—"my dick feels like it got caught in a Waring Blender."

Tortorisi laughed happily.

"No shit," Peter Peeks said. "It was like nothing I've ever experienced in my whole life. Well, I mean, in my sexually active life."

They were half-way up the stairs. Tortorisi stopped, puzzled. "You're talking about sex?" he said. "I mean . . . sexual intercourse?"

Peter Peeks smiled, exposing all those white teeth.

"With *her*? With *Maddy*?"

"The Melon Queen herself."

"You must be insane," Tortorisi said, sobering noticeably. "That's revolting." And then, coldly, "I think I should prefer to sleep alone tonight, Peter Peeks, and perhaps forever."

He went on up the stairs, stepped inside, and locked the door behind him. He was furious and heartbroken at this double betrayal, and it would take him a half hour before he could compose himself sufficiently to be able to write about it—under the guise of the sex life of a female Dean and a randy undergraduate named Paul Parks.

Peter Peeks stood speechless on the stairs. Quel night. He put his hand to his bloody neck and his other hand to his burning crotch and retired, in pain, to his car.

He sat there for a time watching the dark before the dawn. The night was no longer young, he reflected, and there was sadness everywhere. He was pleased at feeling melancholy. He was becoming a deep person.

20

Olga was joyful in her bath. The water was hot, but not too hot, and there were bubbles all around her like in the movies, and she had a little yellow bath pillow supporting her neck. She tipped some perfume, Poison, into the water and a dizzying fragrance rose up around her, making her senses reel. Her mind, however, was ticking over—the word was accurate—beautifully.

Her books until now had concerned themselves with the bored and despairing lives of sterile people. Thanks to her European background, and specifically her time in Paris and The Hague, she excelled at those gray scenes of automatic cruelty.

This new book, she could already see, was to be different. At its heart there must stand an act of utter evil and absurdity, with nothing automatic about it. It must proceed from love gone wrong. It would be, therefore, evil with a human face.

She poured a drop more Poison in the water.

She was filled with joy. How glorious to be a fabricator, making it up, making it happen. How glorious to observe these men and women, complicated beyond their own understanding, with their big desires and their little terrors and—what luck for a responsible writer!—their salvific aspirations. How glorious to be a public disturbance.

She slipped deep into the bath until she lay completely submerged. She blew bubbles, and then slowly she let her nose and then her mouth and then her whole face emerge from the water, her long hair slick against her skull. She felt all the flesh slip away from her bones. She really was a goddess. Up to a point.

There was always failure to contend with, of course, she mustn't forget that. Failure was a constant. The anticipation of failure was even worse, however; it could paralyze; it could cut off the possibility of action and invention. You dealt with failure by refusing to acknowledge it, and by a kind of blind trust in the gods. Daring was essential. We fail! But screw your courage, et cetera, et cetera, and we shall not fail.

An act of utter evil and absurdity. Evil with a human face. At once Zachary Kurtz came to mind. A womanizer. An abuser of trust. A liar. A cheat. A plotter.

Was he really all these things? Well, he was now.

And, most important, Zachary Kurtz had a significant redeeming quality: he loved his son. Fanatically. Who better for an act of evil and absurdity?

There were others, however, who qualified for the job. There was Gil Rudin. There was Rosalie Kurtz, whom she had neglected shamefully. What surprises lay concealed in Rosalie, with her tight red curls and her tight little mind?

Olga felt her own mind turning over, fast and faster, too fast for her to follow it and to process the fine points of all these destinies. What if one of them slipped away. What if Moo were left without a baby? Tortorisi without tenure? And Peter Peeks. What of Peter Peeks?

Her joy began to dissipate and the water began to cool. She should get dried and dressed now and take a few quick notes before she forgot any of it. But instead, she ran some more hot water and sat back deliberately in the bath: an act of faith in her subconscious. You had to trust your talent.

At once she was rewarded with a view of Zachary, apoplectic, strangling his wife. But why? And how would this resolve anything? She made another act of faith and contemplated this unpleasant scene. Zachary was crimson with rage and intent on murder. How interesting and unusual it all seemed. Zachary murderous. Rosalie, not quite believing it, turning monkey-brown as his hands tightened on her throat. So, is this what would happen?

Zachary the strangler? Zachary plotting and skulking and lusting?

She put aside Zachary strangling and went back to Zachary plotting. She was part of his plot, she had understood that from the beginning. And she had her own plot, naturally. It was expected. It was necessary. It was also very simple: she wanted for each of them what they wanted for themselves. And would make sure they got it.

What she must cause to happen—but how?—was the inevitable intersection of their plots. At least for the big people. Marginal people would always remain marginal and must fare for themselves. That's how it was in life and that's why they're called marginal. Though of course she would do what she could.

She got it clear once more in her mind. Through an act of human evil and absurdity, they must all get what they wanted. But by whose act? What evil? Which of an infinite number of absurdities?

Well, it was a start.

She rose from the bath, Venus on the half shell, ready for whatever would happen next.

21

The marginal people became central to Olga's life almost at once, beginning with Moo Wesley Rudin and Leroy O'Shea, who came to her in search of a baby. They were a very attractive couple, white and black in color, blond and afro in hair, and they were so clearly in love that Olga was moved to help them. She had seen their performance at the Kurtz circumcision—the crying and the comforting—and not only had she resolved to give them what they wanted, she had even set about determining how to do it.

"But first," Olga said, "you must have some sherry." They were taken aback, since it was nine in the morning. "Tea won't do for this," Olga said, "never mind the hour." And so she served a good, light sherry and sat down with them to listen.

"We know what you did for Robbie Richter," Moo said.

"He's sane again," Leroy said, and because he loved accuracy, he added, "or at least as sane as he was before."

"And we know you got Betz Rudin away from Gil," Moo said, "that couldn't have been easy." She blushed. "I was married to him, so I know." She blushed still more. "To Gil, I mean."

"We know you can do anything," Leroy said.

"What we want, " Moo said, "is a baby."

They paused, conscious of their marginality, and waited anxiously while Olga sipped her sherry.

"We aren't the big people, we know that," Moo said, "and so we can't make a huge claim on your attention, but . . ." and she left the sentence suspended.

". . . but we've got to have a baby," Leroy said.

They looked at each other and smiled, because more and more they were expressing the same thoughts at the same time. It made a baby seem that much more possible.

"And you can't have a baby?" Olga said.

"We've done everything," Leroy said.

"Timed the period."

"Checked the temperature."

"Stopped drinking."

"Did it five times a day."

"Four."

"Four times a day."

"And the doctors. We've been to every doctor on the west coast."

"They say it should work, but it doesn't work."

"I thought it was Gil, but now he's had a baby with Betz, so I guess it wasn't Gil."

"But the baby's a mess."

"So is Gil."

"So is Betz. She didn't even come to the Kurtz's circumcision."

"No," Olga said, more emphatically than she intended. "The baby is not a mess. The baby is going to be fine, up to a point. Susanna."

They looked up at her, surprised, because everybody knew the baby was retarded. Oxygen, or something.

"In a year," Olga said, "in just over a year," and she was delighted because suddenly she saw that this is how it must be: Betz and Concepcion together, with Susanna healthy and fine, and all their petty rottenness turned toward good. Or at least in the general direction of good. Or wishing good for one another. She frowned. Was she becoming an optimist? A foolish romantic? She frowned more deeply.

"What?" they asked her. "Are you all right?"

"A momentary doubt," Olga said. "I suffer them." She would have to make up for such romanticism by applying ferocity elsewhere. And of course she could do that. Her frown disappeared.

"We want a baby."

"Our baby. Black and white."

"Can you do it? Can you help?"

"Drink your sherry," Olga said, and got up to get a book. "This will sound strange," she said.

"We've been through strange," Moo said, laughing, and Leroy laughed too.

"No, just listen now," Olga said, the stern teacher. "As I say, this will sound strange, but it may work. In Roald Dahl's *Ah, Sweet Mystery of Life* there's a story about the breeding of calves. It's not a very good story. In fact it's more titillation than anything else. But it contains a primitive truth. That the sex of the calf can be determined by whether the mating cow faces into or away from the sun. You get a heifer calf if they mate facing the sun, a bull calf facing away from the sun."

Moo and Leroy were troubled but went on listening.

"It will work for a child," Olga said.

"For getting one, you mean?"

"A girl facing the sun. A boy away from the sun."

They looked at one another. Facing the sun, because they wanted a girl.

"So it has to be done in daylight?" Leroy said.

"In a field," Olga said.

They nodded, soberly.

"We can do that," Moo said.

"Gosh," Leroy said.

They sat in silence for a while, contemplating their future: in a field, in daylight, facing the sun.

"Drink up," Olga said and gave them her copy of *Ah, Sweet Mystery of Life*. "Otherwise," she said, "it's not a very good book."

They left, holding hands.

~

Later, but not much later, Eleanora Tuke rang her up.

"I have to tell you," Eleanora said, "that I thought your work was much overrated. The usual Hague hype, am I right? I read it with an open mind, of course, but it struck me as just more of the same. Same old same old. Otherwise I would have invited you to one of my salons long before this. I mean, you've been here so long that it's almost rude to invite you now, right? Any*hoo*, I took another look at your novels, which really aren't half bad, Olga, and I took a look at what you've done with Betz and Gil Rudin, prying them apart and filing for divorce and all that *property*, my God, not to mention what you've done with Robbie Richter and that mouse Cynthia—talk about the mouse that roared, I mean, she's turning into Frieda von Whatzername before our very eyes—anyhow it occurred to me that you're a lot smarter than anybody thinks and you might be useful even to me, if you can imagine such a thing, and so I'm not only inviting you to a salon, I'm offering to *feature* you. You'd be the main one, I mean. There'll be painters and sculptors, because we collect people very seriously, and there'll be the usual country western singers because my little physicist has begun to fancy himself a singer, well, he writes these crying songs, you know, and there'll be Peter Shaffer and David Hwang because they're in town working on new plays, but *you*'ll be the featured guest. You know how it works: little groups of four and five, all talking about their own things, or about philosophy, we aren't choosy—talk about anything so long as it's deep—and the idea is to bring culture and a *variety* of culture to this city, because otherwise we might as well be in Omaha. I see it as this city's last chance, really. I mean, this is a city that has the *Chronicle* for a newspaper. I ask you. I want us to have a talk about this—culture, I mean—and what I intend to do about it. I'm at a crossroads." She paused at last. "Olga?"

"Yes?"

"So I'll plan on it? Two weeks from today?"

"Alas, no," Olga said.

"What do you mean, alas no?"

"It's a negative expression, indicating non-compliance."

There was silence for a moment and then Eleanora's voice, changed, diminished, saying, "But I need help."

"I don't think I'm your person," Olga said.

"Oh yes. I think so."

"I'm sure I'm not."

"You're wrong."

"Nonetheless," Olga said, ending the discussion in an accent that was foreign but not necessarily European.

She had to move on, quickly, to the others.

~

Olga got out her notebook and made a list of the marginal people. She was surprised to see that some who had seemed big people were well on their way to becoming marginal: Betz Rudin, for instance, and Concepcion, and Maddy Barker. Eleanora Tuke and her nearly non-existent little physicist. Leroy and Moo. And of course Daryl who, though he didn't belong, *would* force himself into it, dragging along with him his flight attendant wife and perhaps even her lover the priest. And finally Peter Peeks. Always there was Peter Peeks. Would so much physical beauty go to waste? It seemed so. Because she could think of nothing to do with him.

The little people. The marginal people. How Foucault would enjoy this philological manipulation.

Then Zachary Kurtz, full of hope, came calling.

~

Zachary Kurtz was wearing his yellow sweater and his tan chinos and his macho tennis shoes. He looked like a butch canary with a mustache.

"Like the outfit?" he said in the voice of Eleanora Tuke. He did a slow pirouette.

He loved his son, Olga noted, *and* he was capable of self-mockery. He had at least two redeeming qualities.

She made him tea.

"You haven't got a beer?" he said.

She brought him some cookies.

"It's noon," he said, ogling her nifty feet. "Let me buy you lunch. We can go to some quiet place. We can have a real talk."

"This place is quiet," she said. "Talk."

"I like those sneaks," he said. "Little footies."

"Talk," she said.

He did. He reminded her that the end of the quarter was in sight, they'd be voting on Tortorisi's tenure very soon . . . .

"And Concepcion's tenure as well," she reminded him.

And Concepcion's tenure as well, he agreed, but that wasn't his point. Tortorisi was the point. He wanted her to promise that Tortorisi would not get tenure, that she'd do everything she could to get him out of here. Okay?

"Out of here," she said musing.

"He'll get tenure over my dead body."

Olga turned this over in her mind.

"Don't say that," she said. "St. Teresa says there is more unhappiness in this world over answered prayers than over unanswered ones."

"I thought Truman Capote said that."

"He thought so too."

"Whatever. I want Tortorisi out of here."

"I can take care of that."

"So you can promise me he won't get tenure?"

"I can promise you he'll get out of here."

"Good," he said. "Okay. Good."

Zachary smiled now, relaxing, because everybody was agreed that Olga could do anything, and he had thought so all along, and now he was convinced of it. He had doubted her for a while, it was true. That was when she'd been trashing Foucault in her seminar, but, according to Peeks, she had come around again and was acting responsibly. She'd get rid of Tortorisi, he could tell just by looking at her. How, he had no idea, but it didn't matter so long as she did it. Good old Olga. He pressed the toe of his sneaker against the toe of her sneaker. Was there an answering pressure? He looked her straight in the eyes, but at that moment she got up from the table and said, "More cookies?"

"Forget the cookies," he said. "They're stale, you know."

"You wanted to talk," she said.

She placed another saucer of cookies before him.

"Talk," she said.

"Robbie," he said. "Robbie has got to be the next Chairman."

"He will be," she said.

He paused. "How can you be so sure?" he said. "What if he goes crazy?"

"He is crazy."

"I mean really crazy."

"Semantics," she said. "In any case, he'll be the Chairman."

He nudged her sneaker gently with his sneaker. She didn't move hers away. He nudged it again. Still no response. He looked at her and she looked back. Deliberately then he tipped his foot sideways and let his toe nuzzle along her ankle and above, rubbing just a little, cozy.

At once there was a sharp crack on his shin as she shot out her other foot in a karate kick that was instant and painful. He yanked his leg away and began to rub it.

"You're crazy," he said. "What's the matter with you, anyhow!" He continued to rub his shin. "You could have broken my leg!"

"I know," she said. "I took care not to."

He could feel a swelling rise on his shin.

"You did that deliberately," he said, accusing. "Why did you do that?"

"You want to know? Truly?"

"Truly."

"You are an utterly depraved human being," she said. "You are selfish, arrogant, intolerant, you connive and cheat, you have no sense of loyalty or obligation. I was convinced for a while that you had no redeeming qualities. I was afraid that you had outlived your heart."

"Really?" His interest was academic.

"It's the ultimate tragedy, I think, to outlive your heart."

"Sounds a bit hyper to me."

"But then I discovered that you love your son. It was a great relief."

"Adam Zachary," he said, "A to Z."

"Because it made you vulnerable."

Zachary rubbed his shin and thought about this. "Look at this bump I'm getting," he said and raised his pant leg. It was not a very prepossessing sight and he dropped his pant leg at once. Olga had not bothered to look.

"Where were we?" he said.

"Vulnerable."

"Funny you should say that, because it's the one thing I'm not. Young Peeks once asked me what I'd like to be in another fifteen or twenty years, and I told him, honestly, that I'd like to be completely invulnerable. And I'm well on my way."

She looked at him, amused.

"Have you been to bed with Peeks?" he asked.

She continued to look at him, but she was not amused now.

"Is he good? Or just energetic? Does he spy for you?"

She looked through him and beyond.

"Who *are* you? *What* are you?" He was moved suddenly, inexplicably to say he was sorry, to say he wanted to start all over again and be a better person, a complete person and not a complete shit, he wanted not to outlive his heart, the ultimate tragedy. But he got hold of himself and regrouped and said, "Be that as it may, we've got to talk about the new Department."

"Of Theory and Discourse," she said.

"Of Theory and Discourse," he said, and he began to feel his old self again.

They talked on and on into the early afternoon and it was agreed—provisionally, Olga insisted—that she would do what she could, that she would do what he wanted, that she would get for him this goddam Department of Theory and Discourse.

For this had she come.

22

Tortorisi paused so that Olga could finish laughing. He was reading aloud to her from his fifty new pages and he had reached the sex scene in the swimming pool, his favorite, and he didn't want her to miss any of it.

"It's terribly funny," she said. "The President? And Peter Peeks?"

"It's me, of course," he said, "not really the President."

"Of course," she said.

"Do you think people will think it's the President?"

"Yes. Isn't that your intention?"

"Well, I don't really want to *hurt* anybody."

"Yes, you do."

"Yes, I do."

"Think about it, though," she said. "The satisfaction is brief, but the hurt is long."

He thought for a minute.

"Could they sue? Would they, do you think?"

"Forget that for now," she said, "and let's just talk satire. There's always the temptation to go too far."

"Yes?"

"Do you think it's essential that the President have only one, as you put it, ball?"

He blushed.

"And that it be withered?"

"It's symbolic," he said.

She looked at him, hard.

"I'll give him two balls," Tortorisi said.

She continued to look at him.

"Plump," he said, "not withered."

"Sometimes less is more and sometimes symbol is too much. I thought you understood that."

"Well, I'm trying," he said. "I'm just a beginner."

"Read me some more," she said, and he did.

Olga listened, marveling.

What astonished her was the way this fat, ineffectual man wrote lean and practical prose. Before this he had written only abstract gibberish and suddenly here he was writing satire, sharp and bitter, perhaps too sharp to be altogether convincing, too bitter to be altogether funny. But he could learn. She could help him. She was astonished too by the evidence he gave of possessing the fastidious economy of the true artist. He combined his own moral failings with the physical idiosyncrasies of his neighbors, and out of the combination he created fictional characters with all the limitations and contradictoriness of life. But what astonished her most was his wit. He was funny. He was ironic. He had, at least in his writing, a keen social sense of the incongruous, the ludicrous, the preposterous, and he could distinguish one from the other. He might, in fact, complete a successful book.

But would there be a second book? Or did he have only enough energy for one? She could see what would happen: his anger would thin down and his work would thin out and his writing would become nasty, hateful. Malice, after all, was not vision. And even his malice, she could see, had little staying power. Tortorisi had the rudimentary gifts of an artist but not the necessary endurance. He would never survive as novelist. What he needed was a medium in which almost nothing was required by way of stamina or intelligence, just malice that had been sweetened to taste, and irony allowed to grow soft on the edges. What he needed was . . . TV? For no particular reason she found herself thinking of Eleanora Tuke. Why?

"So, what do you think?" Tortorisi said, putting down the last page. His face was shining, he looked holy. "Do you think it's funny?"

"I think it's very funny," she said.

They fell silent. There was a post-coital *tristesse* in the room.

Tortorisi straightened the pile of pages he had read from, he leafed through them, he put them down.

Olga sat, doing her thoughts. Tortorisi. Eleanora. Economy. You had to *listen* to your thoughts.

"Is it too mean?" he asked. "Is it not funny enough?" And after another moment of silence, "Am I just wasting my time?"

Olga looked up then and smiled at him.

"Make me a copy of this," she said, "and I'll give it to Eleanora Tuke, and . . . "

"And?"

"And I'll guarantee you the perfect job."

"Tenure?"

"That, too, if you want it," she said with confidence, "but I guarantee that you won't."

She left him then.

Next door at her own condominium, she went straight to the phone. Her thoughts had come together nicely, indeed with the wonderful economy that characterized all her best work, and she could foresee not only the final perfect flowering of Eleanora Tuke but, remarkably, with what ease Francis Xavier Tortorisi's fate could be made to coincide with Eleanora's.

She phoned her at once and was surprised to find that Eleanora Tuke was not altogether pleased to hear from her.

"I'll come to your salon," Olga said.

"I'm not sure about that," Eleanora said. "I'll have to think about it."

"I'll bring a new writer. You'll want to know him."

"Who?"

"You'll *need* to know him."

Pause.

"Because he's new."

"You've hurt my feelings," Eleanora said.

"Yes."

"Nobody has ever refused me before."

"No."

"But you're willing to come now?"

"Yes."

"You *want* to come now."

"Up to a point."

"Who is this new writer? Why do I need to know him? What does he have to do with me?"

"I'll send you his work."

"You've hurt my feelings. Some of us are more sensitive than others."

"Till then."

And thus it was that Olga attended Eleanora Tuke's last salon and introduced to her the newly clever, fat and funny, always entertaining—ta-daaa!—Francis Xavier Tortorisi.

23

Moo and Leroy, fresh from their mission to Olga, were atingle with anticipation and desire. She had given them new hope for a baby and new hope for their life together. Her prescription was unorthodox, even bizarre, but they had been through so much, tried so many painful and embarrassing remedies— all of them futile—that they were willing to try anything, even having sex in daylight, in a field, facing the sun.

Leroy sat in the car with the motor running while Moo ran in to get their copy of *The Joy of Christian Sex*, just for good luck, and when she returned she was glowing.

"They bought my Dick and Jane book," she said. "There was a message on the machine."

Leroy kissed her quickly, and then again more slowly, and then— spontaneously—they eased apart. "We'll save it for the field," Leroy said, and pulled away from the curb with such speed that he scattered gravel for a good thirty feet.

They held hands as they drove up to the foothills.

Everything was coming together for them at last. They were young and beautiful, ebony and ivory, and they were in love, but they wanted more than this. They wanted accomplishment, they wanted status, and most of all they wanted a baby. And now her book was sold, *Dirk and Jahine: An Interracial Idyll*. And Leroy's research on Ma Rainey was coming to a close, and he would have a book too, and tenure. And, best of all, they were about to get pregnant. With a daughter. Life was very good.

In the foothills they took a side-road they had never been on, and then a branch to the left, and then another, and found themselves eventually on a road that dead-ended in a grove of eucalyptus. Just beyond the grove was a pasture and a hill. They had found the perfect place.

They jumped from the car leaving the doors open behind them and sprinted out to the center of the pasture.

"Here?" Leroy said. "Do you think a pasture qualifies as a field? What do you think?"

"Maybe a little higher up the hill?"

They ran a little higher up the hill.

"Okay?" he said. "Okay?"

"Just a little more," she said.

"I'm gonna burst," he said. "Quick!"

She flopped to her back and started to shimmy out of her panty hose. The elastic was caught. The hose tore but she still could not get free of them.

"Jesus," Leroy said, suddenly aware of their exposed situation. "Anybody could see us."

"There's nobody here," she said.

He unzipped his trousers and looked around. He zipped them back up.

"I can't get these damned panty hose off," she said, struggling. They tore again. They were tangled around her knees.

"Leave them, leave them," he said, looking around again. "Jesus."

"Well, how are we gonna do it, smarty, with these things up around my knees."

"I can do it, I can do it," he said, and knelt down in front of her. He just knelt there, however, as if he didn't know what came next.

"Help me with these, goddammit!" She was beginning to yank and tear at them, but still they would not give.

He took one last desperate look around, wrested her knees free of the panty hose, and unzipping his pants, he lunged forward, entered her, and came.

They were silent for a full minute.

"I feel like a fool."

"*You* feel like a fool? You ought to try this with a vagina!"

He rolled off her and zipped up his pants. She pulled her skirt down and her shredded panty hose up.

They continued to arrange their clothing decently, careful not to look at one another.

"Do you think it worked?" he asked.

"I think so," she said. "I don't know."

"We forgot the sun. Jesus. Did we face the sun?"

They looked up into the sky. It was very blue and the sun was very bright. Wouldn't they have noticed if they'd been facing toward it?

"What do you suppose 'facing' means in this context?"

"Jesus," he said.

"God," she said.

Which reminded them that they had not said their prayer. They always said a little conception prayer before and after sex, and so now they said two prayers, one for invocation—a bit after the fact—and one for thanksgiving.

They sat on the grass, uneasy, dissatisfied.

"I don't think we were facing the sun."

"We could do it again."

Leroy stood up and looked around. He sighed.

"Look," he said. "let's do this right. Let's go home and put on appropriate clothes and come back and line up with the sun and say our conception prayer and do this thing properly. Don't you think? It's unbecoming, all this wrestling with panty hose and with just my dick sticking out of my trousers. It looks bad."

"Well, nobody's here to see us," she said.

"God sees," he said.

She nodded agreement.

"And it certainly wasn't much fun," he said.

They drove home and changed their clothes. They put on bermuda shorts and tee shirts, roomy ones that were easy to get on and off, and they drove back slowly to their pasture on the hill. They were much more relaxed this time.

"Shall we bring the book?" she asked.

"Bring both of them," he said. "I've got the blanket and the compass."

They walked hand in hand across the pasture until they found an attractive spot. It took only a minute to spread out the blanket in the bright sunlight, to anchor opposite corners with the two books, and to determine, with the aid of the compass, exactly where their heads should be in relation to the sun. They knelt down. Moo recited the invocation, asking God to assist them in a generative ejaculation and an attractive fetus.

Leroy stood up and looked around, still rather anxious. They were lined up with the sun perfectly. There was not a human sound for miles. Still, he was embarrassed.

"Well, fuck it," he said, and took off his tee shirt.

Moo took off her tee shirt as well.

Leroy took off his bermuda shorts.

Moo took off her bermuda shorts.

He looked at her body, admiring it, and then he looked around one last time. Then they lay down, heads facing the sun, and made love properly, in a Christian manner, with restraint and with purity of intention, more or less. It took a fairly long time.

When they were done, they snuggled for a while and then Moo read aloud the scene from *Ah, Sweet Mystery of Life*, just to make sure they'd got everything right. It struck her as a really dumb scene for a book and she was relieved when Leroy said, "That's a really dumb scene," because they were thinking and feeling in union, which was a good sign. Moo began to feel sexy all over again.

"Let's look at the pictures," she said, and giggled.

Leroy reached for their worn copy of *The Joy of Christian Sex* and at once the book flopped open to Figures 6 and 7, their favorites. On facing pages were anatomical drawings of the aroused internal female genitalia (side view) and the aroused internal male genitalia (side view). These were line drawings, not photographs, and they were modestly executed, with little arrows pointing to the ovary, the fallopian tube, the elevated uterus, the expanded inner two-thirds of the vagina; on the male drawing the arrows pointed to the seminal vesicle, the contracting prostate, the elevated and enlarged testicle, the erect penis. The arrows and the identifications were necessary aids to comprehension since the drawings themselves looked like a Rorschach test.

Moo and Leroy gazed at the pictures shamelessly. They were not really dirty pictures, after all, and the book was a Christian book where all the female genitals were blurry and the male genitals were nice and small. Nonetheless it was a terrific turn-on.

He glanced at her and could see her nipples had grown hard and, though he didn't look down, he could feel himself stiffen. Ordinarily they would have turned to one another, dropped the book, and read no more that day. But a fit of craziness possessed him suddenly and he leaped to his feet and began to dance around the blanket making Indian war cries and shaking his engorged penis at her. Crazed too, she snatched at it repeatedly, missing of course because he was dancing around her and she was in a recumbent position. She squirmed on the blanket. He moved in closer and then darted away. She writhed, reaching out to him. He teased and tormented her. Here it is. There it goes. Lobbling and bobbling, looking larger all the time, it began to turn positively purple. Finally she could stand it no longer and, casting off all the refinements of Christian sexuality, she cried out, "Gimme it, gimme it," and fell to her back, her legs pedaling wildly in the air.

The consummation took a very long time. They felt the earth move—in fact there was a small earthquake, 3.5 on the Richter scale—though Leroy and Moo went right on making love, and the sun dipped lower in the sky, and a soft white cloud appeared and disappeared, and still they went at it. Finally they came, simultaneously and with vigor, and then they lay stickily side by side.

"Thank you," she said.

"Thank you," he said.

"And we must thank God," she said.

"And Olga," they said, at the same time.

They were silent for a while, praising God and letting their sweat dry, and then Moo turned her head and kissed Leroy on the nose.

"We're pregnant now," Moo said. "I feel it."

"With our daughter," Leroy said.

"Maybe we'll have twins."

"Or triplets."

"No, I think it'll be just one daughter."

"We'll call her Moo," Leroy said.

She kissed his nose again.

"No," she said, "we'll call her Olga Moo."

"Olga Moo," he repeated.

"It's only right," she said.

He kissed her nose this time.

"Should we do it once more?" she said. "Just to be sure?"

"Would it be decent? A fourth time? Out here in the pasture?"

She sat up and looked around. The sun was about to dip behind the mountain. She began to feel cold.

"We could do the fourth one at home," she said. "We wouldn't want Olga Moo to catch a chill."

They rose and dressed, slowly, languidly, because they were very tired. Moo gathered up the books and Leroy gathered the blanket and compass. With their arms around each other they strolled across the pasture and into the grove of eucalyptus where they had left the car.

They were greeted by a park services officer. He was huge, with a blond goatee, and he looked like a movie star. A pair of binoculars dangled from his left hand.

"Sir. Ma'am."

"Officer," they said together. Moo turned very red and Leroy turned maroon.

"This your car, sir, ma'am?"

Leroy nodded.

"License and registration, sir?"

Leroy fumbled in the pocket of his bermuda shorts, found nothing, and looked wistfully back toward the pasture.

"It's on the seat, sir." The officer tipped his head toward the car.

Leroy thanked him and opened the car door and retrieved his wallet. He began to burrow through it for his license.

"As a matter of fact, I've already checked the license, sir."

Pause.

"In fact, I've checked everything, sir." He said it meaningfully, nodded in agreement with himself, and tapped his binoculars.

"I didn't want to interrupt you folks, because you're university people obviously and because you're an African-American and Caucasian couple and we have to be very careful not to even *seem* to harass folks like you, BUT . . . are you aware that public nudity is not allowed up here?"

"Well, yes," Leroy said, "but . . ."

"Not to mention acts of a carnal or—excuse me, ma'am—specifically sexual nature?"

"It's not what you think," Moo said.

The officer looked at her and looked at Leroy.

"Well, it's not," she said, and held out to him the copy of *The Joy of Christian Sex*.

"That must be some book," he said, shaking his head, but he did not take it and in fact he moved a little away from her. "I don't want you to think my interest was prurient," he said, and again he tapped his binoculars. "I had to check for crime. You know? You probably remember what Theodore Roethke says about—excuse me, ma'am—about love-making. He says that from a little distance it looks and sounds like murder. So I had to check on y'all. And then, when I saw what it was, I didn't feel it was right to interrupt."

"Well, that's very nice of you," Leroy said.

"Thank you very much, officer," Moo said.

"But you might want to be more discreet in the future," he said. "Some people could get the wrong idea."

He shook their hands and moved off toward his own car, but as he went, he turned and slapped Leroy companionably on the behind.

"Nice going," he said.

24

The park services officer told his barber about the frolic in the pasture and the barber told his wife who told her sister who told her daughter whose Boston College roommate had a girlfriend in California, at the university, in Suzie Sweezie's post-Christian feminist prayer group, and in a very short time—a bit under twenty-four hours, in fact—everybody at the university knew about Moo and Leroy doing it in the pasture, in daylight, starkers. They all began doing it, at least all the undergraduates, but the instructions had been garbled in the telling and now they faced away from the sun so that they wouldn't get pregnant.

Tortorisi had already put it in his novel by the time he and Olga attended Eleanora's salon. In his version the frolic was attributed to Missy and the President's best friend, the Provost, and this was how he presented it chez Eleanora. Eleanora loved it.

"He's too much," she said, fairly shouting her approval. "He's absolutely brilliant and I used to think he was a bit of a turd, but he's not turdy at all. Am I right? Olga? *Rien de turde ici?* You all know Olga. *Medea's Daughters?*"

"It's fiction he's writing," Olga said softly, "one has to remember that."

"Oh, don't be stuffy," Eleanora said. "We'd all *like* it to be true, and Tortorisi's told it very well, you've got to admit that, and so it *is* true. Am I right?"

"Facts are irrelevant?"

"Facts always make a good story, Olga, but you can't let them get in the way."

"Paul de Man thought that too."

"Ugly, ugly Olga," Eleanora said, not altogether joking.

Tortorisi, who all through their conversation had been sniggering his old unpleasant snigger, nervous and apologetic, suddenly let forth a robust, orotund, bellowing laugh, part Pavarotti, part Jim Carrey. It was a glad, emancipated bray of approval, of endorsement. Silence fell for just a second and then everybody, and especially Eleanora, laughed along with him.

"Ugly, ugly Olga," people began to say and the general feeling was that it was a great salon and great fun to be in attendance and Tortorisi was great and of course Eleanora was great and it was so nice to meet that Olga, especially since David Hwang and Peter Shaffer didn't show up, which would have made it really really great.

Shortly after midnight the little physicist made his country western debut. He wore a black leather vest with his initials done in rhinestones, and black leather chaps which set his little crotch in relief, and his guitar was studded with rhinestones too. He wore a ten gallon hat, unfortunately a little large for him, and in a surprisingly sweet voice he sang a series of old favorites: "Rhinestone Cowboy," which he thought of as his signature song, "Cheating Heart," "Jose Cuervo," and Patsy Kline's "Crazy." He closed with an all-stops-out rendition of "Stand By Your Man" which he changed, in honor of Eleanora, to "Stand By Your Gal," after which there was a great deal of applause and some unexplained laughter.

It was a great salon, everyone said, fleeing.

But it was not a great salon, and at the end of the long evening Olga pointed this out to Eleanora Tuke and her little physicist during the post-mortem. They were seated in matching love seats, sipping the good cognac that the little physicist had produced as soon as the last guests departed.

To begin with, Olga said, the food had been poor, and scarce as well. Twenty garlic toasts, and radishes, did not a salon make.

The drink was—how to say it gently—bordering on vile.

The guest list was too eclectic and offered too many and too various contending egos.

The little physicist's country western singing was . . . sweet . . . in tone and . . . to be sure . . . in motive. But it was not an ideal way to end the evening.

Tortorisi had been a sensation, of course, with his readings and his new ingratiating laugh, but he should not be allowed to get out of hand. Here Olga gave him a sharp look.

And the conversation. Olga shook her head. The conversation had been ordinary gossip and, while it remained gossip, people had enjoyed it. But whenever Eleanora and her physicist had scurried about trying to break people up into groups of four and five to talk aesthetics and to be deep together, the conversation had fallen apart. They didn't want to talk aesthetics and few of them were by nature deep. They were merely celebrities, or thought they were, and they wanted to look at one another and flirt with one another and perhaps go to bed with one another. They wanted to know who was, and who was not, wearing underwear. And what kind. And how to get into it. They wanted to hear Tortorisi recite long, funny, scandalous passages from his novel, not because it was literature but because it was scandal. And, more to the point, destructive scandal about the President and Missy and the Provost, who could not even defend themselves.

Eleanora, Olga said, had the salon thing all wrong.

She let that sink in for a minute.

Eleanora cried quietly in her love seat but said nothing in response. This was her hour of lead, remembered if outlived, and she knew she would outlive it and be the better for it. This was her fate and her fate was hard. Meanwhile her physicist tried to comfort her. "They liked my songs," he said, "I don't care what Olga says." Eleanora stopped crying long enough to tell him he was an idiot. He continued to stroke her hand reassuringly.

Olga resumed her critique. What they wanted, these awful guests, was what Eleanora could provide better than anyone else. Didn't she see? They wanted a meeting ground and they wanted to shine and they wanted, and needed, somebody to show them off. A brilliant hostess, with wit and charm and a sense of the outrageous. With clothes to match.

Eleanora, who for a long while had said nothing, perked up here, because in her strapless gown of citron, melon, and strawberry chiffon she knew she was a stunner.

And they wanted to be seen, Olga said. She added, pointedly: "Which means . . . ?"

"What?" Eleanora implored.

"Think!" Olga said.

"Tell me!"

Olga waited, but still Eleanora did not see the obvious.

"Television!" Olga said, and she began to speak in tiny emphatic paragraphs.

"TV."

"Your salon in a box."

"Eleanora on the air."

"With Tortorisi as your sidekick. Give us that laugh, Tortorisi."

He brayed, robustly, on demand.

"See? Can't you imagine it?"

"Television," Eleanora said. "Videotics, of course. But me? I?"

"You'd be the Larry King of the literati. You could have theme shows: Derrida, Hillis Miller, Geoffrey Hartman. You could have Jay McInerny and Bret Ellis and Tama Janowitz. You could have Camille Paglia. All by herself. Think of it! And Tortorisi could be yucking it up at every show."

Eleanora sat up straight. She was on camera. "I could *do* it, of course, there's no question about that. The only question is would I *want* to do it."

"The salon is dead," Olga said. "Long live the salon of the air!"

"I could buy you your own station," the physicist said.

Eleanora patted his knee. "I'd want a network show," she said.

"Maybe I could buy you a network," he said, doubtfully. "Maybe."

Tortorisi laughed, rowdy and appreciative, the sound of big money.

Eleanora was thinking aloud. "I could get to wear *all* my clothes," she said. "I could do my best one-liners. Ugly, ugly Olga was very good, you've got to admit. Am I right? I could celebrate all the super ephemeral stuff before it fades—Nazi surfer theory, the micro politics of identity, sound text—because the important thing about a great intellectual fad is that it doesn't last and you've got to get it while it's hot. So. I *could* do it. The question is: do I *want* to do it?"

That question hung in the air.

"You do," Olga said.

"You do," the little physicist said.

They all began to clap to the beat: you do, you do, you do.

Tortorisi was braying, out of control.

"You do, you do"—and they clapped—"you do, you do."

"I do," Eleanora said, giving in at last, "I do, I do."

She jumped up and down, clapping her hands, shaking her great breasts, and then she spun around and around and around, twirling like a jumbo ballerina while her citron, melon, and strawberry chiffon skirt swirled about her sturdy legs. Her head was spinning and the room was spinning because at last she saw her true fate and it was wonderful: she would teach the chosen few in daylight at the university and, at night, on TV, she would teach the world.

She was to be an academic *and* a television star.

25

"I've neglected you terribly, Rosalie," Olga said, " and I want to apologize."

"Yes?" Rosalie said. She made a face to indicate what she thought of Olga's apology, not to mention her impertinence in suggesting her neglect had been noticed or that it might matter one way or the other. They were talking on the phone so looks didn't count.

"I'm rushed," Olga said, "and we're near the end of the quarter."

"Yes?" Rosalie said.

"To be brief, what do you want? Tell me."

"Want?"

"Want. Tell me. I'll get it for you."

"Money," Rosalie said, and hung up.

26

It was evening, beautifully cool, and they were sitting on the patio behind the Kurtz's house. Zachary had just passed the drinks around and Rosalie had passed around the pretzels and the nuts and they were about to settle in for a good chaw and a chat. They were the power people: the Kurtzes, the Richters, and Gil Rudin.

Rosalie excused herself for just a second so she could check one last time on Adam Zachary. They had moved his crib into the kitchen where they could keep an eye on him and, despite the slamming of the patio door, he was sleeping nicely, a bottle clutched in his fat little hand. She went outside and joined her guests.

"Plottin' time," Rosalie said, singing it out like the foreman at Tara. She sat down and raised her drink in a toast: "Plottin' time."

"Jesus!" Zachary said. "Are you crazy! Consider the Nigra!"

"What?" Rosalie said, and laughed. "There are multicultural police in the bushes?"

"Plottin' time!" Gil sang out, determined as always to annoy.

"Fuck a duck," Robbie Richter said, apropos of nothing, and Cynthia slugged him in the ribs.

"Could we *please* get a grip here please?" Zachary said.

"That sounds like a Raymond Carver title. *Could We Please Get a Grip Here Please*, without a comma before the second please. That's very good, Zacky. I think you've got a future in literature."

"Rosalie, would you let up? Just for a few minutes?"

"Mistah Kurtz," she said softly. That was all she needed to say but, just for fun, she whispered to Gil, "He dead."

"People, come on now. It's almost the end of the quarter and the last faculty meeting is only two weeks away and we've gotta deal with the Tortorisi problem. We've gotta get our strategy straight before the next faculty meeting. Are we agreed on that?" He roughed up his mustache in annoyance.

"Agreed," everybody said, and Rosalie added, "*Sayonara*, Tortorisi."

"Okay. You've heard the latest, of course. He's putting us in a book. He's going to try to make fools of us."

"I didn't hear that." Robbie Richter giggled. "How could anybody make a fool of *me*?" and then he shrieked as Cynthia tickled him in the ribs.

"Or you?" Rosalie said, indicating Zachary.

Gil smiled at her cozily. And to Zachary he said, "What do you have against him, Zack? Aside from the fact that he's a terrible writer and a terrible teacher and a general blight on the aesthetic landscape, what exactly makes you want to exterminate him?"

"He's *fat*. He's a fat fuck and it makes me sick just to look at him."

"Well, at least that's clear," Gil said.

"So we'll deny him tenure," Robbie Richter said. "Agreed? Which means, in effect, that we'll have to call in favors. We should insist on negative votes or, where we can't get a negative, at least get an abstention. I'll contact my people—all the untenured hires—and Gil, you can work the fools, because they know you and like you, sort of, and Zack, well, you'll have to work from the students on up, I guess. And through Olga, if you can. Agreed?"

They agreed.

They were impressed by Robbie's take-charge manner, which seemed to bode well for his future Chairmanship. Unfortunately, he ruined the impression almost at once by dissolving into giggles.

They all looked at one another.

"Oh, what fun!" Robbie said, with a little shriek of pleasure.

Zachary shook his head, despairing, but before he could say anything, Rosalie redirected the conversation.

"A fat fuck?" she said. "Tortorisi is a fat fuck? What does that mean exactly?"

"Don't be a fool," Zachary said, and heard her whisper, "Mistah Kurtz."

"Fools, yes, of course," Robbie said. "But, you know, I can't believe Tortorisi would try to make a fool out of me. First of all, he's not smart enough, and second of all, who would believe it? I mean, look at my books, not to mention my articles and reviews. Besides, this Lawrence I'm working on is going to revolutionize the study of biography. *And* the writing of it. *And* the reading of it, as a matter of fact." He sat back and smiled contentedly. "It's my *chef d'oeuvre*," he said.

"It's true," Cynthia said. "Robbie has been reborn. I think a man is born twice. First his mother bears him, then he has to be reborn from the woman he loves. That's what I think."

Cynthia and Robbie leaned together and began nuzzling.

"Can we get back to Tortorisi and the fools?" Zachary said. "And can we be specific, please. Who's going to call whom? Robbie? Robbie!"

"Oh," Robbie said, snapping to attention. "I'll call the Chairman since, after all, I'll be replacing him soon." And he added, "He likes me."

"The Chairman likes everybody. That's why he's a fool." The new and alarming Cynthia Richter said this, nastily, and everybody turned to look at her. What a complicated woman she was becoming: lust one minute and murder the next. "What's the matter? I can't be nasty?" she said, and of course she had a right to be, just like everyone else, but for some reason they all felt uncomfortable about it. She took a hefty slug of her drink.

They watched her in silence and suddenly they all got serious about their plotting. Gil offered to call Toby and Ron, and Zachary said he would call Stephanie and Mike and David, and so on and so on, and in this way—wives included—they divvied up the votes of the fools.

"Next on the agenda," Zachary said.

"Another drink?" Rosalie said. "Cynthia needs one, Zack, and so does Gil, and *you* always need one."

Annoyed, Zachary gathered the glasses and retreated to the kitchen, where he downed a quick scotch in hopes of improving his mood. Then he checked on the baby, little A to Z, fat and perfect and gurgling in his crib, and he resisted the temptation to pick him up and squeeze him and squeeze him. What a great gift this baby was. His offspring. His eternity. He began to feel loving and tender and then he remembered the drinks he had to prepare and, cursing, he went to the refrigerator and started wrestling with the damned ice cube tray which, like everything else around here, worked inefficiently and only part of the time.

Outside, they could hear Zachary banging around in the kitchen.

"He's got one of his headaches," Rosalie explained.

"He *is* a headache," Gil said, smiling at her. She smiled back. Encouraged, he reached over to brush away a mosquito and accidentally touched her breast.

"How is Betz doing?" Rosalie asked, quick as an adder.

"Yes, what about Betz?" Robbie said. "I've heard she's moved in with Concepcion. Can that be true? Is it true that Concepcion's a lesbian?"

They all stared at Robbie, incredulous.

"Well, is she?"

"Have you been living in a cave somewhere?" Rosalie said. "Concepcion teaches gay studies. She teaches lesbian lit."

"But she teaches Chicana lit too," Robbie said.

"That's because she's Chicana *and* lesbian," Rosalie said.

"Well, what about Roland Barthes?"

"Roland Barthes is *not* a lesbian."

They all laughed because—who knows?—maybe he was.

"Concepcion perhaps," Robbie said, "but *Betz* can't be a lesbian. She was your wife!" He turned to Gil for confirmation.

"I did my best," Gil said, and snorted into the night air, hoping to dismiss the topic.

"I bet you did," Rosalie said. "And I bet she'll do her best now."

"Meaning what?" Gil said.

"Meaning she'll clean you out. Money, money, money."

"Yes," Robbie said. "Will you be losing everything, Gil, or just half of everything? I guess it'll only be half." He sounded disappointed.

"And what about Concepcion?" Cynthia asked. "Will this affect her tenure? I've always liked Concepcion."

"It can't affect her tenure," Robbie said. "Not if she's a lesbian."

"Are lesbians granted tenure automatically?" Rosalie asked. "Why, I should like to know. Tell us about it, Gil."

"Well, it's not automatic," Robbie said. "But who would have the courage to fire one? Isn't that right, Gil?"

Gil had begun to look furious.

"Gil?" Rosalie was enjoying herself. "What's Betz up to these days?"

Gil, embattled, said, "Could we *please* talk about something else please."

"Another Carver title," Rosalie said. "We're all so literary tonight."

In the kitchen Zachary downed another quick scotch before taking the tray out to the patio. He had a dull pain in his chest, and he had sloshed gin all over the tray, but he couldn't slow down, not now, not when he'd finally gotten them to *do* something. He smoothed down his nifty little mustache.

"Well," he said, emerging from the kitchen, "we're moving right along." He passed the drinks, making chat, but before he could sit down and say, "Let's talk Chairmanship," Robbie Richter antici-pated him.

"Let's talk about my Chairmanship," Robbie said, and proceeded to a long list of reasons why he should be Chair, why he wanted to be Chair, and why finally they had to make him Chair. These reasons in-cluded his books, which he named by title and date of publication and recommended with quotes from reviewers, and also his articles, for which he gave only brief journal citations, and then, in turn, his reviews, talks, workshops, conferences attended, his class teaching, his dissertation advisories, his contributions to department commit-tees, extra-department fora, and university panels.

This took quite a lot of time, time enough for them to finish their drinks, for Zachary to bring them new ones, for Rosalie to bring fresh bowls of pretzels and nuts, and for Gil to disappear from the patio on the alleged grounds of having to pee. And still Robbie Richter went on.

Gil knew the house well and was able, even in the dark, to take Adam Zachary from his crib in the kitchen and find his way to Zachary's study, flick on the light, and settle down on the couch, alone, paternally, with the baby cradled against his chest. He had not held the baby in his arms since the circumcision and he was pleased with the new way the baby felt, more substantial, more like the son he had imagined for himself. The baby had his hair and his coloring. The baby was perfect. He began to sing "Rock-a-bye, baby," but he couldn't remember the words, and so he switched to humming. At once the baby opened his eyes—blue, like his own—and gurgled at him and kicked his fat little legs in pleasure. Gil smiled at him and wrinkled up his nose. The baby laughed. Gil bent over him and made smacking noises on his belly and shook his floppy blond hair like a crazy man. The baby laughed and kicked. "Is you my ittle baby boy?" Gil said. "Is you my itty bitty baby perfect boy. I could eat you up like an ice cream cone, yes I could, yes I could, I could be a big giant eater and eat up my baby boy . . . " and he pretended to take big bites of Adam Zachary's belly, and he laughed, and the baby laughed and kicked.

Gil looked up then and saw Zachary, a little drunk and very angry, standing at the door. He looked ready to kill.

"I'll put him back in his crib," Gil said.

Gil said, "I was just holding him."

"Jesus, don't have a stroke," Gil said, because Zachary's color was moving toward purple and for once he seemed unable to speak.

Gil took the baby back to the kitchen and put him in his crib. Then he went out to join the others on the patio where Robbie Richter was still explaining why he could, should, and must be Chairman. Gil pretended to listen attentively.

Zachary appeared at the door, still purple, still furious. Rosalie looked from Zachary to Gil and back to Zachary.

"He's mine," Zachary said to Gil in a choked voice. "He's mine," he said to everybody.

Cynthia looked at Zachary, who seemed ready to explode, and then she looked at Rosalie, who seemed to be hoping he might explode, and Cynthia decided it was time to get out, quickly.

Robbie was still talking and Cynthia batted him, hard, across the chest.

Robbie shrieked. "What?" he said.

"Time to go," Cynthia said.

"But we haven't finished," Robbie said.

"We'll finish at home," Cynthia said, "in the hot tub."

Robbie giggled and said, "You're all invited, of course. Only we go nude, you know. You'll have to go nude too." He giggled again. "It's our only rule."

For the moment they forgot Zachary and his fury and they all stared in silence at Robbie and Cynthia. Nobody wanted to imagine them nude.

"I don't think so," Rosalie said.

"I'm not up to it," Gil said.

There were polite goodbyes. Robbie and Cynthia ducked out by the side stairs and Gil joined them at once.

Rosalie followed them to the stairs. "Jesus," she said, calling down to them, "Stand not upon the order of your going," but they were gone before she could even finish the quote.

Zachary was still standing, furious, in the doorway.

She was fed up with him, he was always like this, ruining everything whenever she was having a good time.

"Do you mind telling me what this is about?" she said.

She said, "You stand there looking like death and you drive everybody out of my house!"

She said, "What a shit you are!" and because he said nothing, she added, "What are you up to?"

"What are *you* up to?" he said. He wanted to say something devastating about Gil Rudin and Rosalie and the baby, *his* baby, but he could not find the words. He could not even find the idea.

They stared at each other for a moment, silent, hating, and then she picked up Adam Zachary and he picked up the crib and they both went into the nursery. They tucked the baby in and gave him his bottle and stood looking at him. Neither said a word. Zachary turned off the overhead light and Rosalie turned on the night light and they left.

Rosalie went to the bedroom and locked the door.

Zachary went to his study and locked the door.

If I had money, I could get out of this trap, Rosalie thought, and was surprised because she had thought she didn't care about money and didn't realize she was in a trap.

Zachary did not think. He pressed his hand against his chest, hard, to stop the pain. And it did stop after a while, but even then he wasn't able to think. Something had gone wrong in his brain. He sat very quietly and after a long while his head cleared a bit and he got out his beloved *Emma*. But he was unable to read. He was unable even to focus.

He was not up to this. He was, for the first time in his life, becoming vulnerable. The baby had made him so. A to Z. Little Adam Zachary. His eternity. And Gil Rudin was—somehow—threatening them, both himself *and* the baby.

Things were going too fast and he could not cope. He must get all this out of his hands and into Olga's. Everything: the Department of Theory and Discourse, getting rid of Tortorisi, securing the Chairmanship for that asshole Robbie Richter.

Zachary leaned forward and laid his head on *Emma* and tried to think calm thoughts. Gil Rudin was not to be trusted. And Rosalie had become a stranger. And the baby, he was terribly worried about the baby. But why?

He had no room left for a calm thought. It was all up to Olga now.

27

For her interview with the Deans, Olga wore her hair pulled back, school-marm fashion, secured with what appeared to be a toy dagger. Her eyes looked large and innocent, her open face incapable of calculation. She wore her yellow dress to confirm the impression of sincerity.

Her manner, however, was all business. She had much to accomplish and in far too short a time.

"A pleasure," she said, a little stiffly, as the Dean of Humanities— "Call me Seton," he said—introduced each of the lesser Deans. There was the tall one she had met at the circumcision party, and the yellow and the black, who seemed always to travel together. They were pleased to see her again, they said.

"A pleasure," she said.

Then there was the gay Dean and the lesbian Dean, a sort of androgynous duo, whose clothes and hair and dress, and indeed even their features, seemed remarkably alike. They could have been a pair of very unhappy twins. Originally there had been only a single Dean for both gays and lesbians, but the lesbians had complained that this was a clear case of penile hegemony and so a lesbian Dean had been appointed, as much like the gay Dean as possible given their sexual differences.

"A pleasure."

The Chicana Dean was not able to attend, Seton explained, because she was participating in an international forum on mariachi, past and future, and would be away for the month. The Dean of Jewish studies would join them later.

"Ah," Olga said.

"Call me Seton," he said again, and gestured toward the conference room.

They all filed in and sat down. Olga looked around, surprised at the room's opulence. It was oval-shaped and wainscoted below, with paintings of former Presidents arranged chronologically above. The conference table was black teak from Brazil, a single sheet, inlaid at either end with a mother-of-pearl scroll, the university symbol that looked suprisingly like a dollar sign, and there were matching chairs of black teak also. Heavy satin drapes covered the high windows.

"Our little room," Seton said, and all the Deans smiled. He opened a worn leather folder and looked at it for a moment. "We have a memo from your Chairman," he said, reading from the folder. "The Dean"—he pointed to the tall one— "the cognizant Dean for the English Department, has brought the memo to our attention and we thought it best to pursue any furtherance of the matter with you personally, since, of course, it's you that the memo concerns. I want to thank you for coming."

"I thank you too," the lesbian Dean said, and she was echoed by the gay Dean, but not by the black or yellow Deans, nor by the tall one. Olga decided they must have their own agenda.

Seton closed the folder and continued, but without his notes. They were all interested in the idea of her staying on at the university as a part-time or full-time member of the faculty. It would be a tenured position, of course. A full professorship. In fact, a university chair, if they could find the money for one.

The black Dean interrupted to point out there was no black chair and the next chair had better be a black chair. Or else.

The yellow Dean smiled pleasantly, but shook his head. He taught psychology and he understood.

Or else they'd raise the roof, the black dean insisted. They'd burn the muh-fuh down. He laughed loudly, menacingly. Just kidding, he said.

The lesbian Dean commented that lesbians didn't want a chair, not yet, and they did not plan on burning down anything. What they would like, she said, was justice and equality.

The gay Dean said, hear, hear.

Seton waited politely until they were done and then he went on. Money was a problem, he explained, because there wasn't ever enough. Had she heard about the money scandals. Yes?

"Yes."

Therefore, Seton said, and in the light of the minority Deans' objections, her appointment would have to be an opportunity appointment, *not* a chair. The money would come from—he paused, thinking—from funds that wouldn't be available to them, to any of them, *otherwise*. It would be found money. Money that wouldn't exist except for the existence of Professor Kominska herself and this splendid opportunity to hire her—Do I say it right? Kominska?—and so he hoped everybody was happy.

Everybody was silent because they all knew that such moneys appeared from time to time, though nobody cared to investigate the source.

"Is that appealing to you?" Seton asked.

"No, thank you," Olga said. "It's flattering to be asked, but I don't think so."

Seton smiled and went right on. It could be a five-year appointment, or a ten-year appointment, or an appointment without term. Of course he would have to send the appropriate papers back down through the English Department, but the Chairman would take care of all that, and, once she was appointed, would she be interested in serving as Chairwoman? Or Chairperson? Whatever? The English Department was very short on people with credentials for the Chairpersonship, and there had been strenuous objections by the young Turks to the appointment of another fool, and, from what he'd heard, Olga seemed to be the happy balance between theory and literature, between Turks and foolishness. Was that right?

"I am a happy balance," she said.

The gay Dean and the lesbian Dean nodded. The black and the yellow and the tall one seemed willing to commit.

"So you'll accept?" Seton asked.

"There would have to be conditions," she said. "There would have to be changes. And still I couldn't guarantee that I'd accept. I would have to do my thoughts."

"Conditions," Seton said. "Changes."

"Change is always good," the black Dean said, adding, with a disarming smile, "for the white boy."

"Pressure, pressure, pressure," the yellow Dean said.

"Conditions," Seton said again, "and changes."

Olga paused to prepare them for this: "The Department name would have to be changed."

"Not call it a Department?"

"Not call it English," Olga said. "English is thought by some to sound too . . . exclusive." Suddenly she seemed to have an English accent.

"It's undemocratic," the black Dean said.

"It's imperialistic," the yellow Dean said, "not to mention xenophobic."

"It's *homo*phobic," the gay and lesbian Deans said together, and for once they smiled.

The tall Dean observed this display of unanimity in silence then, speaking as the Department's cognizant Dean, he said, "I never liked the name, I confess."

"It could be called the Department of Theory and Discourse," Olga said, "or something exactly like that."

"Theory and Discourse," Seton said. "Theory and Discourse. It has a certain ring to it. Yes." Seton was the Dean of Humanities and so of course he already knew about Kurtz's little plot to create a new Department of Theory and Discourse and to get rid of the English Department, or make it a program, or something like that. Some new screwball scheme. Who could care?

"What exactly would such a change mean," he said, "in terms of personnel?"

"Oh, they'll be happy," Olga said, "because nothing will be changed, you see, except the name. It's the words that matter. English will still be English."

"Hey, mon," the black Dean said, "English still be English."

"No tickee, no laundly," the yellow Dean said.

"The Turks would like it, sure," Seton said, "because they're big on words, but what about the others?"

"Oh, the fools care about words too, but they don't care what you call the English Department so long as they continue to teach English literature. So they'll be happy as well."

"They'll be happy," Seton said wistfully.

The black Dean snickered and the yellow one smiled and all the others nodded approval. It was a nice idea: a happy Department.

"That's the first thing," Olga said, "the name of the Department. Then there's the matter of appointments. To tenure, I mean."

"We've heard about that Tortorisi guy," Seton said.

The tall Dean groaned.

Everybody nodded in agreement.

"He writes novels?" Seton chuckled. "Don't worry about him. He's outta here. He's history."

"*Sayonara*," the yellow Dean said, mocking, he hoped, the Japanese.

"Oh, but he has to stay," Olga said.

She said, "You haven't heard the end of Tortorisi."

She said, "He's written a book."

That sounded vaguely menacing and they all stared at her.

"This book is—how shall I say it?—a *roman a clef*." They continued to stare. "About people you will recognize," she said. "People in the academy. This academy. Above the level of Chairman." Seton lurched forward in his chair. "In short," she said, "it's about the Deans."

There were snorts and growls, indicating disbelief.

"We'll sue," Seton said.

"And about the Provost," Olga said.

She said, "And Missy."

She said, "In the pasture."

"Not in the bushes?" Seton asked.

"That too," she said.

The Deans, the Provost, Missy. It was too awful to contemplate what the local papers would do with this. Or the national papers. Or, again, *60 Minutes*.

"But not . . . ?" Seton couldn't bring himself to ask it.

Olga let the question hang in the air.

"Yes," she said finally.

"The President?"

She nodded and all the Deans nodded and Seton lowered his head to the table. There was a long silence in the room, broken by the yellow Dean's nervous giggle. Olga examined her nails.

After a very long time Seton banged his head lightly on the table and, as if that had restored him, he suddenly reared back in his chair and said, "We *will* sue. We'll sue the bastard for every cent he's got. We'll destroy him. We'll murder the son of a bitch."

"String him up," the black Dean said.

"He's a traitor," the lesbian Dean said, but the gay Dean said, "I don't know, he strikes me as kind of *sympathique*."

They all turned on him, but since he was gay they didn't dare hit him.

"We'll sue," Seton said. "That's what we keep that army of lawyers *for*, for Chrissake, to *sue*. They've cost us ten mil a year for the last three years running, and where have they got us? In *The New York Times*, for Chrissake. In *Newsweek*. On *Sixty Minutes*, with that prick Wallace running around putting his face into the President's private life and Missy's clothes closet and photographing the freeking *wine* cellar. It's the lawyers' fault, goddamit, can't they do anything right? Well, let me tell you, kiddos, they're gonna do it right this time. They're gonna nail that sucker. Tortorisi's history. Tortorisi's outta here."

He slumped in his chair, exhausted. Everyone waited.

"It's not going to be easy," Olga said.

Still they waited.

"It's a libelous book. But you can't sue for libel unless you're willing to prove that *you* are identifiable as the libelous character. That everyone recognizes you as this idiot in the book because it's a very good depiction of who you are." She paused to make sure they got it. "He's taken care that you won't want to prove that. You'd be proving you *are* that idiot."

Silence.

"It's a very funny book." She suppressed a smile, and added, "Up to a point."

Seton's beeper went off and he silenced it.

"There is a way, however," she said.

Seton leaned toward her, lowering his voice. "Bribery?" he asked.

"A harsh word," she said.

"Money?"

"Oh no," she said. "Tenure."

"Tenure! Why not money? We can raise it. How much would it take?"

"Tenure," she repeated.

There was silence then and consternation. Seton's beeper went off once again, and once again he silenced it.

"Tenure," she said.

"And he'd suppress the book?"

"Up to a point."

"Which means?"

"Creative revision."

"He'd take us out?"

"Effectively."

"And the President? Will he take him out too?"

"I'm quite sure. I'm certain. I could guarantee it."

"It's blackmail," Seton said, "and it would be wrong."

"It *is* blackmail," she said, "and it *is* wrong."

"Well, now let's be reasonable here. It's only blackmail in a sense," the tall Dean said. "It's really an investment in our future. Or rather, in the future of the university. We can't sustain another scandal."

"We can *not*," the black Dean said, and everybody said no, no, we can *not*.

"And besides," Seton said, "intentionality counts here. Our intention would not be to do something illegal but merely to prevent harm to our university. Nobody can fault that. If you look in your hearts, you can see that our intentions are pure."

"Besides," the tall Dean said, "our intentions are pure."

"That's what I just said," Seton said.

"So we're in agreement then," the tall Dean said.

"But *I* said it," Seton said.

But then the lesbian Dean nearly ruined everything. "I don't like it," she said. "It's . . . I don't know."

"Well, is he in fact gay?" the gay Dean asked. "He looks gay to me, but he's so fat, I don't know."

"I don't know either," the lesbian Dean said.

Seton's beeper went off and he silenced it. At once it went off again. And again.

"It's the President," Seton said. "He's getting antsy." He swallowed, blinked, and said to Olga, "Tenure for silence. God, what a deal." He realized that if the English faculty turned Tortorisi down—and they might, they could—he'd have to overrule them and give Tortorisi tenure on his own *fiat*. And how would *that* look? Still, what could he do? He had to protect the President's ass. And his own. "A deal," he said, and stuck out his hand.

"A deal," Olga said.

A deal, they all said, and shook on it.

They were shuffling to their feet, awkward but relieved, when the Dean of Jewish Studies was pushed through the door in his wheelchair. He wore dark glasses and kept his head tilted at an angle that indicated blindness.

"Visually and physically challenged *and* Jewish," Seton whispered to Olga. "Now that's what I call a *real* catch."

"Shalom," Olga said.

"You're Jewish maybe?" he asked from his wheelchair.

"Up to a point," she said.

He smiled and beckoned her down toward him. He took her hands, felt for her face, and then with enthusiasm tweaked both her cheeks hard.

"Bubelah," he said, and everybody applauded lightly.

Seton hurried them along to the President's suite where the appointments secretary tapped her watch with a long fingernail and glared at them. "You're late," she said, and led them out of the waiting room and down the corridor to the President's office, the Dean of Jewish Studies trailing in his wheelchair. She knocked and went in, holding the door ajar. Seton crossed the threshold on tippy-toe.

Once again Olga was impressed. The President's office was very large and very dark, with heavy Persian carpets on the floor and velvet drapes along one wall. The other walls were hung with tapestries. With the addition of a crucifix, it could have been a chapel.

"Mr. President," Seton began, "I want to present Professor Olga Kominska, our distinguished visitor from . . . where are you from?"

"Abroad," she said.

"From abroad," Seton said. "She's been sharing some excellent ideas with us. Excellent. Excellent."

"You're late," the President said.

He was a different man in his office. He seemed younger, more confident, and distinctly in charge. Perhaps, Olga reflected, it was the big desk that accounted for the difference, or perhaps the office itself, or perhaps simply the absence of Missy. He nodded to the Deans at large and shook Olga's hand vigorously.

"Good to see you again," he said to Olga. "Barbaric scene there, wasn't it, at the Kurtzes. The circumcision?" And to the Dean of Jewish Studies he said, "No offense, it's just a fact. Right?" Finally he turned to Seton. "I had to beep you three times, Seton. Slipping? Getting a little casual? I wouldn't do that, if I were you."

"Oh sir," Seton said.

"I had hoped to hear good news."

"We have good news," Seton said. "Lots."

"And I want to hear it," the President said, "but unfortunately you've kept me waiting."

His appointments secretary appeared at the door, hovering.

Seton, about to be cut off, blurted out: "We're hiring Olga, or at least we hope to, and we're changing the name of the English Department to the Department of Theory and Discourse and—we can't help it—we've got to give tenure to that Tortorisi dork. Okay?"

The appointments secretary moved in, as she saw it, for the kill. "Mr. Schwarzenegger and companion," she said.

"And so you'll have to go," the President said, and turned Seton toward the door. To Olga he whispered, "We'll do this again," and by way of explanation he added, "fundraising comes before everything."

As they passed through the outer office, Olga stared in surprise at Arnold Schwarzenegger and the Secretary of State, deep in conversation with the university lawyers. They all seemed very happy about something.

"Ah," Seton whispered, rising from his gloom, "money and more money."

They reassembled in the conference room to interpret the sense of the meeting with the President—they agreed that *he* had agreed to everything—and to mull over the possibility of changing the names of *all* departments, and to reassure each other that the bargain they had struck was good and necessary, that they had done the right thing, that Tortorisi's tenure was a small price to pay to preserve the name and integrity of a great university.

Well done. Well done. A good day's work.

They all agreed to go out for a drink. All except Olga who went home, eagerly, for a hot and at least symbolically cleansing bath.

Part IV
~

28

Olga was full of sorrow in her bath. The water was hot, but not too hot, and there were suds all around her like in the movies, but she was full of sorrow nonetheless.

It was the nature of her calling that made her sad. That, and the fact that she had just compromised herself by being the catalyst for blackmail and hush money and covert bribery. Crime especially made her sad.

It was one thing to go to bed with Peter Peeks just for the hell of it, because he was young and sturdy and beautiful and empty, but it was quite another to be the agent of corruption. She had appealed to what is easiest and most base in human nature and she had found a ready response in the Deans. No matter that Tortorisi would turn down his tenure at the university, no matter that no blackmail would ever be paid. They had, each of them, been offered the chance to sell their souls, and they had taken it, eagerly, and with a degree of satisfaction, and it was she who had set up the sales booth.

She was accustomed to being a writer and therefore the devil's advocate, but she disliked playing the devil himself. And, clearly, there was something diabolical about all this.

What she liked was the miracle of creation, the way as a *writing* writer, fully launched and credulous, she attracted to herself the events, the characters, the very words, everything she needed and wanted, and they all fit, they all came to her at exactly the right time, useful, economical, serendipitous, perfectly suited to her needs. At the moment of creating all things were given to her, freely, effortlessly. They were forced upon her. Even your enemies, she reflected—if you have enemies, and if you tend to notice them—even your enemies rush to give you aid and comfort and to tell you their darkest secrets to use as you will. Writing was a most intriguingly divine action.

But, alas, diabolical too. Because though she never judged, though she let all of her characters damn or beatify themselves, there was the odd nudge she gave them, the opportunity to sin or praise, the chance to work out their destinies, and it was she who set the balance. She had done exactly that with the Deans and with Tortorisi and . . . . She clenched her fists until her fingernails made half-moons in the palms and the blood began to come, but she stopped then because the blood was merely symbolic. And melodramatic. And, she had to admit, self-indulgent.

She left off thinking and scrubbed her knees hard with her orange fingernail brush, and then her heels and her toenails and the soles of her feet. But there was no point in trying to scrub her flesh away; flesh was of the very essence of the matter. She must accept things as they are. She was a writer, she cobbled together a pack of lies and served it all up for a few moments of amusement—with a moral tincture added, of course, for those who liked that sort of thing. It was not for her to mitigate horror. It was not for her to alter the nature of being. Furthermore, in a real way, she was the daemon of the piece.

Acceptance is all. This is who she is, this is what she does, and this torment is the stuff her imagination feeds upon.

And then, suddenly, for no reason, her subconscious sent up for inspection something it had nurtured down there all day long: the look on Seton's face as he realized Tortorisi's book was about the Deans, the Provost, the President. It was a look of horror and outrage and disbelief. It was a look that said, "Why me, why always me?" instead of the look of wild hilarity that was required. Olga saw herself in that look, and Gil Rudin, and Zachary Kurtz, and she reminded herself that this was a comedy and it was time to get on with it.

She rose from her bath, cleaner, lighter, a better person or at least a more honest one. She accepted what was inevitable and she went forth to make it happen.

29

Gil Rudin was waiting in Huddle and Pilbrick's inner office. There were three places to wait—the outer office, the inner office, and the office proper—and people like Gil, when they had to wait at all, waited in the inner office. The receptionist had brought him coffee and today's copies of *Wall Street Journal* and *The New York Times*, and of course a telephone and a note pad, and she had asked if Gil would prefer the heat lower or higher or if he'd like the air-conditioning. She was only doing her job, but she also had in mind the not-impossible dream of herself as the next Mrs. Gil Rudin. Today, however, he showed little interest in anything she had to offer.

"*Anything* else?" she asked.

He flashed her an appreciative smile, just tinged with lechery, but she could see his heart wasn't in it and so, reluctantly, she excused herself and left him to his telephone and papers.

Gil had arrived early. Usually he liked to keep his lawyers waiting just to show who was employing whom, but this morning had been traumatic for him and by noon he found he had nobody to turn to except his lawyer.

It had started with Olga, that bitch. He had just come out of his ten o'clock class feeling pretty good; his voice had been honeyed, the kids responsive, and he had been absolutely pellucid on the subject of liminality and the hypothetical unconscious. What he wanted now was to tell somebody about how terrific he'd been and, bang, he ran smack into the Olga.

"Gil," she had said, in that arch, infuriating way, as if she'd just been gossiping with Betz and knew all his secrets.

"Olga," he said, doing his best to match her tone.

She burst out laughing.

"What's so funny? I'm afraid . . ."

He was about to say, I'm afraid I don't get the joke, but she cut him off before he could finish his sentence. She reached out and touched his arm with those electric fingertips of hers, fixed him with her hard eyes, and said, "What are you afraid of, Gil? Tell me. What is it you fear?"

He wanted to strike her, he wanted to punch her out. She was to blame for everything. It was she who had convinced Betz to keep the baby. It was she who had given Betz the idea of filing for divorce. It was she who had driven Moo out to pasture with that black bastard and had them screwing in broad daylight. He'd like to beat her up. He'd like to do her, hard, right here on the path and then piss all over her and never stop.

"What am I afraid of?" he asked. He stared into those eyes of hers, leaned closer in, and said earnestly, "With a dick like mine, bitch, I don't have to be afraid of anything."

She looked as if she had been slapped. Her gaze narrowed, she retreated behind her face, she practically disappeared from before his eyes. Indeed, in a moment she was gone.

He had been surprised at how furious he was. He was shaking with rage and he was sweating hard and he wanted to lash out. He found himself repeating her questions. What was he afraid of? What did he fear? Well, he had a question of his own: who the hell did that foreign faker think she was, coming over here, intruding, asking questions, getting everybody crazy? Interfering with his wife! *And* his former wife! *And*, for all he knew, his next wife!

Well, he had put her in her place. He was, it just so happened, afraid of nothing.

He went directly to his office and locked the door. He lowered his pants and his underpants and looked down at his dick. It was a truly excellent dick. It was amazing, really, nice and big, elegantly formed, and very pleasant in color. It was just about perfect. Everybody had said so, always: the kids at St. Paul's, the girls at Harvard and Oxford, Moo and Betz and Rosalie, everybody. Missy had adored it. And Eleanora. And all his teaching assistants. He placed it carefully, lovingly, on his desk. He was estranging it—as Viktor Shklovsky would say—locating it outside its expected environment in order to heighten its singular "dickness." It was buff-colored and handsome against the blue blotter and it smelled—if you could use such a word here—teasingly of sandalwood and myrrh. A splendid, unique dick. It was the center of his being, physically and psychologically. It was the source and agent of his ambitions. It was his conscious and his unconscious both. It really was, in a sense, *who* he was. He had thought about this a lot for his projected study of sexuality, tentatively called *The Phallocentric Universe*, and he had taken extensive notes. Everything began—the whole world—right here between his legs. He paused in his thinking to fondle this most excellent dick and, loyal and dependable, it responded at once. Huzzah!

He was furious still and would remain so, but what he wanted now was to use this superb instrument, to plug it in, to plant a seed, to watch it perform all its clever clever tricks. He tucked it away tenderly, pulled up his pants, and charged out of his office. He was on his way to see Rosalie Kurtz.

Rosalie Kurtz was on the back patio, reclining in a deck chair, taking the noon sun. Adam Zachary lay in a large shaded basket by her side. It was a bucolic scene.

Rosalie had just finished rubbing sunblock 30 on her arms and legs and was starting on her stomach—she was wearing a string bikini—when Gil came around the side of the house, surprising her, and said, "Can I give you a hand there, Miss? Hmm?"

He was being deliberately provocative and Rosalie paused in her work, her hand caressing her belly. She was looking good again, she had her sexy figure back, and here was a chance to use it. She gave him an appreciative sidelong glance. The glance turned at once to amusement when she saw the anger beneath the leer.

"You look like you mighta swallowed a mad dawg," she said, quoting somebody, maybe Faulkner or Flannery O'Connor.

Gil's momentary good mood reverted to gloom.

"*What* is the matter with everybody! I come over here, full of joy and fellow-feeling, just a wee little bit horny, and everybody conspires to ruin my mood."

"A mad dawg," she said.

"You're not gonna get to me with that stuff," he said, moving close to her and standing with his legs apart. He touched his crotch lightly, to get things started.

"And you're not gonna get to me with *that* stuff," she said, but she watched with interest nonetheless.

They both watched.

"Amazing, isn't it," he said.

She looked away suddenly. She seemed angry.

"What?" he said. "Look. Touch it."

"Jesus, Gil," she said, "the baby."

He wilted at the word baby.

He paused, thinking he might still recoup his losses, but decided to give it up. The edge was off. He hadn't really noticed Adam Zachary in his big shady basket—he'd had other things on his mind—but now he moved around Rosalie's deck chair to get a look at the baby.

"He'll smother under all that netting."

"You don't expose a baby to the raw sun, Gil. Don't you know anything!"

He knelt down and, pushing the netting aside, he smiled into the basket. He made soft clicking noises with his tongue. After a while he sat back on his heels and just gazed at the baby.

"Don't wake him," Rosalie said, but Gil ignored her as if he were thinking about something else, and he was. He was thinking through what he could make happen next. Several minutes passed this way. Finally, when he had rearranged the netting to shade the baby, he turned and faced Rosalie.

"He looks like me," Gil said. "The blond hair, the eyes, the shape of the nose. Everything."

"So?"

"So, I think he's mine. I think I'm the father."

"You've said that before."

They were both silent for a moment. Finally, she said, "Well?"

"We could make a deal."

"That's why I hate you, Gil. That's why I broke it off in the first place. You think everything's a deal. You think anything can be bought. And now you want to buy my baby."

"No, I want to buy you."

Silence.

"And the baby along with me?"

"Well, he's *my* baby. It seems only fair I should get him along with you."

More silence.

"You're forgetting Zachary, I guess. Or are you going to buy him too?"

"No, I'm going to buy him *off*."

She laughed because he really believed he could do it.

"I could prove paternity, you know. Easily. Good old DNA. I could sue."

"A mad dawg," Rosalie said.

She was smiling sardonically. The bitch. They were all bitches. Gil felt his mouth go sour. Somewhere in his mind he had evolved a plan, if only he could get back to it.

He swallowed his anger and smiled at her. He sat down on her footrest and ran one hand along her very shapely calf, in a friendly way, nothing sexy about it. He concentrated on feeling sincere.

"Look," he said. "We've been friends," he said. "Haven't we?"

"Oh, come on."

"But we have. And we've made love. And it was really good, wasn't it?"

She was oddly moved.

"Wasn't it?"

She nodded.

"I know," he said. "And we get along, too, there's more than just sex involved here. There's a real attraction." He ran his eyes up her legs and paused there, and then moved to her chubby neck and that cute pouting face, pained now and serious and uncertain, and for the moment he felt something like love for her. He felt that he could do it one more time, one last time—marry, that is—if that was the only way he could get the child.

Consciously, because he could not afford the distraction, he pushed aside the thought that perhaps Olga—the impossible Olga—had organized all this.

He stared deep into Rosalie's eyes. I'm going to marry you, he was thinking, whether you like it or not.

"What are you thinking?" she asked.

"What do *you* think? Do *you* think I'm the father?"

She looked over at the sleeping baby. She didn't have to think. She knew. She had already checked blood-types—hers and the baby's and Zachary's—and had found that Zachary's was incompatible with having fathered this child. The only possible father, then, was Gil. It was a problem.

"You do, don't you."

"It was a mistake, Gil, a fling, everybody makes mistakes and you were mine."

"So you *do* think I'm the father."

If he had been a praying man, Gil would have prayed for inspiration here, but as it happened that wasn't necessary because at that moment Rosalie spoke the magic word.

"Olga says . . ."

"Olga says"—and he leaned close to her, concentrating, getting the voice right— "Olga says, 'What do you want? Tell me. Tell me everything.' Right? Who cares what Olga says."

"Olga says she wonders if I've chosen wisely."

"What *do* you want?" he said. "Tell me, and I'll get it for you." It wasn't clear whether he was speaking for himself now or still imitating Olga, but before she could reply, he rushed ahead. "First, let me tell you what you've got. You've got a little house with a big mort-gage, a short pudgy little husband, and a future of listening to his big ambitions, his plots and his plans, his conniving and his cheating and his famous, endless headaches. He's short. He sweats. He probably smells. He's a brilliant teacher, I grant you that, and he's a very good scholar, an excellent scholar, but think for a moment of the extent of his ambitions. A new Department? With him as Chairman? Once he dumps Robbie, that is. Do you know what that means? He'll be a nanny for all the bellyachers and incompetents and born losers. Everybody who can't hack it will come whining to him. 'I need a re-search assistant. I need summer support money. I need a corner office with two windows.' This is power? This is idiocy. He thinks he's gonna shape some new and dazzling kind of intellectual machine, but what he's shaping is his own destruction. He'll have a stroke before he's forty-five.

"And you?"

"Wait, wait, I'm not done. You also have a son, a baby, who ought to be given opportunities. Circumcision isn't gonna hurt him, but do you want him growing up a Jew? Think about it. This is the end of the twentieth century and we're in the heart of a great academic commu-nity and, even here in Tolerance City where anything goes and the best man wins, even *here*, do you think for an instant that a Kurtz has the opportunities that a Hollywood Rudin has? From St. Paul's and Harvard and Oxford?"

"So that's what you're offering me? A WASP name?"

"And marriage." He leaned close and took her two hands in his. He said tenderly, "And the one thing that will make all the difference."

"Which is?"

"Money," and he caressed her hand.

Rosalie pulled away from him and got up, awkwardly, and adjusted the threads of her string bikini. She stood tall, or as tall as she could, and she gave him a long slow look of contempt.

"Think about it," he said.

She picked up the baby in his basket and walked to the house.

"I'll see my lawyer today," he called after her, and in his mind the matter was settled.

Rosalie closed, and locked, the patio door.

Gil sat there for a few minutes, in the hot sun, thinking of what lay ahead: a lot of time wasted on lawyers, a lot of money wasted on Betz. Still, money wasn't real and the baby was real and he had to get on with his life.

Why, though, was he so anxious? What was he afraid of? He was tempted to take out his dick and examine it again, just for reassurance. He glanced toward the patio door and was surprised to see Rosalie standing there. She slid the glass panel open and stepped halfway out.

"I'll think about it," she said, and disappeared inside.

And so he had done the next, necessary thing. He had come here to Huddle and Pilbrick to make drastic and final changes in his life.

Gil had been waiting nearly ten minutes, and during that time the receptionist had been in and out constantly, popping her boobs at him, twitching her tail. He was getting tired of it. He had no time for sex right now. Women never seemed to know when you were buying it and when it was just a pain in the ass.

She appeared again and said, "Mr. Huddle will be with you forthwith," and sure enough, there was Huddle, forthwith, waddling out to welcome him and pour Southern Comfort on him and, in general, to use up all the oxygen.

"Gi-yul," he said, "my good friend, what a very very lot this is goin' to cost you. Lotta sorrow. Lotta sorrow."

And they settled at once to business.

Gil had been through this before, with Moo, and he knew the prenuptial agreement wasn't worth the water it was written in, he said bitterly, and he was prepared to strike a deal.

"Betz," Huddle murmured, "has hired herself a first rate law-yuh."

So Gil knew it was going to be a costly deal. He'd pay her off, whatever it took, one mil, two mil. She could have the house and Christ knows she could have the effing baby, but alimony was out of the question. He had paid Moo alimony and look what he'd gotten for his trouble, a black husband-in-law and a baby conceived in a pasture.

"But your little Moo is fixin' to marry the colored fella," Huddle said, "so that'll be the end of your havin' to pay alimony. Maybe you could see your way to tossin' in a little extra for Betz."

"Two million is not enough?"

"Two million and five would help her out with her law-yuh fees."

Gil changed the subject. He was going to marry Rosalie Kurtz, he said, just as soon as she got rid of Zachary, and this time he wanted an air-tight, water-proof, bomb-resistant prenuptial agreement, even though he was certain this was the last marriage. This time, they'd already *had* the son.

Let's not rush, Huddle urged, but Gil explained how certain he was that the baby was his, and why, and Huddle said they'd check blood-types first, and then do a DNA search, and then they could talk about marriage. But Gil was having no delays. He wanted the paper-work to begin at once. He wanted the divorce from Betz at once. He wanted to marry Rosalie. He would be forty-two this year and he wanted to get on with his life. Now. At once. Understand?

Huddle looked at him and smiled his rich, southern smile of peace, tolerance, and understanding. And then, completely out of character, as if he were possessed by some demon of personal destruction, he said, "Gi-yul, my friend, what *are* you afraid of?"

At that moment Gil was visited, briefly, by the gods. He heard the voice of Olga behind Huddle's question, and he heard the voice of his hypothetical unconscious answering, and for a fraction of a second he listened. And he understood that what he feared was his non-existence. That he was not anybody. That he was not even money, but only a conduit for money. He looked ahead and for one second he glimpsed not Huddle of Huddle and Pilbrick, Attorneys at Law, but an abyss of nothing, and he knew he was looking into his own absence.

He stopped listening.

He was a rational animal and he preferred a nihilism that knew no terror of the abyss. He snapped his eyes shut against the vision and it was over.

"What am I afraid of?" he said. He threw one arm back over the chair and hitched his hips forward slightly and said, "With a dick like mine, I don't have to be afraid of anything."

"Of course, of course," Huddle said, not the least embarrassed, "and all that money doesn't hurt none either."

They were agreed then on what must be done.

30

It was noon on Sunday, the church bells had bonged their twelve sepulchral bongs, and everybody was content. Or, more precisely, everybody who mattered was content. They had reached the end of the quarter and the exam period that marked another complete turn of the wheel of fortune. Everyone was greatly relieved.

The minority-majority problems, by an unspoken agreement, were momentarily placed on hold.

The unrecognized minorities had elected not to protest anything until spring quarter. These minorities consisted principally of the Born Agains, the Calvinists, the Old Catholics, the Neo-Beguines, and the Taoists, all of whom, being religiously oriented, realized they didn't have a prayer during exam week and were frankly eager for a break from protesting.

The militant minorities, powerful and institutionalized, had put away their placards, their uniforms, their armaments, and had settled down to study at last.

The minority Deans, exhausted from their outrage, were taking an overdue rest.

The majorities—racial, social, psychological, religious—breathed deeply, embattled no longer, or at least not until next quarter.

It was a time of peace and everyone fell gratefully silent, the faculty in particular. No more lectures, no more conferences, no more consoling the bereft and the benighted. No furious students who accused you of failing to appreciate them. No more crises of conscience about tutorials, honors essays, office hours. Hey-ho! Hey nonny nonny! No more academic crap.

The faculty—fools, Turks, hangers-on—all of them foresaw two lovely weeks of rest and study and some brisking about the life.

Chez Olga, however, there was discomfort, discontent, and a pressing sense of incompletion. There were lives teetering out of balance. Fates not yet enacted. Ultimates unachieved. Olga, like academics everywhere, was experiencing the need for closure.

In her way, of course, she was attending to these matters. She was doing her thoughts.

~

At the edge of the campus, chez Richter, Cynthia and Robbie were out on the patio steeping pleasantly in the steamy surround of their hot tub. They were listening with reverence to the solid bong of the church bells when, antiphonally, their door chimes rang and Ozzie sent up a howl of welcome. They exchanged looks. They had known this would happen eventually, they had discussed it, and they had agreed on what they ought to do: they must act out their beliefs, they must confront the world with naked honesty. But now that it was happening, they looked at each other, suddenly shy, and Robbie burst into giggles. Cynthia punched him lightly on the arm.

Ozzie, agitated and hopeful, ran back and forth between the hot tub and the patio door, barking excitedly.

"Fuck a duck," Robbie said, and rose from the hot tub, dripping, and padded through the house to the front door with Ozzie at his heels. He opened the door wide. Naked and smiling, he said, "Come in."

Zachary Kurtz stood there, uncertain what to do. At once Ozzie made a lunge at Zachary's ankle. Robbie held him back with one naked leg.

"You're naked," Zachary said, and he rubbed his mustache the wrong way.

Robbie shook with giggles and his little penis bobbed up and down. He was hung, Zachary noticed, like a gerbil.

"You're naked," he said again, and looked away.

"Don't be a priss," Robbie said, "don't be a prude. After all, we're all made the same."

Not really, Zachary thought, and thanked God it was not so. He followed Robbie out to the patio, batting off Ozzie's attacks as he went, and by a quick unlikely dodge he managed to slam the patio door with Ozzie on the inside. He turned and was appalled to see Cynthia sprawling in the hot tub, her awful tubular breasts afloat on the water.

"Dunk it in," Cynthia said by way of welcome and kicked her feet about in the water, frolicsome.

"Take off your clothes and join us," Robbie said. He stood there, naked and hideous, staring at Zachary. Cynthia kicked up another spray of water, but she was staring at him too. He turned away and saw Ozzie at the glass door, staring. They were all going to watch him undress.

"Let's have a lookie-see," Cynthia said.

Zachary began to grow very red. He was finding it hard to breathe. He was no stranger to nudity and he had the greatest familiarity with those odd moments when the time has come for one or the other to strip down and let it all hang out. He had screwed a teaching assistant in the library stacks, her behind perched precariously on the O.E.D. He had done it with grad students and undergrads on sofas, in cars, in a decorative haystack, in the shower, the bathtub, on the toilet seat. He had done it once in a moving taxi. He had done it with a Madonna Wannabe who preferred to watch his performance not in the flesh but in the mirror propped next to her bed. But never had he felt such obscene attention to the simple business of taking off his clothes.

"Take them off, take them off," Robbie chanted, and he clapped his hands. Cynthia, breasts floating, joined him in the chant.

Zachary removed his shoes, slowly. Slowly he started on his jacket, and then his shirt, and still they clapped their stupid hands and chanted, "Take them off, take them off," until finally in a frenzy Zachary tore off his undershirt, shucked off his pants and his shorts, and stepped out of them, naked.

"Woo, woo," Cynthia shouted, pointing to his wonk, and as Zachary slipped into the hot tub, she gave him a good whack across the chest. "Titties," she said, and it was true that his pectorals were not all they might have been. He covered his chest with his hands.

"Fuck a duck," Robbie shouted, and though there was no room for such sport, he cannonballed into the hot tub, holding his nose and crunching up his knees. He made a terrific splash.

Robbie rose from the water, shrieking, and Cynthia pushed him under. He rose again and, in a surprise move, he wrestled Cynthia under the water with him. They were crazed dolphins, they were baby whales at play, and the water churned wildly and foamed deliciously. They were greatly happy in the tub.

Inside the house Ozzie crooned with abandon.

Depressed, Zachary huddled at the hot tub's edge. He clutched his hands protectively to his private parts and waited for their sexual frenzy to wane. He waited and he waited, but they seemed to be blessed with extraordinary staying power. He wondered what Olga would make of this and the thought depressed him further.

It was Sunday noon chez Richter, Zachary reflected, and he had come over to discuss his plans for Robbie's Chairmanship. He had wanted to help. He had wanted to create something meaningful for the Department. And now here he was, naked, waiting for a couple of insane old people to finish playing grab-ass in a tub while their dog warbled a hymeneal diapason.

This was his life, he understood, this was his reality. And it was too tragic to be borne. He slumped lower in the water and in spite of himself he began to cry.

~

Maddy Barker was at peace and at pleasure. She lay on the bed beside Tortorisi and toyed gently with his cunning breasts. Maddy and

Tortorisi had made up, thanks to Olga, and their new relationship was based on trust and affection. They half expected it to grow into love.

How this had come about was wonderful to both of them. Part of Maddy's new feeling she attributed to revulsion for her actions with Peter Peeks. There were times she woke in the night dreaming of her hand around that disgusting thing of his—she had actually touched it, yuck!—and then she relived the whole foul experience. It was a nightmare she could not shake off and so she had confessed everything to Olga. And Olga, who *must* be partly divine, had listened, nodding, understanding, and finally spoke the healing words. "Go to Tortorisi," she said, "and tell him all."

Maddy had gone to him. And he had understood.

Maddy did not know, of course, that Tortorisi too had been to Olga, not to confess but to squeal on Maddy Barker and Peter Peeks, those whores, to do them dirt, he said, to fuck them over. Olga had chastised him for such language, pointing out that in his proposed television career as laughing man for Eleanora Tuke—and "Salon of the Air" was indeed in the works, thanks to Eleanora's little physicist and his big big money—Tortorisi could not afford to use such coarse expressions. Nor could he afford, actually, to remain single. Advertising executives, most of whom were gay, preferred to show the public a married image. Viewers appreciated it, they thought. It didn't matter what you did privately, or sometimes even publicly, so long as you had a wife around. For photographs, mostly, but for patriotic purposes too. And for the fight against AIDS.

Tortorisi looked puzzled until Olga explained that she was quoting the experts, that these were held truths of the TV industry, and that he would do well to get himself a wife. The thinking, she granted, was retrograde, benighted, and insulting, but the networks had advanced only this far and, alas, it was not yet the Year of the Queer. So he could take it or leave it.

Give a thought to Maddy Barker, she said.

And, she added, keep this is mind: if you're going to bother with a wife at all, you might as well get one who gives you—she paused— pleasure.

Ah, pleasure!

Tortorisi went to see Maddy at once. He was a new man. He would tell her everything.

Maddy descended her stairs just as Tortorisi descended his stairs. They saw each other across the drive and they stood for a moment, gazing. They began to walk toward each other, in slow motion. They walked faster. They ran. She caught him in her arms and held him close and she could feel his wonderful breasts pressed against her own. They rubbed around like crazy, right there in the street. Alone. In public. It was a festival of boobs and they gave themselves up to it.

And now, here they were, only days later, together. They lay on their backs, fully clothed, listening to the church bells toll noon. Maddy pressed her index finger lightly against Tortorisi's nipple and thought how good life was: she had her career, she had peace of mind, *and* she had a man of her own whose breasts she could caress. She looked over at him and smiled.

She was struck then by a feeling she had never experienced before. It was inexplicable. She wanted to do something nice for him. To give him something.

"I promise," she said, moved finally to speech, "I promise I'll never touch you . . . down there."

His breath caught. He was shaken by emotion.

"And I promise," he said, returning her vow, "that I'll never touch you down there. Or up here either."

Naturally they intended to touch other people—lots of them, up here and down there—as often as nature impelled and opportunity permitted. It was only each other they promised to spare.

They moved closer together until their heads were touching at the ear. She cupped his breast tenderly in her hand. They sighed.

They were very much in love.

~

As the noon bells rang out, there was peace everywhere, and among the fools there was peace and a certain degree of jollity. They were having a cookout at the Chairman's place. It was a spontaneous cook-out, there had been no invitations, it was just a custom that at the end of the quarter they all got together for burgers and beer and family gossip.

When the Turks had first arrived, they had been invited to these cookouts, and they had come. But only once. The Turks had found the conversation trivial, the food fattening, the beer disgusting. Fur-thermore that goddam dog, Hamlet, was forever snuffling around their feet in search of a place to pee. It was a geriatric picnic, they said. It was a feast of fools. It was a warning and a threat. They had never come back, any of them.

So the fools had the Sunday cookout all to themselves. They car-ried on as they always did, shaking hands in greeting, kissing spouses, squeezing Sweet Jesus, friendly and—considering their mean age—rather frisky. As always, they were having a good time.

They condoled with each other about rotten children, uncoopera-tive students, the decay of the educational institution. They talked about their vacation plans: Greece seemed to be everybody's favorite this year. They rejoiced at Robbie Richter's return to sanity, more or less, and they laughed unkindly at Zachary Kurtz's plan to supplant English with a Department of Theory and Discourse. It was a hoot, they thought, as so much of the theory stuff was, just more fascist bul-lying from the new right wing. As if books were improved by calling them discourse! They were smart enough, these fools, to know they were missing the point—indeed, deliberately so—but it was fun to puncture balloons and belittle pomposity and, specifically, to call *un sac de merde* a bag of shit. But rancor and indignation never lasted long among the fools. They immediately moved on to practical things: who would water Dave and Sheila's plants while they were away, who would feed Stephanie's cat, who would look in on the Chairman's mother. And who, God help us, would be willing to take over as Director of Undergraduate Studies, the pissiest job of all. And then they free-associated about the latest movies and the opera and the multiple varieties of trash television.

They were a functioning community, full of small rivalries and odd affections and lots of forgiveness. They knew one another and they accepted one another. Mostly they liked one another. This was what the Turks could never understand about them: they were content.

~

The President lay in bed listening to the noon bells and he too was content. He had just made love to Missy and, even if he said so himself, it had gone quite well. She had wriggled and grunted and carried on just like in their earliest days. Moreover, he felt that he had done his share and done it well. It was nice to know that at sixty you were still in charge, you could still man the guns, you could still rear back and say, "Damn the torpedoes and full speed ahead!" Who said that? Wasn't that a quote from somebody? A military man. A swordsman. He smiled at his cleverness. He wasn't losing it. Not by a long shot. He smiled again. Everything was sexual really, when you thought about it.

The church bells began to toll noon.

They had never never *ever* done it in the bushes, he and Missy. That was just loose talk, a vicious distortion of a harmless tussle in the grass. Though, to be honest, he wouldn't mind giving it a try.

The church bells finished tolling noon. Twelve bongs, he thought. He'd like to give Missy twelve bongs like the one he'd just given her.

Missy made it all worthwhile: the scandals, the insults, the betrayals. And the money—good God!—the money! But he put the money out of his mind because here comes Missy from the shower, trailing a small cloud of perfume and the satisfied look of good sex, and—yippee!—he threw back the sheets and revealed himself in all his manly splendor.

"Sit on it," Missy said, "I've got a meeting."

The President waited, exposed, until she left and then he turned over and cried soundlessly into his pillow.

~

The great were accustomed to great sorrows and great delights, which was not so with the little people.

Except for Betz Rudin. Betz had been one of the great, and now, with her divorce in the works, she had moved into Concepcion's studio apartment and had become one of the little. In her new and little life, however, she discovered joys she had never before imagined. She was surprised to feel happy, for instance, and she was astonished to feel something other than rivalry or distrust for the people she loved. She had been accustomed only to the security of money and the constancy of her misery. This love business, especially the cuddling, was altogether new and she was discovering the joy of loving generously: Susanna, Concepcion, even the plump tagalong Suzie Sweezie. She bought them gifts, of course, because it was a natural thing to do. And she said nice things to them. And she did nice things for them. Naturally. What was not natural—for her—was to think about them, and to think about them kindly. She was moved almost to tears by her own thoughtfulness.

Susanna, moreover, seemed to thrive on all the attention. She was eager and responsive; the brain damage, it appeared, had been much exaggerated. They fussed over her and cooed to her and gave her kisses.

They were doing that now as they lay abed. Susanna was cradled in a pillow between Betz and Concepcion. Separate but almost equal, Suzie Sweezie lay curled at their feet, reading from Barthes' *S/Z*. Betz kissed the baby's tummy. Concepcion kissed the baby's forehead. The baby gurgled and kicked her feet in delight. Betz and Concepcion gurgled back at her. And all this time Suzie's thin voice commemorated Barthes' proiaretic code.

The church bells began to toll noon.

Concepcion made the sign of the cross and, frowning piously, recited the Angelus:

> The Angel of the Lord declared unto Mary
> And she was conceived of the Holy Ghost.

Betz and Suzie responded with the Hail Mary, leaving out the part about "the fruit of thy womb, Jesus." Concepcion recited the second verse:

> Behold the handmaid of the Lord.
> Be it done unto me according to thy word.

Again Betz and Suzie responded with the bowdlerized Hail Mary. Concepcion skipped the next two verses, all about Jesus and therefore irrelevant, and she went right on to a concluding prayer of her own devising.

> Holy Mary, up above,
> Fill our hearts with burning love,
>
> Keep us from the world of straights
> Of penises and petty hates.
>
> Make us lesbians, proud and pure
> Make us sweet and kind as you're
>
> 'Cuz you're the one that we adore.
> Give us strength and hear us roar!

It was an anthem, really, and intended for popular consumption, so they were not bothered by the fact that as poetry it was pretty bad.

The church bells had stopped bonging, and a reverent silence hovered over the studio apartment for perhaps a minute, and then the kissing began once more, smack pause smack pause smack, and the reading from Barthes continued, and there was joy unbounded for Betz Rudin.

There was joy unbounded, too, for Moo Wesley Rudin and Leroy O'Shea. They snuggled together, nuzzling like puppies, happy and fulfilled because at last they were expecting. Leroy's black limbs and

Moo's white ones intertwined and they were pleased with how beautiful they looked and they were pleased with each other and they were pleased just to be alive. They feared spoiling all this happiness by marrying but, the risk be damned, they were going to marry anyhow and to hell with Gil Rudin's alimony.

Leroy placed his hand on Moo's pretty belly. Moo placed her hand over his. They traced the likely outline of their baby girl and together, with reverence, they spoke her name. "Olga Moo," they said, "Olga Moo."

The church bells tolled noon. Leroy and Moo untwined a moment, listening, and then they twined back up again. Ebony and ivory. Ivory and ebony. With the baby, floating in her sac, between them. They were very content.

And all the other little people—the lecturers and teaching assistants and the coadjutors—all were content according to their measure. Some, therefore, were only minorly content and others were scarcely content at all. And a few, it must be said, were malcontent. Such was the nature of academe. Such was the nature of life.

And yet the bells tolled equally, for all of them.

~

Chez Kurtz, contentment took another form. It was not sensual or sexual, it did not depend on sorrows great or little, nor on pleasures either. It depended on the tidy satisfactions of a successful business deal.

While Zachary Kurtz covered his parts and dodged the action in the Richter's hot tub, Rosalie Kurtz and Gil Rudin were completing inspection of a draft of their prenuptial agreement. They were sitting on the patio, chez Kurtz, within sound of Adam Zachary in the kitchen, and they were enjoying the noonday sun.

Huddle, of Huddle and Pilbrick, had prepared a document that was, in nearly every respect, satisfactory to both parties. Rosalie was to get four thousand per month for personal expenses during the first year, and a thousand more per month each year for the next ten. Should they divorce after ten years of marriage, she would receive one million dollars. After fifteen years, two million. After twenty years, five million. Two cars, travel allowance, two weeks of R&R—by herself—in spring and again in fall, communal vacations in summer at the beach and in winter on the ski slopes, etc., etc. There followed many pages of clauses that qualified, mitigated, or augmented terms of the agreement pursuant to quality of performance, length of relationship, degree of satisfaction. And all of this—everything—was dependent on (1) the establishment by DNA testing of Gil's biological paternity of Adam Zachary Kurtz, (2) Gil's legal adoption of Adam Zachary Kurtz to proceed with all due speed, since time is of the essence, and (3) in case of separation or divorce of the principal parties, Adam Zachary Kurtz Rudin was to remain in the custody of the legal, biological (*and* adoptive) father, Gil Rudin. The text was literal, comprehensive, and menacing. It pleased Rosalie greatly.

How strange, she thought, that money was what she'd wanted all along and she'd never realized it until prompted by that phone call from Olga. Clever Olga. Clever, clever Olga, with her accents and her trick of looking dowdy one day and gorgeous the next. Everything about her was strange. Her eyes were very strange. And her feet, too. There was something wrong with them, even Zachary had noticed that. There was something troubling, in fact, about almost everything that concerned Olga. Rosalie sat back, contented, thinking these consoling thoughts.

"Well," Gil said, "what do you think?"

"I'm thinking about Olga."

"Dogshit," Gil said, "if I may quote the absent Zachary."

"I wonder what Olga would make of this."

"Why?"

"She's very big on people getting what they want. Or maybe getting what they deserve."

"Is that a threat?"

How quickly his mood could change. She would need her wits about her if she was not going to end up like Betz.

At once Rosalie leaned over and kissed him, even though that wasn't very professional in this particular situation, and she put Olga out of her mind.

"I'd want guarantees for all this stuff," she said.

"That's what this contract is. Guarantees."

"For you," she said, and smiled.

"And for you. You're well taken care of." He returned her smile. "Very well."

"I'd want my own lawyer to look at it."

"Be my guest."

"I'd need to be very sure."

"Of course."

"I'd need . . . "

"You need it? I've got it." He touched his crotch.

Rosalie pretended not to notice.

The church bells began to toll noon. She looked off toward the bell tower and sighed deeply. This was the beginning of her new life. Very full. Very exciting. And by God she was ready for it.

In the kitchen Adam Zachary began to cry. It was time for his feeding.

They got up, together—Rosalie and Gil, Mom and Dad—and went into the house to give the baby his bottle. It seemed a nice way to seal their agreement.

Now all that remained was to break the news to Zachary.

"Think of the headache *that* will give him," Rosalie said, and they laughed, happily, satisfied with their deal.

"Thereafter, they were friends," Rosalie said, quoting something, though she couldn't remember what.

~

Beyond the campus, beyond the sound of those tolling bells, everybody who mattered was content. Even in the City, chez Tuke, there was a moment of content.

Eleanora was hosting a brunch for eight at the Top of the Mark.

She had taken Olga's salon critique seriously, painful as it was, and today the food was plentiful and the drink superb. They were having a fab time, the TV director confided to her, and they were actually getting a lot of work done, decisions made, strategies in place. Schmoozing with an edge, he called it.

The director had insisted on a showdown meeting, because the final money had still not been secured and they could proceed no further until Eleanora's physicist coughed up the cash. But her little physicist had certain problems, Eleanora said. There were certain things he wanted guaranteed she said. There were conditions, she said. Finally—confessing all—she blurted out the truth. He sang country western songs and he was determined to perform on her show.

"Good Christ," the director said, despairing.

So they had decided on this brunch. "My treat," Eleanora said. "Business, but with an overlay of pleasure. The Medicis and the Munsters, so to speak." And, in fact, they were all getting along really well: the director and his two assistants, the three cable executives, Eleanora, and her rich, recalcitrant physicist, who was outfitted today in racing silks and a black eye patch. Tortorisi had not been included because he was only a secondary player and, besides, the director had insisted Tortorisi lose forty pounds—"like today, Babe"—and felt he shouldn't be exposed to food gratuitously. The food, as he had foreseen, was wonderful. The drink was terrif.

"A fab time," the director said, nudging his way toward the agitated question of money. "Absolutely fab."

It was a moment of peace, of confidence, of hope.

The little physicist chose this moment to make his move.

"I'm going to be a guest on Eleanora's first show," he said.

Everybody looked at him.

"I'll sing one of my songs," he said. "Rhinestone Cowboy."

"I've decided," he said.

"But you're the money man, you aren't in this at all." It was one of the cable executives who spoke, and he was merely explaining, merely being sincere. "This is how it works," he said. "You put up the money, we produce the show, Eleanora here hosts it. And that's it. You're out of here. That's all she wrote. Period. End of story. *Fini.*" He paused. "See?"

The two other cable executives nodded agreement, and then the director and his assistants, and finally, with a certain reluctance, Eleanora herself nodded.

"I've got the money," he said, "and I want to sing on TV."

The second cable executive explained it once again, this time in the more technical language of network contracts. The explanation took a long time.

"But I want to sing," he said. "I want to."

The third executive took over. "Pal," he said, "listen. I can explain this to you, not to worry. It's like this. You put up cash and eventually, if you're lucky, you get cash back. Meanwhile you get percentages and you get tax hedges. You get perks. You can even get laid. What you don't get is to be a TV star."

This made an impression on him and he fell silent. Angry, but silent.

Eleanora took over.

"You're famous, darling, but you're famous for bombs. Your singing is wonderful, it is, wonderful. I think it's the best country western in America today, by a white male over fifty, but it's bombs that you're famous for. You are a great bomb-maker and you are a great man. Think nuclear, think Armageddon, and whom do we think of? You, that's whom!" She straightened his tie. "You, you, you!" she said, thumping his chest. "Am I right? So you'll get to sing your songs, and they'll be wonderful, but not on the first show. Okay? Okay. Not on the first show."

"Not any show," the director whispered.

Eleanora shot him a killer look and started up again. "Look, Pookie," she said, resorting to intimacy, "your singing is—how to say it?—caviare for the general. Your singing is too *rare* for educational television. It's too . . ." but she was getting desperate and she was getting lost.

"I don't *have* to fund this thing, you know. I could buy my own theatre if I wanted. I could buy the opera house. I could buy my own fucking network."

"Of course you could, and you may want to some day, but right now we just want to get this show off the ground, Pookie. Pookie, Pookie, Pookins." She wiggled her finger inside his vest. "So let's agree that you'll sing "Rhinestone Cowboy"—she gave a quick, menacing look around the table—"and *soon* too, very soon, but *not* on the first show."

"On the second show?"

"Soon, Pooks."

"I've begun writing a song of my own—'Bombing Along Together'—and I'm going to sing that too."

She looked at him, flirtatious, from under her long lashes.

There was a nervous silence and finally the little physicist gave up and nodded his head in agreement.

They sighed, singly and together.

"A toast," Eleanora said, rising from her chair. "To my little physicist."

They clinked their glasses and drank deeply, because the touchiest part was over and the money was in the bag.

"Fab," the director said, "absolutely fab."

~

The church bells had just began to toll noon, a lingering leaden sound, and Daryl put down the telephone and began to cry. It had been a conference call, the cruelest touch of all, and he would never recover from it. His wife and his best friend. It was a joke. It was a classic joke. Mythic even. Especially when you considered that his best friend was the Thomasite priest in whom he had confided all his worries. "She's above reproach," Father Owen had said, that ecclesiastical shit, "she's Caesar's wife." And meanwhile he'd been bouncing her in and out of his bed.

Daryl sobbed until he had a headache and a stomach ache and then he decided to knock it off.

He got out the grass and rolled himself a joint. He didn't usually do this, he didn't approve of it, but his wife was shacking up with his best friend—a priest, goddamit!—and he just felt like killing himself. Or killing her. Or killing them.

He took a deep drag on the joint.

She was a flight attendant and very beautiful and he had never deserved her, he had to admit that. He wasn't worthy to touch the hem of her garment. He was a lousy lover, he had to admit that too. Any priest was bound to be better, especially when he looked like Father Owen and wore that sexy white robe and cowl. Women loved that stuff. They had loved it all through history, in all the literatures of the world. Go to the priests if you want it done right. Christ, look at Tiresias! He could screw you coming and going and coming again. So to speak.

He sobbed again for his inadequacy and he rolled another joint.

Everything had started out great this morning. He had taken his Adorno to bed, meditating, and suddenly he'd been filled with all kinds of insights, great ones, and he'd sprung out of bed and hit the desk wearing only his shorts, and he'd written for an hour, then two hours, and then, sure enough, the goddam phone rang.

"Daryl," she'd said, with that lilt in her voice that always signalled good news and hot sex, and then he'd heard a whole bunch of clicks and clunks, and then "Daryl," Father Owen said, and an operator or somebody said this was a conference call, please go ahead, and he heard, "Guess what?"

"What?" he said, the complete asshole.

They were in love in Jesus, she told him. They were going to get married and live together and love together in the Lord. Daryl would always be her best friend— "Mine too," Father Owen said—and he would always be welcome at their place in Denver, and they hoped, they *knew*, he would understand.

He finished the joint and lay back on the bed, mellowing out.

She was a ditz. She had never had a brain in her head. And anyhow he had suspected for weeks, for months, that she was cheating on him.

"In Jesus?" he said.

She explained all about Jesus. They were born again in love, and hence in the Lord, and she told him how satisfying it all was and how spiritual too. Father Owen didn't have much to say about this.

"What shits you two are," Daryl said.

"Yours," Father Owen said, "is a natural reaction, Dar. Feel it. Go with it. Experience the pain. It's natural. But in time, I want you to try for a *super*natural reaction. Get what I'm saying? I know you can do it, Dar. You're the real thing." Father Owen had an M.A. in counseling.

There was silence on the line.

"Aw, don't be mad, Daryl," she said. "I *never* wanted you to feel bad."

She went on for some time about how she wanted him to feel: happy. She really did. Truly.

Father Owen joined her in wishing Daryl happiness. Everybody who knew Daryl, he said, wanted him to be happy. He was a great guy. A mensch. A supermensch.

There was more silence on the line.

The church bells began to toll noon, slow leaden bongs that hung in the air, and Daryl, despairing, had put down the phone and begun to sob.

He smoked a joint. He was not worthy of her. And another joint. She was a ditz and a bitch and a whore. He examined his stash of pot and decided he'd better ration it.

He spent a long time rolling a pile of cigarettes. He divvied them up in little piles: two a day for the next two weeks. He rearranged them: four a day for the coming week only. Or would six a day be better? Eight? He tried nearly all possible configurations and then he just scrunched them all together in a single pile.

To hell with her. To hell with Adorno. To hell, as a matter of fact, with living.

He lit another joint and kicked back, inhaling deeply, welcoming the darkness that clotted in his lungs. There was no point in saving up joints. This was the end.

Bugger them all.

He would smoke himself to death.

~

Chez Olga things were looking a whole lot better. It was several hours since the noon bells had rung, and in that time she had put aside her discontent, discomfort, and her sense of incompletion. She had done her thoughts, and now she was writing them down, and indeed it was as if the things she wrote had really happened.

She frisked with Cynthia and Robbie and clutched her parts with Zachary Kurtz. She romanced with Maddy Barker and Tortorisi, cavorted with the fools, suffered with the President, savored the sensory delights of Betz and Suzie Sweezie and Concepcion, snuggled abed with Leroy and Moo and Olga Moo floating in her amniotic sac, and she calculated bargains with Rosalie and Gil. And maliciously—she could not deny it—she toasted the little physicist with Eleanora and Company.

She frowned.

She could not condole with Daryl, she could not include him, and she could not intervene. He was not in this, so far as she was concerned. His fate was out of her hands.

There was much, of course, that remained to be dealt with. A denouement. An act of human cruelty, of love gone wrong. A death by strangling.

Also, there were loose ends. Zachary's foot fetish, what of that? Would it precipitate disaster or just remain local color? And Tortorisi's book: would he rewrite and publish or give it up and just take tenure? She guessed he would rewrite. And Suzie Sweezie? And poor old aging Hamlet? Not to mention Sweet Jesus, and the retarded Susanna and the embryonic Olga Moo.

Which made her think of Peter Peeks. Beautiful, bland, and physically perfect. With a good mind. And good intentions. And, alas, the inability to say no. What of him? Could nothing, *nothing* be done with all these gifts, with all this natural perfection? Perhaps? She would have to see. Perhaps there was still time for Peter Peeks.

This day's work, however, was at an end.

Still, she found it hard to put the work aside altogether. Nor would she. Nor indeed could she. Her unconscious would take care of that.

It was exciting. It was thrilling. Everything she had imagined became—now—a catalyst for action, pushing her forward, compelling closure, as if matters had gone completely beyond her control. The wheels were set in motion, the actors took the stage, the gods, always ready for a show, were watching. Only the smallest gesture was needed to trigger the fatal action.

It was like a tragedy except that the people were not big enough for tragedy.

But were any people, ever, too small for tragedy?

Ah well.

She lay on her bed and fell asleep at once.

31

And so the time had come for the showdown.

It was Sunday afternoon, still, and Rosalie Kurtz and Gil Rudin were out on the patio working on their third gin and tonic. They were a bit nervous at what they were about to do, but the gin nicely dulled their anxiety and in fact gave them something of a lift. The whole mess would soon be resolved, tra-la, tra-la.

They had decided to break the news to Zachary now, this afternoon, and their emotions were running high. Gil was feeling hornier by the minute and Rosalie, to her own surprise, had begun to look forward to the encounter with Zack. She disliked a complicated life.

In her mind Rosalie had been rehearsing Zachary's many faults, the spiritual neglect she suffered at his hands, the sordid nature of his plots and ambitions. Not to mention his sexual hi-jinks with graduate students and his locked cabinet full of novels. She had every right to do what she was doing. She should have done it earlier.

"Let's fuck," Gil said, forcing himself to use that word. He had more complicated pleasures in mind, but he was willing to start slow.

"Afterwards," Rosalie said. "If we're going to tell him now, we'll need our wits about us."

Gil wanted to get on with it. He was a scholar and had work to do.

"He's got to understand that it's all over," Rosalie said.

"How about just a quick one?"

"Clarity. That's the big thing."

"The big thing's right here," he said, touching himself.

"I've got to be clear and definite."

Gil gave up hoping for sex.

"And I mustn't give way to mockery."

"Don't underestimate the power of mockery. You have a certain skill with that."

"I don't want this to be cruel. Just quick. And final."

"Behold, the dreamer cometh," Gil said, pointing toward the stairs where Zachary was trudging into view. His hair was wet and he looked mortally sad and he was fiercely red in the face.

They couldn't help laughing.

"Jesus Christ," Zachary said, "I've just been in the hot tub with Cynthia and Robbie. They're insane. I'm really beginning to think they're insane."

They laughed some more.

"What're you laughing at? What's so funny?"

"They've always been insane," Gil said. "That's their charm."

"But wait'll you hear the latest," Zachary said. "Listen to this."

"You listen," Rosalie said, "we're getting divorced."

Zachary looked at her, reclining in her deck chair, a gin and tonic in one hand, her other hand raised against the sun. He must not have heard correctly. He thought she had said divorce.

"I'm gonna get a drink," Zachary said, "then I'll tell you about it. The Richters have gone around the bend."

"I mean it," Rosalie said. "I'm divorcing you."

Zachary's red face grew redder. He looked at Rosalie and then at Gil and then back at Rosalie. Everything he saw had a red cast to it, as if he were looking through a window pane smeared with blood. There was a terrible pulse beating in his forehead. He felt his arms lift and he thought he was going to strangle her. And then something quite remarkable happened. Something crackled in his brain and he felt the pressure lessen behind his eyes and he thought what a nice thing a gin and tonic would be. He forced a little smile.

"I'm gonna get a drink," he said. "Anything for you two?"

Without waiting for an answer, Zachary went inside the house and poured himself a drink. For the moment he forced himself not to think of those two out on the patio. He poured himself a little more, a double, and then turned to check on the baby. Adam Zachary, little A to Z, lay in his crib inside the kitchen door. He was playing with his toes, but when he saw Zachary, he began to gurgle and laugh, reaching up toward him. Zachary could not resist. He put down his glass and lifted the baby and began to croon to him. He could feel A to Z's heart beating against his own, and he was moved almost to tears. Here was somebody who loved him unconditionally, with perfect trust. Here was the new Zachary Kurtz, writ small, the one thing in his life that mattered.

But, come, come, he was letting himself get sentimental, and that harpy out there wanted to talk divorce, so he put A to Z back in his crib and wound up the blue and yellow carousel that dangled above it. The dinosaur song started up at once and in a minute the baby was reaching up toward the turning carousel, laughing and happy, completely satisfied. There was a lesson in this somewhere, Zachary figured, but he didn't have time to think about it right now. He went outside to join the death squad on the patio.

"*Salud*," he said, lifting his glass to them.

They had been talking together, urgently, but now they were silent.

"Well?" Zachary said. "You were talking, my angel, about divorce?" He waited. And as he waited, he reflected—not for the first time—on the unlikelihood of anything sexual between these two. Rosalie was a nearly sexless creature, and besides, she *did* look like a monkey. Gil was a rutting pig who liked it dirty, everybody knew that. There could be no physical attraction here, so what was it? Anxious nonetheless, he said again, "Well?"

"The baby is not yours. It's Gil's."

And at once Zachary realized it was true.

"No, he's mine," he said.

"Not biologically, not spiritually, not aesthetically."

Gil smiled at this. It was not yet mockery, but she was moving in the right direction.

"And not morally either," Rosalie said.

"Legally, he's mine. I'm the father. He's my son."

"I'm divorcing you. And I'll get custody."

And Zachary realized that this too was true.

"I don't think so," he said, and put down his drink.

"I think so," she said.

"I know so," Gil said.

Rosalie turned to look at Gil who was looking back at her. "Mistah Kurtz," she said, mocking, "he dead."

Zachary lunged at her. At one moment he was standing there looking at her and at the next he was on top of her, ready to kill. His fingers tightened around her throat, his thumbs pushed against her larynx, his whole weight bore her down.

The chair collapsed and they tumbled to the patio deck. She rolled over, clawing at him, but he thrust himself up on top of her and pressed down on her neck, hard, with his thumbs. She dug her fingernails into his wrists and began to thrash the deck wildly with her heels. Zachary bore down harder.

Gil sprang at him finally, grabbing at his shoulders, trying to pull him off her, trying to make him release his hold. He swatted Zachary in the head, he pulled his hair, and then, catching on, he pressed his own fingers deep into Zachary's throat.

The church clock began to sound the hour and for a second they stopped where they were—Zachary with his hands at Rosalie's throat, Gil with his hands at Zachary's throat—and the bell tolled slowly, one, two, three, four.

Zachary rolled off her.

Gil let Zachary loose.

Rosalie lay on her back, gasping, trying to call for help, though no sound would come.

Zachary crouched, kneeling. He could see only black and he had a terrible pain in his chest. He felt strangely free.

Gil sat hugging his knees.

~

The bells finished tolling and even their echo faded. One of those strange disturbing silences settled on the patio and, it seemed, on the campus too, and on the world. A long silence.

The fools, at their cookout, paused and looked up at the sky. "Like in *The Cherry Orchard*," Sweet Jesus said, "you know, the sound of a string snapping?"

Across the campus Robbie and Cynthia Richter leaned together fondly, waterlogged in their hot tub.

And in Faculty Terrace Olga, in her bed, turned restlessly. There was something troubling her, something was not as she had supposed it to be, but she was not conscious enough to give it thought, She twitched, she clutched her pillow, she waited to sink back into her dream. She had been walking, she thought, through a meadow somewhere in France. In south-west France. In Armagne. Lambs were frisking about her, running ahead, darting back—there was a baby lamb too—and she was taking them to the river for a wallow. They were innocent and stupid creatures, nothing but appetite, and she was responsible for them. She was full of hope because her work was almost done. And then something had gone wrong. The lambs had been frightened, something violent had occurred, but the worst—the strangling—had not happened after all.

Olga woke and sat up straight in bed.

She had been dreaming—no, it was a nightmare, horrible, un-real—but she was awake now and her heart was racing. For no reason at all, it came to her that Zachary would not strangle Rosalie, fine though that might be. Some other thing had to happen, something more horrible and more deeply human, but what? She was used to these enormous changes at the last minute, but they exhausted her nonetheless. She shook her head to clear away the nightmare and, thinking kind thoughts about the troubled Kurtzes, she yawned and in a moment fell asleep once again.

~

On the patio at the Kurtz's house all remained silent. Rosalie had sat up finally, clutching at her throat, and she sat staring at Zachary. Zachary crouched, his head in his hands. Gil sat back, leaning on one elbow. After a long while he got up and handed Rosalie her drink.

"Take a sip," Gil said, "it'll help."

She sipped the drink, choked, and took another sip. "You bastard," she said to Zachary. "You tried to kill me."

Zachary looked up at her. He settled back on his heels and gave her a long inquiring look. There was a veil of something obscuring his vision and he tried to pull it away. He plucked at it. But the veil, whatever it was, was in his mind and not in his eyes.

Rosalie looked back at him.

Gil rose, righted the fallen deck chair, and sat in it.

Rosalie tried to get up. She got to one knee, swayed as if she might fall, and then dragged herself to her feet.

She stood there. Gil sat. Zachary knelt.

They remained as they were for quite a long time.

~

Across the campus, in Faculty Terrace, Olga whimpered in her dream. There was another disturbance among the lambs. But she couldn't see what it was. And she couldn't move to help. Events had been set in motion and they would unfold as they must.

~

Zachary and Rosalie and Gil kept their positions. They must have been thinking, but their postures gave no evidence of thinking, nor did their expressions, nor anything else. They were just there, stationary, sculptures for a garden of stone.

When it happened, it happened instantaneously, and all in a rush.

Gil made a dash for the kitchen and the baby. Rosalie, stunned, was a second behind him. But already, Zachary had risen from the deck and was hurtling past her toward the kitchen door. Gil slammed it and threw on the lock just as Zachary struck the door full force. There was the high bright sound of shattering glass and the tinkle and crash it made striking the tile floor. Zachary was cut, bleeding from his shoulder, but he reached through and unlocked the door. He was inside now and crazy.

Gil had snatched the baby from the crib and backed into the alcove between the sink and the stove. The baby, terrified, began to wail.

"Give him to me," Zachary said, but before he had the words half out, Rosalie was at him, pulling him away from Gil and the baby.

Zachary flailed out wildly, struck her with his elbow, and sent her staggering.

Gil stepped forward to help her and Zachary caught at the baby, tearing him from Gil's grip. But Gil was too strong and too quick for him. He spun Zachary around and grabbed the baby beneath the arms and began to pull.

Zachary had the baby by the waist and began to pull in the opposite direction. The baby screamed in terror, and Zachary, frightened, let him go.

Gil whirled and crashed against the stove, the baby safe in his arms.

For a second there was silence.

Zachary, frenzied, pulled open the drawer where the knives were kept and pretended to reach for one.

Rosalie shouted to Gil, warning him. Gil spun around. And Zachary made one last lunge for the baby, grabbed him from Gil's arms, and snatched him free.

But then, in possession of his child at last, clutching him close, with the baby's small head tucked in against his bleeding shoulder, Zachary turned to make a dash for his study. He stepped on a shard of broken glass. He lost purchase and felt his foot shoot out. He went down. Hard. He crashed to the floor, and the baby, shrieking in terror, tumbled from his arms.

The baby was silent, open-eyed. The baby made no sound. He was fighting for breath.

Zachary froze as the little thing struggled out of shock. The baby gasped suddenly, choked on a sob, then screamed long and loud. But Zachary did not hear him screaming and did not see his puckered face flush red with life and rage. He saw a small dead baby, little A to Z, wounded, bleeding, and he was to blame. He saw himself for what he was, a destroyer, a casually evil man. It was too much.

Rosalie picked up the baby and automatically, the good mother, began to rock him in her arms, to smooth his head and his hair and his shaking body. The baby was terrified, of course, and he was hysterical, but he was not bleeding and he was not hurt, so far as she could see. Everything would soon be all right.

"It's all right," she said, "it's all over now." She took the baby out on the patio and Gil followed her.

Zachary, stunned, got up and limped off to his study. He locked the door. He was dizzy, confused, and he was doing the next necessary thing, whatever that was. He unlocked his desk drawer and took out his worn, beloved copy of *Emma*. His head was pounding and the pain in his chest made it nearly impossible to breathe. He sat at his desk as if he intended to read, but the pain, the pain! Still, he was not dead yet. He sat there for a very long time until eventually consciousness returned. He smoothed his little mustache as he made his resolve. If he got through this, *when* he got through this, he would start a new life, with some dignity to it and some semblance of generosity. With his son, little A to Z.

There was another onslaught of pain, hot and liquid, starting in his chest and expanding to fill him up. It took over his entire body. It became who he was. He lay his head lightly on *Emma* and waited for the pain to pass. It was a deadly pain. It would kill him surely. And it did.

His dying was quick, as deaths go, and his body was already beginning to cool by the time Rosalie and Gil got the baby quieted down, and back into his crib, and had themselves another drink.

And then they were seized, giddy, in a kind of possession. They stripped one another, quickly, frenzied, and sank to the patio deck and made love. They were long and fierce about it, and it was very satisfying, and when they were done, they lay there listening as the church bells rang out five leaden bongs, one two three four five.

~

And in Faculty Terrace Olga woke, refreshed, remembering nothing of her dream. She felt quite good, actually, and was ready to get to work, to plunge ahead, to make yet another act of faith in her small gift, in her great hope: to create one good thing.

She was ready now to capture and subvert the mysteries of the faculty meeting. Ah Derrida! Ah humanity!

32

The faculty meeting scheduled for Tuesday was postponed and they buried Zachary Kurtz instead.

The burial was a quiet one—family only, and a few close friends—but a large memorial service was planned for Friday. Zachary was a mere forty at his death, but he was widely known among the avant-garde and he had a fanatic following among students. Even some of the fools thought well of him.

For the Friday commemoration the grieving widow set the agenda. Gil Rudin was scheduled to read selections from Zachary's work, the Israeli MendiCantors were to sing and perform choral odes from *The Song of Songs*, and it was whispered that Derrida himself would speak. Indeed word had circulated that the title of his text was "Old Bottles, New Wine: Textual Inebriation." Distinguished guests had been invited from Berkeley and Irvine and from as far away as Cornell and Hopkins and Yale.

By Thursday night the guests had begun to arrive and by Friday excitement was high. Everybody kept running into old friends and enemies, the California weather turned balmy and breezy, and the occasion was becoming a kind of idealized MLA meeting, but without those annoying conferences.

The Chairman had scheduled Zachary's commemoration service for 3 p.m., to follow directly upon the final faculty meeting of the winter quarter. It was a crisis meeting and he looked forward to it with some hope and with much dread. With hope because he would soon be rid of this hideous job, and with dread because who could guess what would happen when you got these thirty people together in one room? They checked their brains at the door. They came in naked of wit and impoverished of spirit. They turned into vicious children, rancid and perverse.

If only Olga were attending, the meeting would be so much easier to manage. It was true that Olga's standing among the students had slipped of late—she had only questions, they discovered, she had no answers—but the faculty, for varying reasons, still held her in some awe. The Chairman in particular admired her way with difficult people and he would have been glad for her help at this meeting. Since she was merely visiting faculty, however, she did not qualify to attend, not even by special invitation, and so he entered the arena completely on his own.

Worse still, he had it from Olga herself that Maddy Barker and Eleanora Tuke had threatened to square off and fight to the count—the metaphor from sports, surprisingly, was Eleanora's—on the subject of Tortorisi's tenure and Concepcion's as well. But tenure was the least of it, since this was the meeting at which they must do the year's big business. They would elect a new Chairman. They would discuss, thanks to the Deans' insistent meddling, the delicate issue of changing the Department name. Or, if things got crazy enough, they might be forced to abandon the English Department altogether and declare themselves a Department of Theory and Discourse. This was the day the Lord hath made: indeed, it was the very day Zachary Kurtz had planned for his intellectual takeover.

If Zachary hadn't suddenly up and died, the Chairman wondered, would somebody have tried to kill him? *Should* they have tried? One of the fools? Olga? He had the comforting thought that Olga was behind Zachary's death somehow, that she had killed him off metaphorically, and so he'd had no choice but to die for real.

Zachary was dead but his ideas lived on—in the Turks, in the Tuke, in the lesbians and gays and the multiculturalists—and the Chairman simply wanted out. He yearned for the end of his Chairmanship. He longed to lay down the white man's burden. He had just enough energy left, he figured, to get himself through the next two hours. Then, fuck them all, *le deluge*.

~

The meeting began in a surprisingly subdued manner. The fools arrived, as always, with their brown bags of sandwiches and Cokes, their plastic containers of salad and fruit, their smelly hard-boiled eggs. They ate rapidly and talked very little—their usual behavior at faculty meetings—but there was something distinctly different about them. As if they were embarrassed by Zachary's death or awed by the possibility that they might soon lose the name of English. Whatever the reason, their quiet bred a corresponding quiet among the Turks, who drifted in singly and together, hostile and suspicious, visibly worried at the silence of the fools.

Robbie Richter arrived. His face was flushed and he was carrying in his arms a huge pile of orange folders.

"One for you, and one for you, and one for you," he said, moving from person to person, making to each a formal presentation of what turned out to be his dossier. The opening pages contained a list of his publications and a description of his projected *Life and Works of D. H. Lawrence*. There followed transcripts of all Robbie's grades, from graduate school on down through kindergarten, lists of prizes and awards, letters from teachers and students and absolute strangers, and a note from his psychiatrist testifying to his fine mental health. "And for you, and for you, and finally for you," he said, presenting the Chairman with the last of the dossiers.

The Chairman studied the folder for a moment, recognized its purpose, and began the meeting. "Robbie is running for office," he said, "so we'd better get this thing under way." The fools smiled and put away their brown bags. The Turks sipped their coffee. They seemed uncertain how they should feel about Robbie Richter now that Zachary had gone to his rest.

"I can't bear it," Robbie said, squirming in his seat, "I'm so excited," and he let out a small shriek of pleasure.

The first order of business was the tenure votes and so the Chairman, according to custom, asked Tortorisi and Concepcion to leave the meeting. They could wait outside in the quad, he said. Or, if they preferred, in the church with the restless spirit of Zachary Kurtz. Then he apologized for saying this, it was a dumb thing to say, he certainly did not mean to mock the dead. He was nervous, he explained, because poor old Hamlet was not feeling well. And finally he said, "Go. Just go."

They would consider Concepcion's tenure first, the Chairman said, because that seemed the less difficult of the two. He called on the tenure committee for their report.

The extramural evaluations of her work had been excellent, the committee announced. Her probing studies of Villanueva, Viramontes, and Portillo-Trambley, viewed from the perspective of Barthes' five codes, had broken new ground in Chicana criticism. Her writing on New World Lesbian Poetry set a standard for gender studies. In sum, her scholarship was superior and her teaching was superb. A letter from Suzie Sweezie was read aloud as testimony to Concepcion's extensive and valuable influence on student life at the university. Everybody seemed ready to vote her tenure.

Maddy Barker, however, had a problem.

"I have a problem," Maddy explained, and it turned out to be a moral problem. Was Concepcion *really* the best we could do? Yes, she was Chicana. Yes, she was lesbian. Yes, she knew her Barthes. But Barthes? Really? Wasn't he getting just a little passé? Wasn't there some danger that in the life and pursuit of theory, Roland Barthes—and with him, poor Concepcion, for whom she felt deep concern—was about to be left behind? Part of the fascination of literary discourse today, Maddy explained—turning toward the fools, who could not be expected to know this—was the short-lived nature of theory itself. Styles in theory were changing faster than styles in clothing. That's what made theory so exciting, as Eleanora Tuke herself so often said. Here today, gone tomorrow. Could Concepcion keep up? Or was she doomed to be merely a Barthes clone? Maddy had fears about this. She was profoundly worried. It was a moral question. Tortorisi, she added, was another question altogether.

One of the fools said that he thought fashion should be left for the clothing industry and that the concern of an English Department should be something more enduring and dependable—like literature, for instance, like books. Some of the other fools nodded and some just smiled, but then Eleanora Tuke rose to speak so everybody fell silent.

"First, the dress," Eleanora said, and she turned in a slow circle so they could all get a good look. Her dress was black, for Zachary's memorial service, and it was cut very low in the back—indeed the back was merely a vast expanse of Eleanora's white flesh—with a huge red rose mounted just above her behind, a touch of whimsy. "It's Escada," she said, finishing her pirouette and settling down to business.

"Now. Maddy, as usual, has had excellent things to say, even though I can't agree with all of them. She is, as we know, a colleague of promise and ambition, and she is right to worry about Concepcion's ability to keep up. And keeping up is everything: we live in an electronic world, a video world, if I say so myself, and we can't hang back with the techno-peasantry. The most exciting things today are going on in videation."

Eleanora continued on for some time about video acrostics and virtual poetic reality and sound grids. And then, when everyone was lulled into semi-consciousness, she suddenly reached her surprising conclusion.

"We are going to promote Concepcion to tenure, no matter what. That's a given. She's a Chicana and a lesbian and a good scholar in a minor field, as Maddy says, but let us not forget that she *is* a Chicana and she *is* a lesbian. How many of us can claim that? Am I right? I'm right. So we'll promote her. My point is this: we cannot promote Concepcion unless we promote Tortorisi at the same time. Tortorisi adapts and changes. Tortorisi is tomorrow."

There was a stir among the fools. They all knew about Tortorisi's book and they couldn't wait to get a look at it. They loved this kind of thing.

"But we can't consider them together," the Chairman said. "These are separate tenure cases."

"What does videation have to do with *either* case?" one of the fools said. And he added, in the silence that followed, "And what does promoting Concepcion have to do with promoting Tortorisi? What on earth is the connection?"

"Besides," Maddy said, as if she were following up on an earlier point, "besides all that, Concepcion's is the work of a second-rate scholar. You can't compare her stuff to the work of a creative genius like Tortorisi."

Eleanora, of course, heard none of this. She had learned long ago that if you listen to people's arguments, then you have to deal with them, and you never got anywhere that way. She simply closed her mind and did battle.

"If one, then the other," she said. If Maddy could win tenure for a fellow lesbian, then by God she herself would win it for Tortorisi. "It's only fair," she said. "Am I right?"

"You're arguing for the same thing," the Chairman said, "you both want Tortorisi." He smiled hopefully but the two women ignored him.

"You just want him for your TV show," Maddy said.

"You just want him because you sleep with him," Eleanora said.

Maddy gasped, speechless.

"Am I right! Am I! Am I right!"

The Chairman tried to interrupt. "But it seems to me," he said, "that you both want him. For tenure. So what is the problem?"

Eleanora looked at him and Maddy looked at him and then they looked hard at each other.

"I don't sleep with him. I have never slept with him in my life." Maddy paused for effect. "We're going to be married."

The fools had long since fallen silent, but this new revelation silenced even the Turks. Marriage? Maddy Barker? What was the university coming to?

"We're in love," Maddy said.

"Some lesbian you turned out to be," Eleanora said.

"It's the life force," Robbie Richter shouted, "you can't deny it! The life force will spurt up! It just, it just, it just . . . *spurts!*"

There was applause for this. Robbie stood and took a bow, and then he repeated it all again. "*Spurts!*" he shouted.

In the brief lull that followed Robbie's hysteria, one of the fools attempted yet again to deconstruct the situation. He pointed out that since Eleanora and Maddy both wanted to give Tortorisi tenure, albeit for apparently differing reasons, perhaps everybody could agree to go ahead and vote, give him his damned tenure, give Concepcion hers, and get on with the meeting. And if it were possible to get a look at that book Tortorisi was writing, so much the better. He'd heard it was a howl.

The Chairman was about to ask for a vote when Gil rose and stood there solemn, silent, impressive. To even the least of them, he looked like money.

"Tortorisi?" Gil said. "What would Zachary Kurtz say about that?" He stood there, letting them think. "I ask you," he said.

They could hear the clock ticking.

"I ask you," Gil said once more, and flicked back his floppy blond hair.

Robbie Richter could not stand the silence. "We can't do it," he said. "Zachary always said that Tortorisi would get tenure over his dead body."

"Well?" the Chairman said. They all looked at him to see if he really meant it. "Now's the time."

Some of the fools laughed—the blackness of the humor be damned—and some of the Turks complained that Tortorisi was dull and fat and only wrote novels, but time was dragging and everybody was getting bored with the idea of Tortorisi and Concepcion and the mood was turning to violence or compromise, it was not certain which. The Chairman waited for one more second and then decided to test the winds.

"Olga says," and he paused while they all fell silent. "Olga says that if we vote Tortorisi tenure, he'll decline it and go quietly. If we don't, he'll sue."

Everybody liked that: a threat, something practical they could deal with.

"But will he really go?"

"Olga says."

"And he won't sue?"

"Olga says."

"And it would free up a salary?"

"It would," the Chairman said.

"More scandal," Robbie shouted. "The life force!"

But they were all tired of the life force by now—their own salaries were involved in this, not to mention the good of the university— and so reason prevailed and the threat of violence passed in a rich spirit of compromise. They would give Tortorisi tenure and he would give it back. And then they could hire somebody new and attractive. And forget about him.

They voted. While the votes were counted, Eleanora rumbled in the background about Maddy's careerism, Maddy's 'big' offers from little schools, Maddy's ruthless climb up the ladder to the undistinguished middle of her profession. Lesbian, my ass, she said. Maddy's a lesbian only when it's politically correct. She's as straight as anybody. By then the vote was tallied.

It was a divided vote—Gil held out until the end—but a good one. A runner was sent out to bring back Concepcion and Tortorisi, who were greeted with applause and hand-shakes and congratulations. Everybody seemed happy for them, and in a short while everybody *was* happy: it was one of those odd things that sometimes happened at English Department meetings. The Chairman could begin to see a happy outcome to all this.

"Now me, now me!" Robbie Richter shouted.

Time was passing rapidly—there was only a half-hour left before Zachary's memorial service—and the Chairman decided he must speed things up. They still faced major business: the Chairmanship, the Department of Theory and Discourse, term closure.

"A couple more items?" he said. "People? Please?"

He looked hopelessly around the room. His colleagues, fools and

Turks, simply continued talking. Eleanora complained. Concepcion was burbling away in Spanish, and Tortorisi was swelling up like a puff adder. And Robbie Richter continued to scurry about asking for votes, pressing his case, saying "Me!" Only Gil Rudin sat quietly, withdrawn, a sullen smirk on his handsome face.

"What should I do?" the Chairman asked.

"Resign," Gil said.

"I resign," the Chairman said. He shouted, "I resign!"

Everybody cheered.

Robbie took this as an invitation to begin his campaign speech.

"Well," he said, modest suddenly, "I think I should explain to you who I am. Who I expect to be. Who you expect me to be. Today's question then, is this: who is Robbie Richter?"

"No, no!" one of the fools shouted, and some of the others took up his cry.

"I want to tell you about Robbie Richter the scholar, Robbie Richter the teacher, and Robbie Richter the man."

He launched into the history, nature, and attendant circumstances of Robbie Richter the scholar. He had been born of poor but worthy parents in Utica, New York. He went on from there.

The Turks couldn't believe this was happening. Even with their considerable experience of Robbie, they were convinced that this was some kind of high academic satire, and they listened, keen to get the point. They listened very hard. The fools, however, knew Robbie was serious and cheered him on to a quick conclusion.

Robbie was showing no interest in haste. He was caught up still in Robbie the scholar, and he had traced his academic progress through the intricacies of *The Hardy Boys* and *Green Mansions* and on through Barbara Pym and Joseph Conrad, with a gloss on the reviews of his own ground-breaking *The Glow and the Haze: Conrad's Aesthetic Strategies*. He felt he should pause here and ask for audience response to his work, he said, but he knew time was pressing and so they'd have to forego that pleasure until some later occasion.

One of the fools shouted for him to tell them about Robbie the teacher, but Robbie said no, he was not to be rushed. He had to tell them first about his emergence into the spirit and blood of D. H. Lawrence, his acceptance of his psycho-sexual identity with this man of vision, his revolutionary discovery of the penis.

"I thought *I* had discovered the penis," the Chairman said, and all the fools laughed because there were only five minutes left and everybody was turning silly and now they were going to talk about penises?

They were, if Robbie had his way.

"Listen, listen!" Robbie said. "The penis is the still point of the turning world." He gestured delicately in the direction of his crotch. "Here is my mind! Here is my heart!"

"The new Chairman!" the Chairman called out, and the fools began to chant, "Huzzah for Robbie," and the Turks, scandalized, tried to make for the door. The fools blocked it and somebody shouted, "Robbie for Chair! Robbie by acclamation!" and somebody else shouted, "Robbie for penis! Robbie for still point!" and everybody kept on shouting until finally Robbie agreed to keep silent and be the new Chairman.

"By acclamation," the Chairman said for the official minutes of the meeting and "by acclamation" was duly recorded.

Again they were all crowding for the door.

"The Deans," the Chairman called after them, "want us to decide on the name of the Department."

"English," the fools shouted.

"Theory and Discourse," Eleanora shouted.

"Theory and Discourse," Tortorisi said, because now that he was leaving, he didn't give a shit.

"No, never," the fools shouted, for the sake of form. They didn't really care very much.

"Do it for Zachary," Gil Rudin said, "for at least a year."

And so it was agreed that just for the year they would call it the Department of Theory and Discourse in memory of Zack. So that he could have, in death, what he had wanted in life. More or less.

~

The commemoration service for Zachary Kurtz was everything Zachary could have hoped for. Derrida did not make it after all, but Gil was in excellent voice and read Zack's work beautifully. The Israeli MendiCantors were remarkably upbeat. And the widow Kurtz, babe in arms, bore her sorrow well.

"He had those headaches," she said, "always. And a bad heart."

And that was the last day of winter quarter.

33

"To tell you the truth," Peter Peeks said, "I'm a little disappointed."

Olga turned on her side to get a better look at him. They had just made love, and it had been very satisfactory, so she was surprised to hear he was disappointed.

"In our relationship," he said.

"Tell me," she said.

He thought for a while and she watched him thinking. His smooth brow was untroubled as ever, his eyes were clear and bright, his mouth turned quite naturally toward a smile.

She felt a tug at her heart or perhaps it was a tug at her conscience. He was perfect physically, perhaps perfect in other unexamined California ways, and she had made nothing of him. And now it was too late.

She sighed with disappointment, with resignation, with the resolve to do better next time. But this time, and it was Peter Peeks' only time, she had failed him.

"I guess I wanted . . . more," Peter Peeks said, marveling that he had found the exact words to express what he felt. "Just sort of more."

And so they went for a midnight swim, which seemed to satisfy Peter Peeks, and Olga was left to pack up her life and her books and her thoughts and, in a sense, disappear.

She slept soundly, without dreams, without disturbance.

In the morning a cab was waiting to take her to the airport. Daryl had insisted that he would drive her, that he needed to talk to her about his wife, that he was a desperate man.

"You're not in this, Daryl," she had said. "It's sad, but it's true, and I can't let you in at this late date." She added. "It wouldn't be good for you." She added, pleading, "You'd regret it forever."

She had lied to him about the day of her departure, telling him Sunday rather than Saturday. She had ordered a Yellow Cab under Tortorisi's name. She was ready to go as soon as the cab pulled up. What a surprise then to discover her driver was Daryl.

He put her bags in the car and held the door open for her.

She got in without saying anything at all. He said nothing in return. They looked at each other in the rearview mirror.

After a long while Daryl said, "Are you doing your thoughts?"

"I'm doing my thoughts," Olga said.

They drove on in silence.

Her thoughts were tidy and, for the most part, a source of satisfaction. The little people had all been taken care of. Moo and Leroy and Olga Moo. Betz and Susanna. Concepcion and Suzie Sweezie. And Hamlet, poor old Hamlet, who had died quietly in the night. And the big people too. Maddy Barker and Tortorisi and Eleanora Tuke: theirs was an electric, an electronic connection. Cynthia and Robbie Richter and Ozzie; a psychosexual one. Rosalie and Gil and little Adam Zachary; a modern kind of love. Everybody thriving. Everybody getting what they wanted or what they thought they wanted. Even the Deans. Even the President and Missy.

But not Peter Peeks, of course. Her most egregious failure.

Nor Daryl.

Daryl looked at her through the rearview mirror. She wore a black silk suit, very severe, and her long hair was pinned back in a knot. As he watched, she pulled a broad black hat tight over her brow, a sort of Spanish motif, and slipped dark sunglasses over her eyes. She had become a movie star.

He longed to speak to her. He longed to say, "I'm going mad, I'm going to kill, I'm going to destroy my life," but in her own peculiar way she had made it impossible for him to speak and he could say nothing.

He tapped the steering wheel.

He felt beneath the front seat for the screwdriver he had placed there.

He looked at her in the mirror.

They drove among the lion-colored hills, green now after all the rain, and they passed between the mountains, and they descended, silent still, to the metal drone of the airport.

She was nearly done with her thoughts.

The cab pulled smartly to the curb—there was a place ready for them, a porter waiting—and Daryl helped her out of the cab. He gave her bags to the porter.

She shook Daryl's hand and she could feel him trembling.

"I'm sorry," she said.

"I know," he said.

She turned from him and his fate was sealed.

Olga passed through the doors to the terminal, trying not to see the priest in his white robes and the beautiful flight attendant leaning on his arm, but she did see them, and she saw Daryl come running at them, the screw.driver held high in the air, plunging down deep into the soft breast of the flight attendant, and she heard the screams, and she saw the blood as Daryl stabbed and stabbed and stabbed his faithless wife, but there was nothing she could do about it, she had told him from the start that he was not in this at all, and she continued on the way to her flight, doing new thoughts, taking on new accents, pursuing her odd vision of charity and justice, pity and fear, and—she hoped—a kind of joy, joy at the end.

She walked briskly, cutting through the crowds of men and women busy at desire. She could be seen, if they wished to see, but she was disappearing even as they looked, fading, fading, until she was no more than a mote in the eye of the last beholder.

And then she was gone.